GIVE A

Witch

A CHANCE

COLETTE RIVERA

Content guidance for Give a Witch a Chance can be found on the author's website coletterivera.com/content-guidance/

Edited by May Peterson

www.maypetersonbooks.com

Cover design by Ink & Laurel Design Studio

www.inkandlaurel.com

ISBN

Print: 978-0-473-65841-0

Kindle: 978-0-473-65843-4

1

OWEN

*T*he cafe wasn't haunted. There was no way. Hauntings weren't real and neither were ghosts. The muttering coming from the walk-in had a perfectly logical explanation. I just couldn't find it.

As I grabbed a couple pork shoulders off the shelf a disembodied chuckle mocked me so quietly I could almost tell myself it was imaginary. I closed the walk-in door and returned to the kitchen, ignoring the eerie voice.

No. Scratch that, there was no ignoring. There was no voice, because that was impossible. *No one was here with me.* Sure, I had this lingering childhood desire for supernatural things to be real, but that was only a fantasy and I knew it.

Stress was my very real, very not-ghostly problem. I'd recently lost a kitchen hand, who'd moved home unexpectedly for personal reasons. Covering the cafe's cooking without help most days left me exhausted. I was hearing things, letting my imagination get away from me.

I tried to ignore everything unexplainable as I prepped the meat to be slow cooked. Our carnitas torta was one of the most popular menu items and I was behind on prep for tomorrow.

As I worked alone in the cramped kitchen, a muffled voice in my office caught my attention. It sounded like someone was having a heated discussion. Maybe on the phone? Odd. No one was supposed to be in there but me.

The unmistakable sound of a sob made me pause. I wiped my hands on my apron and went to the door of the glorified closet-turned-office.

"Tristan?" I called, giving the door a loud rap with my knuckles.

Tristan was my business partner at Coffee Cat Cafe and the only one likely to be in the office. I hadn't seen him slip past; he must have come by while I was in the fridge getting the meat.

Another sob emanated from the room. Tristan and I were best friends, practically brothers. If something was wrong, standing dumbly outside wasn't an option. I opened the door.

The office was empty. A chill ran down my spine.

"Owen!" Tristan's frantic voice called out from the front of the cafe.

I left the inexplicably empty office feeling weary. He damn well better be calling, if I was imagining that too, I was more exhausted than I feared.

Tristan practically ran into me in the narrow hall. "The sink in the bathroom is overflowing and I can't get the water to shut off!" He was drenched, black Coffee Cat T-shirt plastered to his chest, jeans dripping.

"Shit." At least this was real. "How did your hair get wet?"

We hurried to the bathroom.

Tristan wiped sopping black curls from his eyes. "The thing kinda exploded. I don't know what happened."

We entered the bathroom to find no overflowing sink, only a massive puddle on the floor.

"Huh." Tristan met my eyes with a confused shrug. "Guess I

got it turned off after all." He grabbed a mop, but I took it off him.

"Go upstairs and dry off. I'll cover the register while you change."

Tristan shivered. "Thanks. It's way cold in here today."

After he left, I checked the tap and piping under the sink. Everything seemed fine. The weird thing was, the water wasn't turned off at the valve on the wall. If the sink was overflowing, I didn't see why it stopped. Nothing looked like it'd exploded.

Bathroom mopped, I hurriedly switched the meat on to slow cook and went out front to take orders.

"Thank god. Did Tristan get swallowed by the toilet?" Tess, my best barista, muttered as I joined her behind the counter.

There was a small rush of customers, enough to make covering orders and coffees frantic for Tess on her own. She quickly got to grinding beans and frothing dairy free milk as I took payments and handed people pan dulce from the glass display cupboard.

At least everything out here was normal, not flooded or plagued by disembodied voices. Not that you'd be able to discern a disembodied voice from the rest of the noise, but whatever. The sun was shining in through the windows, lighting up my colorful little cafe. Most of the seats were filled with satisfied customers. We were almost sold out of pastry. By all indications it'd been another successful day. I should have been happy but couldn't shake my uneasiness.

Tristan was right, it was cold in here despite the sun.

I let myself entertain the idea the coffee shop was haunted while I boxed up the last of our polvorones. Coffee Cat didn't seem like the type of place a paranormal presence would take up residence. My cafe was cozy and inviting, not your classic haunt, but then again what did I know about haunts? Maybe dim and spooky was a stereotype. For all I knew, ghosts liked the ambiance created by mouthwatering aromas and a well curated, pop-centric playlist.

I shook off the thought and served the next customer in line. I'd figure out what was causing all these weird issues and be secretly disappointed when it was something boring like a radio and screwed up water pressure.

The bell above the front door chimed.

I did a double take, stomach flipping at the sight of the woman walking in. Aria Belmonte was a ghost from my past, an apparition I'd never expected to see again outside memory.

Not after twelve years.

It was like she'd walked out of my teenage dreams, the picture of casual summer comfort in jean shorts and a loose cotton T-shirt. Her sunglasses were nestled atop her head, amongst long brown hair, silver rings glinting on almost all her fingers, catching the sunlight. Her brown skin sported a few tattoos I remembered and a few I didn't.

Aria wore a distracted, thoughtful expression as she glanced around my cafe. She bit her bottom lip and an ill-advised flutter took over my insides.

Stop looking at her lips. What the hell was wrong with me? Seeing the person that shattered my heart should have set my pulse going in anger, not excitement.

I'd imagined this reencounter a thousand times and lust had never featured in any scenario.

Nerves replaced my silly flutter of attraction. Suddenly I was a lonely teen, not a successful business owner. I froze like the younger me would have. I had the urge to hide. Not do this. Avoid this reunion forever.

Get a grip Owen Sanchez. This doesn't have to be a big deal.

The last time I saw Aria was at an awful high school party. It wasn't fair such a muddled memory was the last we had of each other.

Aria hadn't spotted me behind the counter. She was preoccupied with an over large canvas tote bag. Aria rummaged around the depths of the bag, pulled out a deck of cards held together with a rubber band, then plunged her hand back in.

I turned my attention to another customer and waited for her to get to the front of the line.

Aria extricated a wallet from her bag as she reached the register. At last she looked up. Her recognition was immediate, soft brown eyes going wide. The bag slipped off her shoulder. She scrambled to catch it, unable to look away from me, and half the contents of the tote went crashing to the floor. The loud clang of a metal water bottle made her jump, sunglasses going askew.

Aria tore her eyes from me and ducked down, grabbing at the items rolling around the tile floor. She stuffed her cellphone, an honest-to-god crystal, a small wooden box, and what looked like a pouch of potpourri back into her canvas tote.

She straightened, red in the cheeks and looking like she too had seen a ghost.

"Hi," I said, a wide grin taking over my face. I couldn't hold back a chuckle at the improbability of us, here, after everything.

Aria bristled and narrowed her eyes, as if annoyed by my amusement.

I hadn't meant it at her expense. "Sorry, you surprised me," I said with a more tempered expression.

"Surprised is one word for it," she said in a clipped, business-like tone. "You work here?"

"Obviously." I could have told her I owned the Coffee Cat Cafe, had started it from scratch three years ago and been featured in *The Independent* newspaper twice for my baking, but I didn't need to brag.

Aria's opinion shouldn't matter anymore. No one had ever hurt me like her. That should cancel out everything else.

Aria was having no trouble displaying her displeasure at my unexpected appearance in her day. Any of my amusement, or hope this chance encounter would go well, vanished like a burst bubble.

"It's been a while," I said to fill the silence.

She looked at the menu on the wall behind me, as if it could help her avoid me. "Yeah. How've you been?"

We were best friends all through high school, then more than friends. She was my first love, my worst heartbreak. We were everything to each other, and I had no idea how we went from that to nothing overnight. No clue why she ghosted me.

I could never have walked away from anyone the way she'd cut herself out of my life. But all that was a long time ago. Her reluctance to reunite shouldn't have hurt.

"I've been great," I said, deciding to project confidence. Aria didn't get more of my emotions. She didn't get to know what happened after she left, when I needed her friendship most and she was nowhere to be found.

Aria forced herself to make eye contact. She gave me a tight smile. Something about me must still bother her. I had no idea what.

I was going to ask for her order, get this interaction over with, but couldn't help prying. "Where'd you go all those years ago?"

Aria looked at me as if begging me not to make her do this. "Owen, I'm actually in a hurry to meet someone."

Now wasn't the time or place for this conversation, sure, but I didn't kid myself thinking I'd see her again after today. This was it, and Aria didn't want to give us a chance at even the tiniest resolution. Fine. Neither did I.

"Never mind. What's your coffee order?" I looked at the register with more focus than necessary as I rang her up.

Aria ordered an extra-large cold brew and slipped over to

wait by the espresso machine at the end of the counter. She took out her phone and didn't look up.

"I'm back!" Tristan skidded into me in his rush to take up his place behind the register.

I caught him by the now-dry shoulders to stop him losing his balance. "Right. I need to get back in the kitchen."

I'd like to say I hadn't looked back, had walked off to do my job without giving Aria another thought. That I hadn't lingered half a beat too long before turning away. But of course I had.

She didn't look up from her phone. I didn't say goodbye.

2

ARIA

our days ago.

BOREDOM LED me to rearrange the crystal rings I'd been wearing in the same configuration for years. Which finger the rings were on didn't make a difference to my spell casting ability, so I took them all off and moved them around, taking my time to consider all the new possibilities. I'd almost found a satisfactory arrangement when I knocked a ring to the floor. It bounced out of sight, disappearing under a nearby shelf.

I was alone, not to mention concealed in my fortune telling nook, so I used a quick summoning spell rather than get up to search for the ring. The remaining crystals heated against my fingers as I said the incantation, and the wayward ring zoomed toward me. I caught it and slid it onto my left index finger.

"Aria, you could have warned me!" Clara shouted from the front of the magic shop as the bell above the door clanged, singling her arrival. Her timing was enough to give me a heart attack.

I managed not to trip on the overlong black tablecloth as I stood from my fortune telling table in a hurry, and poked my head out of my lair.

I was at work, in a Mortal magic shop filled with card tricks and illusions, not a real magic shop. The place was owned by my seventy-one-year-old friend Clara Dalton. She came bustling in and threw a stack of letters onto the counter with enough force that a few fell to the floor.

I stayed shrouded in the rainbow beaded portière and gauzy curtains that separated the fortune telling area from the rest of the shop. "Warned you about what?"

"This whole row of buildings has been condemned."

"*What!* How was I supposed to know that?" *Condemned*— what did that mean for us? For the shop? For my room upstairs?

"You're a psychic, Aria. You should have known. Really, if I'd ever been tempted to believe you could see the future, my hopes would be dashed." Clara gave me a look of mocking disappointment.

She'd always been too skeptical to believe my abilities were real, which was the only reason I'd set up in a Mortal shop to begin with. Clara thought my psychic ability was nothing more than keen observation skills, personability, and an endless well of bullshit. My actual ability to bullshit was abysmal, so I appreciated her faith in me.

Sadly for both of us, real-deal psychic Witches like me can't actually see the future.

Still, I might have seen something like this coming, just knowing how things went for me. I'd been rolling along on luck for years, through chance, not magic. My life had fallen haphazardly into a good place for once. I was employed by a friend and able to use my psychic ability to help Mortals in small mundane ways. But my luck had run out. Again.

"What are we going to do?" I asked.

"There's nothing to do." Clara pulled a bottle of gin and two glasses out from under the counter and poured herself a drink. "The city has been sending notices for months. We have to be out by the end of the week. Drink?"

I shook my head and Clara put away the second glass. "But how have we not heard until now?"

"You know I don't check the PO box. And to be fair, these were the only letters in there. I wasn't expecting anything, so why bother checking?"

"But what about my room?" I asked, feeling panicked.

"I know, Aria. I'm sorry. You'll have to be out by the end of the week too." Clara looked genuinely sorry but that didn't chance the fact that everything was screwed. "I'll help you any way I can."

Business at Clara's magic shop was slow, hence my boredom when she wasn't around. Lack of customers meant it wasn't anywhere near a profitable business, but Clara gave the impression this place was more of a hobby for her. I worked here, occasionally minding the register when Clara was out, in exchange for room and board rather than a paycheck. My only income was what I earned from my fortune telling customers. Fortunes were solely my venture, not part of the shop before I arrived.

Clara and I preferred things slow. When I didn't have my own customers the two of us hung out, playing with magic tricks, Clara scandalizing me with stories of her youth while I pretended to have a life half as rich as hers. But the not-so-traditional arrangement meant I was in a tight spot. My client base wasn't the most robust, just enough to cover what I needed, and working for accommodation didn't fill my bank account with savings.

There was no way I'd be able to scrape together a deposit or rent, even if I could find a place available in a week's notice.

Money didn't appear out of thin air. Magic didn't work like that, unless you were up for breaking the law. And I wasn't.

"Will you find a new space for the shop?" I asked.

"No. I think this is the end of an era." Clara helped herself to another measure of gin. "I'm thinking of going to live with my sister in Arizona."

Unlike me, Clara had more than two friends and family she liked talking to. Truth was, I didn't get out much, and had *making friends* on my list of incomplete life goals for the past half a dozen years or so. But I was mostly fine with it. I walked on the beach every Sunday evening and had a long-term relationship with the library.

Now I was losing even that. Well, not the library. Some things will endure. But I was losing Clara and the shop.

"I called my sister on the way over here. A new plan is already falling into place. She wants me to join her salsa class," Clara continued after a hearty sip, acting as if recreational dance was a justification worthy of crossing state lines.

"We have salsa dancing in SoCal," I said. Or maybe whined.

"But their instructor is a babe. I like nimble men who can move."

It made sense; Clara could move. She had grace and presence. A performer at heart.

"Come with me," Clara said, and the scary thing was, she meant it. She wouldn't bat an eye at me tagging along and making two sisters into a trio.

"What? No."

"Why not? It will be fun. You'll like my sister, she's a hoot."

Clara cared. I'd always known, but this offer made it apparent in a new way. She was a genuine friend, and I had no doubt I'd like her sister, but it was too much. I couldn't bear it not working out. I couldn't add Clara Dalton to the ever-growing list of people I disappointed.

"Really, I can't. But thank you for the offer." I squirmed in an anxious hot flash of gratitude.

"Suit yourself, Aria." Clara saluted me with her glass, apparently not at all offended by my decline.

This, however, left me fucked. I had nowhere to go.

Home was a non-option. I wouldn't be turned out, so my crisis was somewhat self-imposed, making me feel like a privileged idiot. But I *couldn't* go home. The folks and I didn't get along.

My parents also ruled out turning to my twin brother Luca. They hovered around him like gnats, and I hadn't talked to Luca in almost two months. It would be a dick move to only call him up when I was out on my ass and in need of a favor. I'd turned into the most terrible twin.

Some might say I'd been avoiding the Witchy world since high school, and so what if I had. I wouldn't be forced back.

It looked like I was going to have to dig deep and call my other friend. Jenn. She was the reason I'd moved to a ritzy beachside town, far too expensive for a partially employed psychic.

Jenn was an ex-girlfriend. We met when I lived in LA, did the, well two hours isn't really long distance, is it? We settled into commuter-dating until I'd moved up the coast and in with her. Then an almost-respectable length of time later we broke up. I'd been stranded then as well, but was already doing fortunes at Clara's and she took pity on me.

After a few years of happy quiet, I'd come full circle. There was no way in hell I was asking to move in with Jenn and her new(ish) current girlfriend, even temporarily. But she might be able to help me out.

JENN CAME THROUGH. Luckily for me, my ex was a softie who managed a suit of local properties owned by her family. After a few days of coordinating back and forth I had an interim solution.

Kind-hearted Jenn had some like-minded tenants willing to help a girl out. There was an apartment with a spare room and a sole occupant who didn't mind having a random move in. Jenn vouched for me, with a warning not to disappoint her. Again. I might be many things, but a pain to live with wasn't one of them. So Jenn gave the guy a discount on his rent in exchange for me taking over his spare room. Not indefinitely, just long enough to get on my feet.

I was feeling okay about the arrangement until about ten minutes ago.

I exited the Coffee Cat Cafe and didn't look back. Hadn't I had enough bad luck? Owen Sanchez was exactly what I didn't need, now or ever. I hadn't been prepared to see him, and I hadn't handled it well.

Jenn was meeting me at the apartment upstairs to hand over the key. I lurked by the building's side door, waiting and hiding from view of the coffee shop windows. What were the chances it was the same building where Owen worked?

Whatever, it wasn't like I was moving into the coffee shop. I'd just never be able to revel in the convenience of living above a place selling cold brew and conchas. I already planned to avoid Coffee Cat like the plague. It wouldn't be hard to organize my non-existent schedule so I could come and go from the apartment upstairs while they were closed.

This course of action was not dramatic, it was necessary.

I refused to let my thoughts dwell on Owen, even if I was tempted. I couldn't take what happened with him on top of everything else. I had to move forward, not fret about our past.

Owen was also an ex. More importantly than that, we'd been

inseparable as teenagers. But what happened between us wasn't your standard youthful drama. After years of resisting, and knowing better, I'd tried to Tell Owen about magic.

Like most other things I attempted, I failed. Owen didn't believe me. He might not even remember exactly what I said all these years later. We hadn't been sober at the time, and I always used to tell him ridiculous stories.

As a Mortal, Owen didn't know about magic or Witches. Most Mortals don't have a clue, and never find out. This enforced secrecy was part of a system of laws Witchy society put in place to protect Mortals from unfair, magical exploitation. I broke the law trying to Tell Owen when we were kids.

If only I'd stopped there, but instead I'd been on a roll of bad decision making.

That one night resulted in consequences that followed me around for the next twelve years. I wasn't allowed to be in contact with Owen as per court orders, and here he was making coffee and asking me where I'd gone like he still cared.

Never mind that I wanted nothing more than to go back inside the cheerful little cafe and talk to him. I couldn't, and so I was hiding outside.

Knowing Owen was downstairs, just out of reach, was going to hurt. On the bright side, it might motivate me to get my shit together and find my own place to live, far away from here.

3

OWEN

*P*art of owning a coffee shop is acquiring a few regulars. This was objectively a good thing, but then there were patrons like Max.

We were getting ready to close for the day and our resident writer, Max, was still typing away. He was a middle-aged nondescript white man with a graying beard and lots of opinions.

"I'm not convinced he's *not* writing about us," Tristan whispered to Tess and me, as we worked behind the counter, cleaning and adding up the day's takings.

I agreed, but wondered if our suspicion was down to Max's demanding personality, and tendency to say uncomfortable things, rather than any real threat the man was watching us. At the moment he had his earbuds in and was paying us no attention. The cafe was otherwise empty. I'd just flipped the "closed" sign, but we usually let Max linger until the mop came out.

"He always makes notes after talking to one of us." Tristan paused in wiping down the display cabinet. "Today—out of nowhere—he said I'd make a good serial killer. Like what does that even mean? It's the weirdest insult framed as a creepy compliment I've ever received, and that bar tragically isn't low."

"He was just making fun of your three-first-names-name," Tess said.

Tristan and I stared at her blankly.

She rolled her eyes. "Listen to a podcast. It's like a serial killer thing. Max looks like he'd be into true crime. Maybe you're in his next book, Tristan."

Tristan glowered, something cutting likely on the tip of his lounge.

"I doubt Max meant anything by it," I said, cutting him off. "He's rude, but I wouldn't worry."

We all glanced over at Max and for once, he reacted like he could feel our attention.

"Oh wow, look at the time." Max stood, entangling himself in the wire connecting his earbuds to the computer. He packed up in a hurry, as if he didn't linger past closing most days. "Mr. Sanchez, Mr. Taylor-Tomás, Ms. Tess—" Max nodded at each of us before turning to the door. "Good day."

"Still no hyphen," Tristan called after the door closed and there was no chance Max could hear the correction for the hundredth time. "I could kill that reporter for printing my middle name."

"Wait!" Tess grabbed Tristan by the arm. "You *are* a serial killer."

I returned to the kitchen, leaving Tristan to tell Tess she could go screw herself. The dough was proofing for tomorrow and the only thing left to do was clean.

By the time the counters were pristine, I was exhausted. We needed to hire more staff. I worked six days a week and loved this place, but it wasn't any sort of picnic.

Tristan and I had done well as a new business. He did a lot more than run the register, even if he liked to downplay his role in Coffee Cat's success. Tristan knew more about marketing than I ever cared to, and recently lined up a feature for us with a popular foodie influencer. We'd been deemed delicious and grammable.

Grammability was all down to Tristan. He'd pushed me to decorate the cafe in a bold and colorful style, walls in golden yellow, red and blue, with accents in fuchsia thrown in for good measure. We featured local, mostly queer, Latinx artists' work on the walls, and I'd always wanted there to be a sense of community. For staff and patrons. Somehow all the little details came together. It was a vibe for sure.

I was excited to share this place in the upcoming feature, but ever since we lined it up, things were falling apart. Okay, not falling to ruin, but there'd been so many small problems. People quitting, the plumbing, a power outage, the damn voices. I couldn't have MyFavoriteEats showing up to wailing walls and exploding sinks. That wasn't the kind of viral content we needed.

Someone laughed as I put the cleaning supplies away. It wasn't Tristan's bubbly laugh or Tess's cackle. The sound was sinister, like it had been listening to my thoughts and was mocking me.

Yes, sleep. I needed it. Twelve hours work-days were not where it's at.

I trudged out front to see how Tess and Tristan were faring with the rest of the close-down.

"What's wrong with your face?" Tess threw a cleaning cloth at me. It hit my chest and fell to the floor.

I scrubbed a hand over my short beard. "My face is the same as always."

Tess retrieved the cloth from the ground. My gaze flitted over to the window, where I'd last seen Aria. Of course, she wasn't there now.

"You're frowning," Tess said, playfully swatting me with the cloth. "It's not a good look for you. I'm the one who makes moody hot, remember?"

I laughed and she gave me an affectionate glare. "Is that a new tattoo?" I asked, spotting a geometric design under her left ear. Not that I was changing the subject.

"It's not that new." Tess swept the multitude of fly-aways off her neck and attempted to wrangle them into her ponytail with the rest of her coarse black hair in order to display the tattoo.

"She's got a new one on her wrist," Tristan said as he wrung out the mop.

Tess had so many tattoos I could be forgiven for not noticing. In addition to being my best barista and good friend, Tess was a tattoo artist. She'd been apprenticing back when we'd first met and I'd eagerly offered up myself as a canvas.

She and I had a similar attitude to ink. I liked the idea of adorning my body with art, expressing things boldly and out in the open, and I liked the beauty of it. Floral and botanical designs were my favorite. The garden of my childhood home was painted on my arm, all the care my father put into plants long dead here with me for everyone to see.

I thought of the small tattoos on the back of Aria's knuckles. She'd gotten them back in high school. I'd found it so terribly cool her parents let her get them before she was eighteen. But she wasn't the reason I got into ink, it had nothing to do with her.

I was annoyed at myself for remembering how excited I'd been when she showed off the simple black symbols. I'd thought she was a badass but teased her anyway. *Astrology isn't silly*, she'd insisted, dismissing me.

Aria had always believed in the unrealistic power of things. She had always demanded to read my palm and tried to give me advice based on transiting planets. It'd been fun, a way to flirt. I'd been captivated by her casual, confident touches. Though I'd teased her relentlessly, I suddenly remembered how much I'd actually believed her.

Aria was the root of my superstitious nature, now I considered it. I'd almost completely forgotten. I might have stopped thinking about her so much over the years, but the seed she planted had stuck. I never really believed, but Aria had always made it seem like otherworldliness was possible. I had no doubt she believed in a strange sort of magic back when we were in high school. I wonder what she thought now. Surely she'd come to her senses.

Tristan and Tess had turned to bickering. I stifled a yawn and went to check the register.

"No, I don't think I'd look good with a nose ring," Tristan said as he went around putting the chairs back down now the mopping was done.

Tess trailed him, an evil glint in her eye. "You'd look so hot. Please? Your just so—"

"Stay away from me."

I opened the register, it was empty. "Come on guys. You need to remember to shut it down once you do the banking."

"I did shut it down," Tess said. "Money and receipts are in the safe."

"No you didn't. It's still turned on." I powered the register off and watched the screen fade to black. Right before it popped back on again.

Okay, that was weird. Maybe the software was updating? But there was no message on the screen. I turned it off again.

It came back on.

"Oh, fuck sake." I turned it off. "Did you guys have any issues with the register today?"

They confirmed they did not. Great, we could be having technological issues too. I didn't need this.

Job done for the day, my friends departed, still bickering, leaving me to glare at the register.

I guess it wasn't really a problem if it didn't want to stay turned off. I had more important stuff to worry about. I shut it down one more time.

It clicked back on.

With a grumble I opened the cabinet under the counter and pulled the plug. The screen stayed lit up.

Residual electrical flow? Techno-ghosts?

The back of my neck prickled. Someone chuckled, I could feel them looking at me. I knew no one was here but I turned around anyway. The wall mounted menu and chalkboard we used to list the day's pan dulce stared back at me.

The cafe wasn't haunted. It couldn't be. Maybe I'd have believed it twelve years ago but I wasn't some dumb kid taken in by Aria's nonsensical stories anymore.

I plugged the register back in and went home.

4

ARIA

*A*fter several trips across town moving my things, I arrived at my new place for good. I parked across the street under a lush jacaranda tree, pleased to see the Coffee Cat Cafe was closed. Ignoring any trepidation I felt about meeting my new roomie, who'd been absent all day, I gathered my remaining two boxes and headed to the apartment.

There was a keypad on the exterior door, leading to an entry housing the back door to the coffee shop and a stairwell leading to the apartment. I let myself in and ascended the stairs.

As I unlocked the apartment my psychic sense told me someone else was already inside. My ability didn't allow me to read a person's thoughts, only emotion and intentions. I wasn't probing for information on the other person as I walked in, only passively feeling my surroundings. The other person in the apartment appeared to be in the kitchen. I planned to slip past, to my room, put my stuff down and maybe hide a while before saying hello.

I crossed the bright living room. The space was dominated by windows, half open to let in a meager breeze. The rest was constructed in pastel. Sky blue curtains fluttered lazily, a colorful rug covered the wood floor, and a pale, salmon pink couch dominated the room.

"Hey," a voice called out as I almost reached the hall. "You must be my new—"

A shirtless man filled the doorway to the kitchen. Fuck, no. A shirtless *Owen Sanchez* filled the doorway to the kitchen.

We both froze, unable to compute what was happening. My mind rebelled. *Come on.* How had my life crashed and burned to leave me here? With him?

Owen was annoyingly hot. Did I mention he was shirtless? Wearing nothing but gym shorts. Okay, it was a hot summer day and the air conditioning wasn't on, but still. If I could manage a T-shirt, so could he. But why would he with all that smooth dark skin adorned with eye-catching tattoos? I hadn't even realized I had opinions on the perfect amount of chest hair until now. Owen was stunning, as evidenced by my stupor. I teetered on the inappropriate edge of lust.

He had a full sleeve in black ink on his left arm, and a partial from his right shoulder to elbow. He'd filled out since we were kids, gotten taller too. Owen had been short in high school, now he was a more average height, slightly taller than me.

A tattoo on his hip begged my eyes to wander lower. It was tucked suggestively beyond the waistband of his shorts. I refused to be so drawn. My eyes rejected all things pointing south, including the trail of hair leading from his belly button. My eyes climbed up. Owen's brown chest gleamed. Good god, was he sweating? What had he been doing in the kitchen? Push-ups?

Fuck, his nipples were looking right at me.

I made eye contact with his, uh, eyes. Owen had dark brown, almost black hair, tight curls cut close, fade impeccable, a short well-groomed beard, and the same dark brown eyes I remembered. He was more refined than the boy I used to know, but I wondered if he smiled and laughed the same. A stupid thing to think about. Owen was far from smiling. He looked unsettled.

"Aria?" He crossed his arms, causing them to flex. "What are you doing here?"

My arms ached and I set my boxes on the ground between us. "I—Jenn said you'd be expecting me?"

"*You're* her ex who got evicted?" Owen looked like he was considering laughing. Or maybe crying in exasperation.

"Well, I didn't know *you* lived here." I crossed my own arms. This was a disaster. "What? You work downstairs and live here?" For someone who'd been doing the exact same thing I shouldn't have sounded so incredulous.

Owen straightened. "I rent the entire building. I own the business downstairs."

Crap, he was successful. I mean, great for him, but I hated being made to care I wasn't.

"Why the hell would you agree for a rando to move in?" I asked like this was all his fault. Successful people didn't house weird strangers for Jenn. My new roommate was supposed to be a faceless, average, uninteresting someone. Not Owen.

"I—I—" he sputtered. "Who cares. You can't live here. Jenn didn't say it was you. Not that she knew about us. I was just helping her out, and never liked living alone."

"Have a friend move in like a normal person!" I felt myself going red in embarrassment and anger. Trust Owen to admit something real like that, humanize himself. I didn't need to sympathize with any pangs of loneliness. See any of myself in him. How dare he.

I couldn't see Owen Sanchez, let alone live with him. Being barred from contacting Owen was a harsh punishment I might have been spared if I'd stopped at trying to Tell him. But I went around the party trying to Tell all our classmates. The Authority Witches deemed me irresponsible—which, get in line, everyone in my life agreed—but this was serious, and they had a lesson to teach me.

Telling a Mortal about magic meant they were no longer protected by ignorance and could be magically influenced, or fall victim to any number of manipulations. You didn't get to Tell people just because you wanted to, it was more complicated than that.

What if I was in trouble just being near Owen, even though I hadn't planned this reunion? Did the court already know? Avoiding the Witchy world all these years might catch me out. The monitoring spell they'd cast on me was still active, but I had no way of knowing how the Authority responded to broken court conditions when the original crimes were so many years ago.

I swiped my hands over my arms as if I could wipe the damn spell off.

"Lucky for you I didn't get my own roommate, Aria. Are you really that hard up for housing? What's going on with you?" A crack of concern broke through Owen's frustration. I hated it.

I looked around the room, desperate for escape. How rude would it be to walk back out the door without another word, and did I care? A quick introspection showed, crap, I cared. Still. About Owen and not hurting his feelings. I didn't want to go, even though I knew I had to. I'd used up all my cold IDGAF energy in the coffee shop, leaving me trapped in this infuriatingly cheery living room.

"You into fitness now, or something?" I asked, pointing at a work-out bench and neatly stacked weights in accusation. I needed to talk about anything but what was going on with me. I needed to rile myself up, or piss him off, until I was kicked to the curb.

"What? That's—I don't have time to get to the gym. I dunno." The concern disappeared from Owen's face. Good. "I had all my work-out stuff in my spare room, until *you* moved in." Owen walked around me and picked a shirt up off the floor. He put it on.

Thank the stars for small miracles.

Now he'd looked away from me, Owen didn't look back. His mouth was a tight line.

I shouldn't have wanted to rub the frustrated creases from his brow. I needed to leave. Living here would never work. On top of all my Witchy restrictions, we had mounds of history that couldn't be ignored any more than it could be rehashed.

Owen leaned against the back of his couch, facing me but focused on his bare feet. "God Aria, what happened with us?"

"Nothing. There is no us. I didn't—I can't—" How could I explain ghosting him when trying to Tell Owen things is what got me in trouble to begin with? What I did to him twelve years ago was unforgivable. My greatest regret. The fact I had no choice in the way I left him only made it worse. It was still my fault.

"You're seriously going to stand there and not tell me what happened? Not explain why you left? Did you really walk out of my life and not look back? Never think—"

"Of course not. I'm sorry. I messed up. Okay? But you're right, I can't just stand here like it was nothing. I won't do this to you. I'll leave." I picked up my boxes as if this was everything, even though there were a dozen more in my room.

"So you're just going to run off? Again. Can't you talk for like five minutes?" Owen looked up at me. I hated seeing hurt and confusion in his face, especially knowing I put it there.

"There's nothing to say." I couldn't look at him, focusing instead on the centering candle in my open box. I really needed to light it, get my shit together.

"Right." He huffed. "Must've made a big deal out of nothing."

I didn't want him to do that. Minimize us. But I'd left him no choice. "Owen—"

"So you have somewhere to go?"

"Yep." I shifted the boxes, trying to project confidence.

Owen raised his eyebrows, catching my lie. "Just stay here tonight if you need to. Okay?"

"You don't have to do that."

"I'm not such an asshole that I'd let whatever kid shit rule my better judgment. I told Jenn I'd help and I will."

The smart part of me knew I needed to run. If the Authority could tell I was around Owen again, they wouldn't overlook the infraction. But another, more wistful part of me was tempted by this unexpected opportunity. If I could stay and make even the tiniest bit of what was broken between Owen I right, then Owen deserved that. I was already here, and likely in trouble for it, what if I made the most of the situation before I caught the consequences?

What happened with Owen broke my heart. Leaving him and not saying goodbye wrecked me. I wanted a second chance, even if I had no idea how to go about fixing anything.

I put my boxes back down and Owen gave his head a shake. A tiny grin on his lips. "Maybe you'll realize talking to me isn't so bad, Aria."

"Maybe. I'll stay tonight, two nights tops. Then be out of your way. I've got to line a few things up." Looked like the twins were getting back together after all, lucky Luca.

"Sure, if that's all you need."

I could have made my exit, hid in my room and avoided him until I could flee, but against the odds I was committed to more. "Owen, I didn't want things to end how they did. I am sorry. It wasn't—my choice."

"Your parents said they sent you away?" He sounded resigned.

"Yeah." I nodded, unable to tell him more. Leaving against my will should have been too melodramatic to be believable, even without the magical context, but Owen had met the Belmontes.

Owen's brow furrowed. "But why? Even if they sent you away, *you* still ignored me. I was worried at first. Luca was weird and wouldn't talk to me at school. I went to your house when you wouldn't answer your phone. Your dad said you were gone. Told me not to come back. But I tried to call you—"

"I know." Each missed call and text from Owen had sparked anxiety and sadness in me.

"We weren't that far off eighteen," Owen said, frustration rising. "Was your family really calling the shots all this time? You couldn't even call? Not that summer? *Never again?* Where did you go? Did they banish you to Siberia? Or like, fucking Narnia?"

"I've heard they don't have cell service in Narnia."

Owen rolled his eyes, no doubt disappointed in my non-answer and trying to hide his hurt. It was all a lie. My parents hadn't banished me anywhere. I didn't know how I was ever going to make up for something Owen didn't understand, or know was in the realm of possibility.

"Owen, if there was a point I could have called, by then it hurt too much." This was mostly true. The pain was real, the loss of him still hurt, but I wasn't ever allowed to call.

Owen pushed off the couch. "I'm going to shower and meet a friend for dinner. I'll see ya later. Unless I don't."

His words stung. Owen left me lost and regretful, staring blankly at the cheery couch and wondering if I'd ever get over him.

5

OWEN

*C*offee Cat had a milk crisis. It started when Tristan took the morning milk delivery as he'd done a hundred times before. Only this time Tristan erupted into an alarming string of curses.

I rushed outside to see what the problem was.

"The milk was all right here." Tristan insisted as we stared at the empty driveway behind the cafe.

"Where could it have gone?" I asked.

"Maybe the driver took everything back." Tristan didn't sound sure but what other explanation was there? The milk hadn't vanished into thin air.

"You saw him unload it?" I'd say it was too early for this shit, but I'd been here since four. Seven a.m. was late morning for a baker.

Tristan looked like he wanted to pull his hair out. "Yes. I saw the guy unloading the last crates of oat and soy. I went inside to check the space in the fridge, rejigg a few things. Then I came back out, and it was all gone."

The call to my supplier to complain didn't go well. The driver insisted he delivered everything as usual, and seeing as the milk was no longer in his truck, his boss was inclined to believe him. There was nothing left to do but go out and buy more milk, paying the marked-up price from the supermarket.

The worst part was, I believed Tristan and the driver. Meaning the milk had vanished. Crates of six different milk varieties couldn't be stolen from our back steps in a matter of minutes. There was no other explanation, unless the driver was in the black market milk trade, which, no.

I found myself checking the back driveway all morning, hoping the crates would turn up again. They didn't. By midmorning I was glad. Imagine if everything reappeared as mysteriously as it'd disappeared. The whole thing freaked me out.

Scared of milk. Honesty, what the fuck? I tried to ignore it and get on with my day.

"Did you hear that?" I asked Tristan as we sat on the steps out by the cursed back driveway having a break before the lunch rush.

He paused in eating a yellow polvoron almost as bright as his fluoro nails. "Hear what?"

"I thought I heard someone talking behind us." I glanced around. No one else was back here.

We sat in silence. A voice wafted on the wind, words indistinguishable and almost breathless.

"There!" I sat up straight, a shiver running down my spine. "What was that?"

Tristan wasn't concerned. He gestured with his pastry to the building in front of us. "Maybe someone in there is talking."

A window was open, but it was too far away. Across the driveway, beyond an overgrown planter box, and up two stories. The voice I heard gave the creepy impression of whispering in my ear.

Was I being fanciful? Maybe it was just a neighbor talking,

but then what about the milk? I deflated, exhausted by the unknown.

"There's been a lot of weirdness around here lately," I said.

My voice wasn't exactly steady, a detail Tristan must have picked up on immediately. He put his polvoron down on a napkin and brushed the crumbs from his hands. "What's up?"

"Everything's screwy. The milk, and the bathroom sink. That power outage last week. The cafe is crumbling. And I keep, um, hearing things. Voices from nowhere. Getting weird feelings."

"It's just bad luck, Owen. Don't stress, nothing's crumbling. I must've screwed up with the milk this morning. Somehow. I dunno. But all this little stuff—you worry about the cafe, I know —but we'll be fine." He put his arm over my shoulder and gave me a little shake.

I leaned into him. "It feels like the cafe is haunted."

I'd only ever admit a silly fear like this to Tristan. He was more than family, had been for a decade and then some.

"You think the cafe is haunted because you've heard strange voices?" Tristan asked.

"Sounds ridiculous, I know."

"Maybe. Or you're worried and projecting?"

I pulled back a little to look at him. "Projecting what?"

"You go through stress cycles, Owen. Don't think I don't notice. Your cafe is doing great. These small setbacks will be okay. It's not going to tank your business. And I know this is more than a business for you. Is it haunted, or are the reasons you created this place heavy at times? You're emotionally attached so it makes sense you're freaking out a little. In the end it's just a cafe, and mysterious sounds or voices are what you're making them."

He was right. My need for Coffee Cat to endure was about more than career goals or money. This dream was fueled by memories. Had I been personifying my problems, wishing the cafe was haunted, because if hauntings were real, maybe other things were too? That thought gave me a twinge.

"I mean, voices coming from someone next door, or like anywhere in a busy cafe, makes way more sense than it being haunted." Tristan gave me a reassuring smile. "The only ghosts are ones you've put here. You know, metaphorically."

"God, I have metaphorical problems now?" I attempted to laugh. Jumping straight to ghosts should have been embarrassing, but Tristan and I had seen each other in all states of dumbassery. This didn't even make the top ten.

Tristan retrieved his polvoron and stood. "I've got a meeting at one. I should get going. Need to put on a professional shirt." The black Coffee Cat T-shirt suited him, but he only worked here part time. Freelance copywriting was Tristan's primary career.

"You good, Owen?" He pulled me up.

"All good."

"Now, if any ghosts give you a hard time—" Tristan gave me a mocking grin.

"I'll be sure to send them your way."

I returned to the kitchen to make tortas for the lunch crowd. I had a kitchen hand on deck today and felt much better for it. No mutterings or ghostly giggles disrupted me. Tristan was right, I was worrying for nothing, and the milk man could piss off.

ARIA WASN'T HOME when I finished work. Part of me expected her to have vanished like the milk. Not magically, because both milk and Aria need to stay within reality, but her up and leaving would be more believable than her staying.

A knock on Aria's door, then a quick peek inside revealed all

her boxes were still in residence. She should be back this
evening.

A thrill of anticipation wound through me, which was
annoying. Was I so pent up I couldn't ignore her physical
appeal?

My dating life dwindled after opening the cafe. I didn't
mind. I wasn't a relationship guy; hook-up apps were all I could
be bothered with these days, and sometimes not even that. So
yeah, it had been a while. No big deal. A longer than usual
stretch of going solo didn't mean I should get the hots for the
first person to cross my threshold.

Except Aria wasn't just anyone and that was a big part of her
appeal. And the problem. I was upset with her but those feelings
didn't seem to stick when I remembered kissing her, how sweet
and damn near magical it felt. She wasn't my first kiss and I
wasn't hers, but it was a first *something*. The first time physical
connection had lined up with deeper longings.

Aria and I hadn't gotten further than kissing back then, but
we were old enough that it'd been hot, frantic, experienced
kissing. Great, now I was thinking about all sorts of intimate
things. Things I'd wanted to do with her then, only we never
had a chance. No way in hell was I going there now, even if
teen memories were making me lusty like I hadn't been in
ages.

Expert at casual though I was, I could not indulge with Aria.

She refused to admit she'd cut me out. No matter what her
parents did, she could have tried to reach out, and there was no
hiding she hadn't. On some level she must have agreed with
them, that I wasn't suitable or worthy of being in her life.

I was mad about her utter rejection, but it was an old, spent
sort of anger that slipped away quickly once I'd walked away
from our unsatisfying reunion. My mom had left before I could
remember her, so in some ways kid me always expected people

to leave, and when Aria did, I got over it. Eventually. I refused to stay hung up on this now.

I bummed around the apartment as memories of Aria flooded my mind. I wasn't waiting around for her, I just didn't feel like doing anything productive. Besides, I couldn't risk her coming home while I doing a work out. Her reaction yesterday was all too satisfying.

Too much good came before the bad to have simple feelings about Aria's reappearance. I wanted to show Aria being back in each other's lives didn't have to be a big deal. It was only a few days. If we could both relax and let shit go, maybe we could be friends again. Or at least be civil, catch up, act like adults.

She'd been my friend first, before my girlfriend, and maybe I'd always valued friends over romantic connection. The return of a best friend was a good thing, a rosier lens through which I could view the present situation than the resurgence of an ex.

Aria shaped my high school years. I wasn't a loner and had other friends, but high school had been about newness and new people. Aria and Luca turned up like these cool alty kids that didn't give a shit. They weren't popular, but they didn't need to be. There was something else about them.

I remember seeing Aria in a worn blazer and jeans, drinking sprite before the first day of school even started. Soda in the morning. Fourteen-year-old me couldn't imagine being so contrary to what I was *supposed* to do, or not do, and then waste that rebellion on something as inconsequential as soda.

Freshman year I had almost all my classes with her. The first day was an exponentially mounting thrill. Every time Aria walked through another door and sat down I felt stupidly lucky. By the last period I said hi, and sat next to her. She said she'd worry I was following her, except I was too much of a goodie, always arriving to class first.

We were paired up for a social studies project in the second week. She immediately invited me over to her house, with a warning; it was borderline creepy, and her parents wouldn't let kids in a bunch of the rooms because they were pretentious, power tripping jerks. As an upside she said they had the newest PlayStation. I couldn't boast anything interesting about my own home, so off we went.

The Belmonte's house was weirder than advertised. It sat up on a hill, set back from the road, hidden in the trees. Nothing like your typical East Bay family residence. Aria, Luca and I took the bus from school, hiked up the hill that was their front yard, and entered what was somewhere between a mansion and a quirky museum.

The Belmontes were rich, I wasn't. Nothing showed that better than a three-story house with seemingly countless rooms. Sometimes I thought familial wealth was the only principle on which Aria's parents judged me, the inherent flaw that kept them from ever tolerating me.

That first visit to the house, I was in awe. Luca drifted off without a word as Aria led me to an attic room filled with bean bags, couches, the largest TV I'd ever seen, and all the gaming consoles. It was the only part of the house that looked close to average. Everything else was antique and oddly foreign, but not in a way I could align with any culture I knew.

Aria and I watched cartoons, her interest in the school report minimal. My default state at that age was constant chatter, a trait Aria encouraged. She showed me how you could look out the attic windows and see into the backyards of the houses down the hill. She liked to make up stories about the people living there full of curses and betrayals and silly imagination. I joined in enthusiastically. When the cartoons and peering out the window got old, we gamed. The Belmontes seemed to have everything that wasn't magic or fantasy related, because *those games were boring*, Aria's words, not mine.

I went to her house every day that week and worked on the project while watching TV and spying on the neighbors. Every day Luca wandered into the attic like clockwork, half distracted by a textbook, and changed the channel to some soapy teen drama. The Belmontes probably had other TVs in the enormous house, but Luca and Aria lived to dissect the show together, and they included me in the ritual without question.

Luca had a huge crush on the lead bad boy, his main motivator in watching the show. I didn't see the appeal and preferred the bookish guy playing someone's hot older brother in college. One day I said so. I'd never told anyone I liked guys before. Their smiles and simple agreement, yes college-boy was indeed hot, was thrilling.

I hadn't thought about it as coming out at the time. But I knew there was a reason I'd told them before anyone else. Eventually I talked about crushes, regardless of gender, and the twins just seemed to get me, with less question than I'd posed for myself. Aria was bisexual too, and I'd thought that was cool. I was grateful now, knowing how lucky it was to have these experiences be freeing. Their magical attic world gave me room to figure myself out and voice it in a way that was never replicated elsewhere.

Aria and I grew into best friends. Luca was always an enigma. He fostered a gothic mystique and didn't talk to anyone at school unless Aria was around. But she and I shared secret fears and stupid jokes, everything, like we were immune to the usual high school drama and gossip. I was sure we'd be like that forever.

If we could get back to even a fraction of what we'd been like back then, it'd be a friendship worth the decade of silence. That closeness and caring, understanding of someone else doesn't just disappear. Milk, sure it vanishes. Not what Aria and I had, it just got buried and forgotten.

6

ARIA

I vacated the apartment for the afternoon and went to the beach. I didn't know what time Owen would get home and I wasn't planning on waiting around to find out. I needed a firm course of action before I talked to him again.

I walked along the hot sand until I found a respectable piece of driftwood to sit on, then buried my pride in the soft white sand along with my toes and called Luca.

"I think you have the wrong number." His face filled my screen, not looking at me but somewhere off to the right.

"Is this a bad time?" I asked.

Given it was a weekday afternoon, Luca was at work. He was busy typing, and while some people might have let me go to voicemail, Luca would never pass up an opportunity to do everything at once. As a Witch-lawyer practicing magical law, my brother was very busy, very successful, and very annoying.

"Good a time as any." His dark eyes flicked to the screen and away again.

Luca's familiar face was a more severe version of mine, but we were unmistakably twins. Same brown skin, same eyes, same tendency to grimace and hide our smiles. He kept his hair shorter, in waves down to his shoulders, while mine was halfway down my back.

"I was wondering when you were going to call, Aria."

"It hasn't been that long." I cringed. For us it was a long time. We used to keep up a constant barrage of texts and late-night calls, telling each other everything. Now we had less and less in common, less and less to say.

"I could've called too." He turned his attention to me fully. "I've been busy."

"You? Busy? No way."

A muscle in his jaw ticked. "There's nothing wrong with having a full schedule. You should try it."

"How about I fill my time by visiting you?"

Luca was thinking about smiling. The lines around his eyes gave him away. "Yeah, great. When abouts?"

"Tomorrow?"

His expression went from pleased to suspicious.

"And by visit I mean, can I stay with you?"

"For how long?"

I pretended to consider. "Oh, however long—"

"I mean obviously that's fine." Luca rubbed his eyes. "Will you tell me what's going on?"

I focused on the magical tattoos adorning his fingers. We had matching ones on our knuckles, but I'd never added to my links to celestial power like Luca had. "Nothing is going on. My job at the magic shop ended." I gave him a brief update that did not include Owen.

"Actually, it'd be a good time for you to come back to the Bay Area." Luca perked up, which was worrying. "My firm's about to open up their internships."

"So? I'm not a lawyer."

"No shit." He rolled his eyes. "They're looking for at least one new, entry level psychic. I might be able to convince them your 'alternative' work history is an asset. You've had experience in the community if nothing else. It's paid of course. A good—"

"Luca—" I interrupted him. "No. You know I don't want to work for the courts narking on people for lying."

"You'd be working for us, not the courts or the Authority. It'd be client interviews, evidence gathering, that sort of thing. You'd be great. You're good with people. There's so much more to your psychic power than you're using."

"Doesn't mean I have to use it," I snapped.

"Oh-kay—" Luca drew out the syllables, clearly trying to stay patient with me. "But you have no job. No money, and no house. It'd be a perfect jump start."

"I don't want the job. I don't want to be given a position because you're my brother when someone else deserves it. Someone who actually wants it. I don't want to snoop around in people's emotions in the name of the law. I don't want to be within spitting distance of a courtroom."

"Okay. *Sorry*. Please continue to read fortunes like the fake, Mortal version of a psychic. Continue to pretend you aren't a Witch."

"I don't do that. I use magic all the time. I broke these sunglasses yesterday. Can't even tell, can you?" I didn't mention needing to look up the simple spell in the grimoire app. Thankfully Witches had embraced the modern age, because my skills were underdeveloped.

My psychic ability was an uncommon, natural gift with very specific and lucrative uses in the Witchy world. Psychics could always see true intentions. We were human lie detectors that couldn't be fooled. It was an ability you could ride all the way to the highest positions in the magical courts, if you were ambitious enough. The fact I chose fortunes, more interested in helping Mortals than catching people out, was deemed a waste, and our parent's biggest disappointment.

Luca sighed, no doubt unimpressed with my sunglass fixing ability. "Aria, I'm only trying to help." He sounded too weary for someone as young as we were.

"Then let me sleep on your couch."

"Well, that's not going to be possible—"

"What? Because I won't take your stupid job? I'll get my own. You can't—"

"*Because* I'm not living in my condo anymore."

"Oh." I deflated. "Why?"

"I sold it. I told you last time we talked. I needed a change."

I shifted uncomfortably on the driftwood, arm complaining about holding the phone aloft. "You never said you were moving."

Being out of touch with Luca sucked. We'd been very twinny growing up. Magic twins were a whole thing, with opportunities for linked power and such. It was never me, it was always us, and no one thing tore us apart. We just drifted, slowly over time. Even after the disaster with Owen, when I changed all my plans and abandoned Luca to take the lawyer path without me, we were solid. Now he'd moved and hadn't told me.

"I'm sure I told you last time we talked, Aria. Looking for a new place is taking a while. I might put an offer on a house in the city. I'm not sure."

"Where are you staying?"

"At our parent's house. The commute isn't bad."

The silence was tense. The bright sun turned cold. My hope died. I would not go home for anything short of the apocalypse, and maybe not even then. I hadn't lived with our parents since high school and my visits were fewer and further between. Our parents were likely to be around for another hundred years, there was no need to spend every second, or indeed every decade together.

"Scratch that visit then," I said.

"Come on Aria, it'll be okay." Luca couldn't say it convincingly and went back to his emailing, or report writing, or whatever he was working on.

"So mom and dad won't have opinions on my failure to hold down a job in a Mortal magic shop?"

"I didn't say that." He wrinkled his nose. "If you took the internship, they'd stay off your back."

"No." I let my arm fall, tipping the phone so Luca had a view of the sky, and stared grumpily at the ocean. "I'll work something out."

"Do you have any other options? You called me after all."

I righted the phone to find Luca looking at me with concern. "I have a place, it's not ideal. I'd rather have been with you."

"You can be. If you change your mind—"

"Yeah, yeah." I waved him off. Like that was happening. "Let me know when you have your own place again."

"I'll send you a link for one I'm looking at. Talk soon." He tapped his screen and disappeared.

Curse the stars, I was stranded with Owen. He was the lesser of two evils when faced with family time, and any forced re-entry to my old life.

While I initially worried being in Owen's presence would land me immediately in magical hot water, no Authority Witches had popped up. I glanced around the beach to check, again. Surely they'd have come by now. Maybe the monitoring spell had lapsed. It'd be so like them not to advertise that.

Whatever the cause of this one stroke of good luck, I was determined to be gone from Owen's apartment before my past mistakes, or the Authority, caught up with me. All I needed was a little more time and a plan.

7

ARIA

I unlocked the apartment door to the sound of laughter. Owen's voice volleyed with someone else's in the kitchen. Not in the mood to meet any of his friends, or have fun, I tried to slink passed.

The tempting aroma of searing spices wafted over me like a snare.

"That you, Aria?" Owen called.

Damn it.

I edged into the kitchen. It was a long narrow space with a table tucked at the far end. The windows were thrown wide, letting in the early evening breeze. A crow cawed outside. Owen stood at the stove while another man busily washed lettuce in the sink.

"Glad you're still here. This is my friend, Tristan." Owen poked the man in the side. "*This* is Aria Belmonte."

Tristan turned to face me; he had sharp eyes and a sharper nose. A shrewd expression cut elegant lines into the soft brown features of his face, which was framed by a tumble of loose black curls. He was taller and slimmer than Owen, and managed to stand in a way that conveyed both contempt for, and challenge to, my presence.

"Hi—yeah, so—enjoy your dinner." I made to duck out.

"Why don't you stay?" Owen turned the sizzling chicken over in the pan. "I got enough for three."

Of course he did. How considerate.

"Thanks. In that case, how can I say no?" I hadn't quite hit a joking tone.

There was an awkward silence as the two men turned back to cooking and I hovered by the fridge. Tristan seemed to know something of me, which wasn't great. He might be here as a deliberate buffer. Like: *help, someone I liked, and now hate, from high school has invaded my home!*

Something brushed against my bare shin. I yelped and only just managed not to lose my balance as a sleek black cat wound its way between my legs.

"Meet Piña. This is her house, I just buy the cat food," Owen said.

"You have a cat?" I shifted my legs away from it. "You never used to like cats."

"I'd never spent much time with one," Owen corrected.

"Piña is *the* coffee cat. You can't not love her." Tristan opened a cupboard, pulled out a bag of coffee and shook it.

The cat crouched, tail twitching as Tristan extracted a single bean. He tossed it to the floor where it skidded to a halt under the table. Piña pounced and swatted at the bean, sending it flying back across the room.

Owen nudged the bean with his toe. "She was here when we moved in. A stray living out back. I didn't have much choice in keeping her, she wouldn't leave."

"Because you were feeding her," Tristan said.

"She looked hungry. I should have thrown her out after she snuck in the cafe and knocked over a whole bowl of pineapple filling," Owen said without conviction. "Don't worry, she hasn't infiltrated the kitchens since we opened. I take health code violations seriously, especially furry ones that lead to ruined empanadas."

Oh, now I was thinking about the sweet empanadas Owen brought to school. The customers were spoiled if he used his dad's recipe in the cafe.

Piña determined the coffee bean defeated and flopped onto her back, twisting her body this way and that.

"Cute," I offered in an attempt to pretend I was entertained.

I wasn't heartless, but I couldn't say I was thrilled about the cat. They could sense magic, and contrary to popular belief, they weren't fans. Cats yowled and hissed when they encountered active magic, generally making a scene and calling attention to Witchy activity.

"Careful," Tristan said in response to my dry tone. "Owen might be criminally nice, but if you don't gel with the cat, you won't be staying."

Tristan definitely didn't like me staying, not that I could fault him.

"Piña and I can cope for a few days." Owen looked adoringly at the cat as she abandoned writhing on the floor to rub up on his legs.

Crap, crap, crap. Now I had to win over cats and protective friends. And Owen.

"About that. Would it be terrible if I stayed longer than a few nights?" A winning smile would have been well played here, but I knew my limits. I went for not-actively-frowning.

Tristan gave me a shameless assessing look. I wanted to glare in return, and felt the expression tug at my facial features as I resisted.

Owen didn't catch our silent exchange as he kept an eye on the cooking food.

"I hit an unexpected snag today," I continued, turning away from Tristan. "I need more time to—uh—get some money together." And find a new place, but one step at a time. Worst case scenario, I'd harass Jenn again. Her girlfriend might kill me, but that could be for the best. I was shaping up to be quite a nuisance.

Owen set out three plates and cutlery, careful not to trip on the cat underfoot. "You can stay as long as you need, Aria. No problem. I'm honestly surprised you're not running away." He smiled exactly like he used to, all dimples and bright eyes. His comment wasn't nasty, though it could have been. Instead he was teasing me.

Playful teasing, not flirty teasing. I didn't want him to be flirty.

I pretended he wasn't sending me spinning down a hopeful path full of longing. "Not until I have a few things in order. Then I'm planning to make a normally paced exit, no running."

"I don't know—" Owen came past me to turn off the stove. He brushed by, not touching but close enough I felt the heat of him. "You might want to run once you realize what I'm like now."

"Uh—" I stood frozen as the two of them dished out the food. I wasn't watching the muscles in Owen's shoulders flex under his T-shirt or wondering *what he was like now,* how different the man might be from the eager, open teenager I'd known. Not at all.

Owen and Tristan sat, and I was forced to join them. "I'll be out of here in a week or so." This was optimistic, but if my plan for cash didn't pan out, I had an only somewhat dodgy back up plan. "Thanks again for letting me stay."

"I made a deal with Jenn. It's really not a problem."

Right, I was a ticket to discounted rent, and Owen was perpetually kind. He'd never go back on a promise to anyone, no matter how small. He wouldn't enjoy having me here. His sweet smiles and attentive eyes were his default, not specific to me. It didn't mean anything.

My two companions ate in amicable silence. Funny how their ease didn't extend to me. I was restless and annoyed they could sit here so casually, enjoying the quiet while I stewed, too aware I was on the outside looking in.

"How'd you and Owen meet?" I asked Tristan when I couldn't take it anymore.

"I found him languishing drunkenly against my dorm room door and took pity on him," Tristan said as Owen let out an exasperated noise.

What did you even say to that? "You two went to college together?" was what I came up with.

I'd planned on coming down here for Mortal college, and simultaneous advanced Witching night school. Instead, I'd discarding the entire career path my parents had set out for me.

"Tristan saved my ass, is what he did." Owen glanced at me, then down at his food. "My dad died and I—wasn't doing well. That particular night I'd decided to get wasted, then get laid. I dunno, to cheer myself up maybe. I don't really remember. It was all stupid and I was spiraling. I went home with Tristan's roommate, but we were both way too drunk for anything, so that ended that. Apparently taking myself home was beyond me and I just laid down in the hall."

Owen pierced a tomato with his fork, eyes down. I was sick with sadness. I had no idea Mr. Sanchez had died.

Owen and his dad were a two-person family that never felt small. I'd been your typical pain in the ass kid with no time for adults, except for Mr. Sanchez. From the moment I met him he talked to me like I was a whole person, not just a kid. Every time I came over he asked me to tell him a story. I never declined and he never seemed to care if it was a recount of my day at school with

Owen, or some nonsense I made up. It was like he figured out I liked to tell stories and fostered that part of me without making it a big deal or a chore. Owen and his dad had a strong relationship I'd been jealous of at first, until they brought me into the fold.

I'd missed Mr. Sanchez, not like I'd missed Owen over the years, but knowing I'd never see him again cut into me and left me shocked. Nothing justified that loss.

I offered my condolences but the words I choked out weren't enough. "I'm so sorry. I should have—" My words fizzled out, feeling inadequate.

Owen looked up at me, guarded and unreadable. "It was a long time ago now. Barely a month after I started classes. I'd have dropped out if not for Tristan."

Tristan blustered. "All I did was guide you across campus and tuck you into your own bed. How was I supposed to know that sort of drunken wandering cements a lifelong bond? I mean, I wasn't going to leave you on the floor."

That wasn't their whole story, no way, but I didn't feel I had any right to ask.

"Your valor was commendable," Owen gave his friend a private smile.

Tristan squirmed in response to Owen's sincere gratitude. I knew the feeling, no matter how distant the memory.

"So uh, Aria, what do you do? Like, I know you're jobless, but what's your thing?" Tristan focused his attention on me.

I was grateful for the jarring subject change. I should have been there for Mr. Sanchez's death, but no amount of talking about it, or apologizing, was going to change the fact I missed supporting Owen in his grief. It was more than a decade too late, and shitty didn't begin to cover how I felt.

For some reason, instead of letting me flounder and suffer in that knowledge, Tristan had reached out and saved me, even though he didn't like me. No wonder he and Owen stuck together.

I cleared my throat and pushed everything down to deal with later. "I'm a psychic. I do palm readings and fortune tellings. The magic shop I worked in closed."

Tristan laughed. "Oh, no. You're serious?"

"I can see it." Owen was bright and open again. His quick recovery from such a heavy subject showed how long ago his loss was. He'd grieved and continued on all in the time we'd been a part. The gulf between us felt enormous. "Aria used to read my palm all the time. Always helped when I was having a bad day."

High school me hadn't minded the excuse to hold Owen's hand, but more than that I liked being able to share any bit of magic I could with him.

As a psychic Witch working with Mortals, I used my real ability to guide my clients. This was somewhat tricky—it was unethical to use psychic ability on anyone without their consent, and illegal depending on what you do with any information you glean. I never read anyone without their knowledge. The Mortals who sought my services could still consent to me using my power on them, even if they don't know its exact form. They believed some form of mysticism is in play during the discussion, and I always told them they were exposing their true selves.

"Aren't fortunes the sort of thing you grow out of?" Tristan stole an olive off the salad on Owen's plate.

"I leaned into it. I'm not going to sit here predicting your exact future, or tell you when and how you'll die, or when you'll find love. I'll guide you to find your own future and help you see what you need to get there." Small, inconsequential kindnesses sold to Mortals for pennies and it'd become my life's work. I pushed some chicken around my plate and contemplated eating it.

"Oh my *god*, it sounds like you believe in it." Tristan was fascinated. And mocking me.

"Lots of people do. Astrology, for example, is very popular. People pay for chart readings all the time."

"So popular you're out of work?" Owen moved a few more olives over to his friend's plate.

I pushed my half-eaten food away. "I'm not out of work. I do readings online." I didn't, but I couldn't stomach them seeing me as a complete failure like everyone else.

It shouldn't matter if Owen and Tristan thought my work was silly; in fact it was better if they did. I wasn't usually defensive. It didn't matter if people were skeptical. What I did wasn't for skeptics. Caring about other's opinions was counterproductive. Why should I start caring now?

"Astrology isn't even a psychic thing," Tristan challenged.

"True. I never said I only had one trick. Both tools work in similar ways. Assisting understanding of people, or yourself."

"Is *this* why you like astrology, Owen? It all makes sense now." Tristan's eyes swept over me, up and down. "Okay. Come one Aria. Try and guess my sign."

"That's not how it works." Owen had gone a tad red in the cheeks.

"No, it's fine." I crossed my arms and stared at Tristan. He made a show of brushing his hair back, blinding me with glaring yellow-green nails.

The Mortal idea of astrology overlapped with actual magic, which is why I lumped it in with my practices. Celestial objects were natural sources of magical power, and asserted minor influences on people. A Witch could enhance their magic by connecting to their stars, draw on their astrological signs, and turn them into powerful conduits. Luca and I didn't have our stars tattooed on our knuckles for aesthetics.

But none of that would help me guess Tristan's sign. I made myself relax. "Do you give me permission to see your inner self?"

Tristan bit back a laugh and agreed. I let my psychic sense out and gave him a gentle once over. I didn't need to know his current emotional state but I got a glimpse of his amusement and suspicion of me. Not suspicion about my abilities, but me as a person in Owen's life. I ignored it and felt for the faint celestial influences tugging at his being.

"You're a Pisces." I could have dug out his moon and rising sign too but that would border on too much. I didn't need them thinking I was actually psychic, as backwards as that was.

"That's right! How about that?" Owen gave Tristan a shove in the shoulder.

He was having fun, so much like we did as kids. I'd forgotten Owen liked being my believer. For the first time in years I thought about the two of us up in the attic playroom at my parents' house. How we'd laid on the floor looking at the stars through the skylight and I'd pointed out constellations before dragging him outside for a better view.

We sat down in the field behind the house and I lost myself in telling the stories of the night sky. Some of it was based in astrology, some of it was from my magic academy lessons framed as legend, some of it I made up. Stories helped me share my magic self with Owen without revealing the truth. Owen reveled in every word. Looking at the night sky was our ritual, he added his own stories to mine and so we created our own world, a little bit magic, a little bit real, and all us. Ours.

The twinge of pleasure brought forth by Owen's reaction as we sat around the table was dangerous. Tempting in a way that had nothing to with his handsome face.

"Lucky guess." Tristan pointed his fork at me, brandishing a leaf of lettuce. "How do I know you didn't see my tattoo?"

"What tattoo?" I looked him over, not see anything immediately.

He held up his right wrist. Two small constellations and a date in Roman numerals looked back at me. A Pisces and a Taurus. I glanced at Owen. He showed me his right wrist and sure enough the two were matching.

"You're right. I saw the tattoo," I lied, rolling my eyes like I didn't care.

I wasn't jealous they were such good friends. That would be disgustingly selfish. I'd never wish for Owen to have gone through the last twelve years without someone strong and constant in his life, especially after his dad's death. I only wished I could have been part of the fray. My own mistakes took that possibility away and I didn't know if I could ever get it back. I'd love a friend like Tristan in my life, but I was never able to make friendships last. I was fine with leaving the rigid Witchy-world behind, but hadn't built the life I longed for amongst Mortals.

Tristan gave me a look like he had me all figured out. "I won't be asking you for lottery numbers."

"I wouldn't give them to you if I had them."

"Now that I'd believe—" Tristan's snark was interrupted by a crashing boom from below.

Owen jumped up. "What was that?"

"The cafe!" Tristan was as worried as Owen. "But like, nothing should be *exploding*!"

They fled the kitchen as the floor rattled. I caught up to them at the front door.

"Wait!" I called. "You're going down there?"

"I'm not going to sit around while my cafe falls to shit." Owen was already hurrying down the stairs, closely followed by Tristan. Never mind that it could be dangerous.

"Why would it be falling to shit?" My question was ignored.

I trailed behind them. What did they expect to find? Commotions like this couldn't be normal. That boom didn't sound like anything minor, let alone something two regular guys should investigate on their own.

If there was actual danger maybe I could—what—save them? With my Witchy powers? Shit, that was a joke. I wasn't Luca, or even half as competent. Even if I was sneaky enough to get away with magic around Mortals, I'd need to look up any appropriate spells on the grimoire app. Using the phone I'd left on the kitchen table.

Owen unlocked the cafe's back door and opened it. "Why does it sound like a rushing river?"

We stepped cautiously inside but saw nothing to explain the noise.

"If it's the bathroom sink again—I *swear*," Tristan grumbled, heading for the closed bathroom door.

Owen flipped on the lights. Nothing in the front of the cafe looked out of place, so I followed him into the kitchen. The gushing sound got louder.

The room was brimming with magic. I almost gasped aloud. Okay, I'd been contemplating the need for heroic magic as a partly-fantasy-mostly-worry thing that wouldn't ever happen. I had in no way expected actual fucking magic to be down here.

"Aw shit," Owen shouted, coming to a stop.

A haphazard pile of crates sat by the back door overflowing with, wait, was it *milk*? I was more concerned with the magic in the room than the mess on the floor but why would *this* be happening? Where was the milk coming from? That many containers didn't make a raging river. Luckily there was a drain in the tile floor so the milk wasn't yet overwhelming us and flooding out the whole cafe.

"How the hell did this get here?" Owen turned to me, a look of confused shock on his face.

"I wouldn't know." My fingers gently clasped his elbow and pulled him back. The milk was almost to his toes.

A soft chuckling sound wound through the air around us. Owen looked over his shoulder and scanned the room.

Tristan hurried into the kitchen. "You've got to be kidding!"

The amount of liquid flowing from the crates and covering the floor had to be magically enhanced. An endless fountain of dairy free alternatives. Where was the magic coming from? There was no one else in the building with us. And I knew Tristan wasn't a Witch, I'd have been able to feel his power.

I reached out with my magic, in a sort of abstract way, to see if I could glean anything else from the mess in the kitchen. I wasn't adept at analyzing active spells, but something was better than nothing. As soon as I made contact with it, whatever it was, it stopped. The magic vanished.

That wasn't normal.

The three of us stood, stunned as the milk slowly stopped flowing and made its way down the drain. I probed the room with my magic and found nothing.

"Someone's messing with us," Tristan said, jarring us all out of bewildered silence.

"That's one way to put it," Owen said as he and Tristan began to clean up the mess simultaneously, working together with practiced ease even in this bizarre scenario.

"It's one hell of a—prank." I edged around the residual milk so I could reach the cartons.

"It's screwed up," Tristan said. "Theft, then this?"

"Was anyone other than us here when the milk was delivered this morning?" Owen peered inside a soy milk container looking like he was unsure of what he'd find, but must have seen nothing. He threw it away.

I helped gather up empty cartons double checking each item I touched for signs of magic. A spelled object shouldn't lose all traces of tampering immediately, I was pretty sure I remembered that much from introductory magical forensics. But everything felt as mundane as it looked.

"Tess came in while I was out back. I think." Tristan tipped a whole crate's contents in the trash.

"She wouldn't do this." Owen was adamant. He also looked close to scared. He shouldn't have been. Right? From his point of view this was just a shitty prank.

"Has something been going on at the cafe?" I looked between the two men.

"No." Tristan shook his head. "Just a bunch of small mishaps."

"This is not a small mishap." Owen gestured around us.

Damn right, and had they forgotten about the loud booming?

"Okay. Yeah. But like, what even is this?" Tristan threw a container aggressively at the trash can. "A fucking joke? A break in? Revenge for—milk related dissatisfaction?"

Owen gave Tristan a pointed look. *What did that mean?*

"No, Owen. Even this is just—I dunno—maybe we need a security camera."

Whatever this was, it was magic. I wondered if Tess could be a Witch. Magic like this didn't pop up out of nowhere. Fuck. I didn't need malicious, completely weird magic against Mortals happening while I was around. I was dubious of the Authority's position on me around Owen as it was. What if they thought I was responsible for this? That was reason enough to run, but I couldn't leave them. Owen and Tristan couldn't deal with a magical milk attack by themselves.

We mopped the floor, took out the trash and gave the

kitchen a once over. I came back from putting the cleaning supplies away to find the two of them muttering.

"Haunting is ridiculous," Tristan whispered. "Nothing reappeared. This is like, vandalism. It's totally explainable."

"How did they get in?" Owen whispered back.

I froze. A haunting. I hadn't considered that. It could explain why the magic fled from me without a trace. It wasn't just magic but something sentient. *Well, that isn't good.*

"Who has keys? Look, I'll call a locksmith for tomorrow. Change everything out. Get cameras." Tristan pulled out his phone and began typing.

Owen stroked his beard looking at the clean tiles where the milk had spilled. How the hell had his mind jumped to a haunting? He couldn't believe in anything like that, not really.

I'd never come across an autonomous paranormal presence before. They weren't really ghosts as such, more like a ball of motivations and desires that moved between planes. Hauntings were rare and way outside my expertise. If you could say I had expertise in anything, beyond finding myself constantly underprepared.

I walked over to Owen. "What other small mishaps have happened?"

He tried to hide his weary expression with a smile. "Oh, bad luck with the plumbing, electrical problems. Tristan's right, it's nothing major."

I didn't need to be psychic to see Owen was holding back. Still, I didn't challenge him. Owen couldn't get any closer to believing in hauntings or magic. If he found out about magic now, with me back in his life, I'd be in trouble for a lot more than breaking my court mandated restrictions. That Owen was this close to belief was a serious complication, and my own damn fault after spending our teen years whispering stories in his ear.

"Okay. If there's anything I can do, let me know." I hoped he could tell I meant it.

Owen reached out and tucked a stray lock of hair into place behind my ear. "Have you improved your cooking skills in the last twelve years?"

"Uh—" My eyes were locked on his. All sorts of distracting, warm feelings pooled inside me. "My cooking skills are about the same. I can still make a killer cup of tea."

We stood very close together. I thought he was about to touch my hair again when he dropped his hand to my shoulder instead. "You're hopeless."

Owen was even better looking up close. The details of his face drew me in. Each line in his forehead, and at the corners of his rich brown eyes, were a part of the man he'd grown into. I wanted to run my hands along his rough cheeks, feel his beard against my skin.

"I'm not hopeless. I was very serious when I said you'd only catch me cooking in an alternate timeline."

"How have you managed to eat all these years without me around?" Owen squeezed my shoulder.

I'd never met a Witch that bothered learning to cook anything involving more than two steps when we had spells for that. Still, home cooking had its own magic. Meals with Owen and his dad were among the greatest of my life.

I barely resisted pulling Owen closer. "Cup of noodles works on the same general concept as tea. Boil water. Pour water."

Owen chuckled, rumbly and unrestrained. He sounded different, yet made me ache with the familiarity.

Tristan cleared his throat.

I jumped back, Owen's hand falling from my shoulder.

He ran his fingers through his hair. "If you'd learned to cook, you could help me in the kitchen. We need a kitchen hand for a few shifts a week, but I can't say cup of noodle skills are up to my standard."

"I have interviews scheduled for that position this weekend." Tristan came to stand directly next to us.

"Oh, good." Owen nodded half-heartedly.

I poked at the counter beside me. "That's for the best. I'd be a liability."

"No more than problematic milk." Owen gave me a smile that didn't quite cover up the worry lining his face.

We left the cafe and trooped back upstairs. I took a moment to ask the cosmos to allow whatever was going to resolve itself, quickly, quietly, and without my involvement. The stars made no answer.

8

OWEN

*W*ork on Saturday was uneventful after the milk break-in of Friday night, not that lack of issues put my mind at ease. The problems at the cafe spun through my mind all day and into the night, everything feeling more and more sinister the longer I lay awake in the dark. I still had no idea what had caused the explosive sounds.

I managed to doze fitfully in the early morning and woke late on Sunday, for the first time in years, still mulling over ways to prevent problems without knowing the cause. Tristan was right, everything was explainable no matter how weird, but the possibility it was something else nagged at me. A puzzle I couldn't solve. A worry I couldn't put to rest.

I showered appallingly late, standing under the hot water yawning and lost in thought. There was a moment during the milk disaster, when laughter ticked my ears like an unwanted flirt, uncomfortable and jarring. It happened as Aria and I watched the flowing mess in the kitchen. If the sound was more than a moment of my own making, she'd have heard it too. Only, she hadn't reacted, so I tried to let it go.

I turned off the water and toweled myself dry. As I tidied up my beard, I noticed a crow land on a branch outside the open window. It cawed at me, making eye contact and cocking its head in that creepy, twitchy way birds do. My overactive imagination told me the look in the bird's eye was not normal. It had opinions, secrets, and devious intentions.

Crows were definitely something I associated with hauntings, but if I were Tristan, I'd put that down to fiction and not look twice. Even Aria wasn't as mysterious as I remembered. The way she talked about fortunes at dinner was grounded, and though I had flashbacks of feeling swept up in fantastical stories as a kid, it was nothing like that now. Maybe it never was as magical as I made it out to be.

The crow cawed. It was just a bird, not doing anything out of the ordinary. There were dozens of the damn things around on a daily basis.

I opened the bathroom door, mind stuck on crows with evil eyes, and collided with Aria.

She squeaked and pushed herself back off my chest, the fleeting pressure of her hands on my skin lingered like a burn. My hold on the towel slipped but I managed to save myself some decency.

"What are you doing here?" Aria went red and directed a look of outrage at me. She wasn't making eye contact but looking somewhere around my midsection.

"I live here." I adjusted the towel, worried it might slip lower.

Aria wore cotton sleep shorts and a T-shirt. Her hair was unbrushed, she was rumpled and had marks from wrinkled sheets on her cheek and arm. "Why aren't you at the cafe?"

"We're closed on Sundays. I can't work every day of the week. You wouldn't be attempting to avoid me, would you?"

She made eye contact, her expression losing its hard edge. "No."

Aria was noticeably absent yesterday, though Tristan said she stopped in the cafe while I was busy in the kitchen. I wasn't disappointed we hadn't crossed paths, it was just nice to see her now.

The ghost of her touch still lingered, maybe she'd run into me with more force than I first thought. Why else would I still be thinking about it?

"You realize living here means we're going to run into each other," I teased.

Aria's eyes skittered down my chest again, almost involuntarily. "I was just surprised."

Teasing her more was tempting. Instead, I stepped out of the bathroom doorway. "Enjoy your shower."

"Sure." She watched me for a second before quickly ducking into the bathroom, her reaction delayed, like she was distracted by me.

I made my way to my room and flopped down on my unmade bed. I found myself smiling, all preoccupation cleared from my mind. Aria couldn't keep her eyes on my face if her life depended on it. I wasn't all that fit, but I did okay. Either way, it'd been too long since anyone looked at me like that.

I closed my eyes and imagined Aria pulling me close. That touch would burn even brighter than the impression she already left. What if I'd let the towel fall—I sat up like a shot. Not a path I should go down, even in my mind. Great, now I was blushing, alone in my room, trying to ignore the perkiness of my cock.

What the fuck was wrong with me? Okay, nothing was wrong with me. That was extreme. Aria was gorgeous, especially when she wasn't sinking all her energy into hiding her every thought, but I needed a clear line and not to cross it. I couldn't seem to help flirting with her and that was fine if she was up for it. I'd always loved drawing out her reactions, the private smiles we shared. Imagine adding intimacy, the things I could draw out of her then.

No, it was best not to.

I made it out of my room eventually. My day was thrashed. Sleeping late and laying around weren't my preferred activities. I brewed coffee, chemex style, ate some toast and went to the living room.

Aria was sitting on the floor, boxes spread around her.

I sat down on the couch with my mug. "I expected you to be out."

"I'm not avoiding you, Owen." Aria didn't look up at me. "I also don't want to intrude. We each had our own things to do yesterday. There's no law saying you have to hang out with roommates."

"Okay." I sipped my coffee, worried I was making this weird. I'd expected us to spend some time together, but she was right.

If Aria felt the weirdness she didn't react. She was busy counting decks of playing cards and black and white plastic magician's wands. She noted something down on her phone.

I regarded her array of items over my mug. "What are you doing?"

"I'm selling the merchandise from the magic shop online. Clara—the owner—gave it to me to try and help with funds. I mean what else was she going to do with it?" Aria set a crystal ball on a navy-blue throw blanket and switched it on. Multicolor lights throbbed faintly. She took a picture with her phone and examined it.

I set my coffee down on the side table. "Do you want a hand?"

"Huh?" She looked up at me.

"I can take pictures too."

"You don't have to. I'm sure you're busy. Have a life, or plans or something."

Aria had never been great at accepting help. Once upon a time I'd been the only one she went to. Thinking we'd get back to that palace was unrealistic, but I could offer this small favor.

"I don't have plans today, and I'm too disoriented from sleeping late to get my morning together." And to be honest, morning was minutes away from being over. I scooched off the couch, sat on the floor opposite Aria and picked up some giant metal rings.

"I've already listed those. Here." Aria pushed a box to me with her foot. "Take pictures and text them to me. I'll do the listings and descriptions."

"I don't have your number."

"Yes you do, it's the same."

I opened the box to avoid looking at her. "I deleted it."

"Oh right. That's—normal. I, um, here—" Aria tapped away on her phone and my pocket buzzed.

"You kept my number and never called?" I opened Aria's text; it was nothing but a crystal ball emoji.

"I keep everyone's number," Aria said in a rush. "I probably still have Sophie M's number from algebra. And Luca's friend Jo. I even kept my parents' numbers to warn me when they're calling."

Aria turned off the crystal ball, put it carefully back in its box and took a picture of that too. When she was done, she looked at me. "Are you going to take pictures and text them to me, or not?"

I got to work, wondering if she really had Sophie M's number or if it was all bullshit to cover her display of sentimentality. Was keeping my number evidence she cared, or hadn't cared enough to need to delete it?

We made good, if silent, progress and soon everything in the boxes was photographed and listed. Aria disappeared down the hall and returned, arms full.

"Oh good, there's more," I said, looking into an open box of books.

"You're free to go." Aria sat next to, rather than across from me and leaned her back against the couch.

"No, I enjoy—" I picked up a book. "*Balloon Animals for Beginners.* Is that even magic?"

"Eh, party magic adjacent." Aria opened her box and groaned. "Wanna trade?"

"No." I leaned in to take a peek.

"You know you want to catalog a box of fairies." She pulled out two balls of tissue paper and unwrapped a couple of small wooden figurines with wings and flower crowns.

"Is every one of those different? That's going to take forever." I recoiled from the box.

"Please, it'll be so much fun." Aria nudged me with her elbow and flashed a grin. It was devious, and deployed with treachery, but stunning all the same. The smile reached her eyes, lighting them with playful promises.

I leaned in. "I don't know. A favor like that, is it worth my while?"

"I'll tempt you." Aria waggled the fairy at me.

"Yes, you do." I hadn't meant to say it, especially in such a low I'm-thinking-naughty-things voice. Aria's reaction was worth it. She looked straight to my lips. Her smile turned soft and natural. I wanted to taste it more than anything.

"At this rate we'll get nothing done," she said as she turned her attention back to the box.

"That doesn't bother me."

"No, you're enjoying spending time with me, aren't you?" Aria challenged.

"Sure. Why deny it?"

"Because after all this time you shouldn't."

"No? Should I be sad and pining? Not over it?"

Aria's smiles were gone. "That's not what I meant. You just don't have to like me after everything."

"Obviously I don't have to. It also doesn't have to be a big deal."

"But it was." Aria looked devastated for half a second before she schooled herself into grumpy indifference.

Our past hurt her too, and I didn't like that. I wanted to wrap her up and whisper comforts, even if I wasn't sure they were true. She'd had the power to shape our history into something better if she'd wanted.

I shrugged, not knowing if the gesture was convincingly casual. "It was a big deal at the time. Past tense. Now we're here, surrounded by all your weird stuff, having fun. What's the problem?"

"Everything. The way you look at me. The way it makes me —" Aria started off her statement stern, but a blush bloomed on her cheeks, and by the end she sounded wistful.

"Yeah? Well, at least I can keep steady eye contact. Unlike you."

Aria's mouth parted in outrage, but her vision slipped down my body. Again, that reaction she couldn't quite control.

"I'm sorry if I've made you uncomfortable," Aria said.

"You haven't." I set my book up and took a few pictures.

"Good." She let her gaze linger.

A slow, lazy grin took hold of my face. I held her stare until she looked away. Down at my arms. It was disgusting how smug that made me.

What were my reasons for resisting this again?

As we worked in silence I was aware of every shift in Aria's movement. She made no effort to maintain distance, and sat close enough we brushed elbows. It shouldn't have been as thrilling as it was, like I was innocent and experiencing mutual attraction for the first time. Which I wasn't. I was pent up and letting it all out with Aria was a seductive thought. A dumb thought, but seductive as hell.

"What are you thinking about?" Aria asked.

Damn. What had my face been doing? "This isn't as bad as I thought."

"Yeah. We're almost done with these boxes."

Not how I meant it, but okay.

I might have panicked when Aria showed up and thought I needed Tristan as a buffer to hide behind, but I was looking forward to spending time with Aria. I knew she was only in my life temporarily this time, and could handle myself accordingly. There was no danger in these flirty feelings when I didn't expect her to stick around.

Aria's phone buzzed. I left her to check her message and got on with the photos.

She pulled on my shirt sleeve. "This is Clara." Aria showed me a picture of an older woman dancing. "She didn't waste much time. Look at that silver fox."

The pair looked like they were having a good time. "You two were friends?"

Aria responded to the text message. "Yeah. Working together might have been the best job I've had."

"How long have you lived in town? I'm surprised we never crossed paths."

Aria set her phone down and unwrapped another fairy. "I'm not. I had a set routine the last three years. It's not like I was going out bar hopping after Jenn, and evidence suggests you don't go to the library. Your life doesn't overlap with most of the people in this town. I'm no different."

"I'm not much of a bar hopper either. Maybe we should go out. Push our boundaries."

"I suppose going out could be fun. Spend time with friends." She made a pinched face, like the idea was complicated. "Clara was the one with the social life. I'm not so inclined."

Well that was me shut down, and honestly, her words came as a surprise. Aria and Luca kept small friend circles in high school, but Aria itched for more. She was social and outgoing, always looking for connections with other kids that somehow never panned out. I didn't know what held her back, or kept Luca from ever socializing with anyone that wasn't part of the night classes the Belmontes made the twins attend. But the way Aria was when she was younger, I'd have thought her adult life would be full of people.

"Not inclined?" I gave her an arched brow. "You were tempted once. Remember how you hunted out parties at the end of school? Determined to get that classic teen experience."

Aria didn't smile at my playful tone. "Yeah well, I was an idiot. I should have listened to you."

She'd schemed for weeks as I tried to feign disinterest. In Aria's mind, we had to get to A Party before graduation. My main priority had been making out any chance we got, but the idea had taken hold of Aria and she wouldn't let it go. That silly mission was our last.

I shouldn't have brought it up. Aria looked defeated by the memory. The party itself hadn't been awful, but the event had turned sour with time. It'd been the end of us and I didn't know why. Maybe that was why I mentioned it. I couldn't help probing for a little more clarity on what happened with us, despite my insistence that our past wasn't a big deal.

Since we were both thinking about it, I pushed on. "What happened that night? Was there something I said—" —*that made you never want to talk to me again?* I couldn't manage the last part out loud. Aria's parents shunning me was one thing, but I couldn't shake the feeling I missed the moment when Aria decided to agree with them.

It had to have been that night.

We showed up at the house of a guy neither of us knew and blended into the crowd. It was all exciting and yet nothing special. Beer and booze, kids we didn't like or talk to. We got drunk, and got silly. Aria was making up stories as usual, but nothing drastic happened. Only one awkward moment when Aria got into it with some of the other kids, talking nonsense and then telling them off for laughing at her, or maybe for laughing at me. I could barely remember what anyone had said, it was so long ago.

Then Aria's dad showed up accompanied by a guy I'd never seen before, both of them dressed in suits and ties like they'd come straight from the office at eleven o'clock at night. They marched Aria away and didn't say anything to anyone else, me included. I didn't see her again until she showed up in my coffee shop.

Aria twirled the wooden fairy in her hand, at last answering me. "It was nothing you said, Owen. My parents sent me off, the party was the last straw. You know how controlling they could be."

"You never gave in before. We always found a way around them. I guess I thought that wouldn't change."

The Belmontes' reaction to our small act of teen rebellion was outrageous, but in line with their personalities. Looking back, Mr. and Mrs. Belmonte were odder than I appreciated at the time. I wouldn't put anything past them. They'd campaigned against my presence in Aria's life as our friendship grew over the years.

It's an uncomfortable thing to know how much someone disliked you, and not have them try to hide it. In the end they must have gotten under Aria's skin. Maybe cutting me out was easier than dealing with whatever was happening amongst the family. It wasn't just me her parents had strong opinions on.

"I shouldn't have given in. I regret it." Aria looked everywhere but at me. "But I couldn't face calling you. I'm sorry I—ignored you. There's nothing more to it than that. I didn't know how to break up with you, so I did it with silence. *Ugh*, that sounds selfish."

I brushed a loose curl back as it fell to hide Aria's face. She looked heartbroken, much more so than I felt in this moment. "We were teens, badly was the only way to do breakups at that age. I won't pretend it was okay, but I'd rather let it go. You've apologized and that's enough."

"Sure, Owen," she said without conviction. After a shared look we turned back to our work.

I'd always wanted a smoking gun I could point to when, in reality, nothing specific had ended us. I'd lived with the idea there was more to the story for so long, it was disorienting to know I'd had the pieces all along, but talking about it now helped. Our end had been nothing more than teenagers unable to figure out how to balance family pressure, and failing to face difficult conversations. I'd processed that years ago, there was nothing new to grieve here. We really could move forward, and even reconnect if we wanted.

"You've lived here since college?" Aria asked after a while. Her manner reluctant like it was when I first joined her in the living room.

I latched onto her question, determined to make up for lost time, get on with seeing if friendship was possible. "Yeah. I had no desire to move home after dad died, and anywhere else felt out of reach. Tristan and I went North those first few college summers. Stayed with his uncle in the city. Living with them made the Bay Area feel like a different place. It helped, but in the end neither of us wanted to live there long term."

"Owen—" Aria took my hand and squeezed it. Then dropped it abruptly.

"It's okay, Aria. But I can't talk about my life here without bringing up my dad. He's the reason I am where I am."

"I'm sorry—"

"Really. You don't have to be. It wasn't your fault he died."

"No, but it's not that simple. I do have something to apologize for," she insisted.

I sighed. "Feeling bad for not being there doesn't do us any good now."

Aria stood up. "Acting like nothing matters doesn't make it true, Owen." She turned and walked away.

I scrambled to follow. "I can't help it if you feel guilty."

Aria turned on me. "Don't worry about my guilt. Stop pretending what happened between us isn't a big deal. Or that my actions didn't affect your life."

"Why? Why can't I, if I want? I was so mad at you, Aria. But I'm over it. Moved on. I don't want to drag the past back up. I'd rather none of it mattered."

"But it did matter. You were so important to me. Don't pretend it was nothing."

"If I was so important, why did it take twelve years and an impossible situation for you to talk to me?"

Aria let out a strangled, frustrated noise. "I can't do this!"

"Yeah? You going to leave? I knew it."

She looked livid. "If you want me out, just say. Don't goad me into going."

"I wasn't." Shit, maybe I was, and *that* wasn't what I wanted. I closed the gap between us. "What are we supposed to do here? Cling to the past? Be upset about this forever?"

Aria sniffed and leaned into me. I folded her into my arms and held her. She was trembling, her breathing erratic. I stroked the back of her head and felt the tension leak out of her until she started to cry.

"I'm such a a-asshole," she blubbered into my neck.

"Uh, why?"

"I was trying to—to—about your dad. Now I'm making it all about me."

"Okay. Not an ideal framing of the situation." I stroked her hair again. "But you only just found out he died. For you it feels fresh. He loved you too, you know. And you're right, you not being there mattered. Everything mattered—our relationship ending the way it did was heartbreaking—but then my whole world disappeared. Can you blame me for trying to cope? I moved on and don't need to relive it. All I wanted was an explanation as to what happened with us. You gave one. Let's call it done."

"I can't blame you for moving on." Aria pulled back and began wiping her face with the sleeves of her T-shirt. "God, I'm the worst. I just couldn't stand us meaning nothing to you. I'm sorry I missed your whole life."

"Not my whole life. Shit, I'm only thirty."

That made her laugh. Good.

I had no interest in guilting Aria for not being there to support me after my dad's death when she didn't know what I was going through. And I didn't want to talk about the worst of what that loss did to me. That part of my life wasn't only about Aria and me, so I didn't feel I had to share it.

Aria's absence was undeniably tied up in my dad's death. She played a part in the loneliest period of my life, but someone more alone than me came along and thought to care. Sometimes that meant so much it hurt, and it had nothing to do with Aria. Tristan saw what eighteen-year-old me needed and he gave it freely. His instinct was to find something worthwhile in me when I was a hopeless, painful mess. He helped me before we even got to know each other. That was what I focused on when I looked back, not ways Aria would have helped, not wishes or what ifs. When you need family you find it, and when it's something you had to make yourself you never let it go.

I'd moved on from Aria's absence, even if I'd questioned it until now. Standing here in the hall, her cheeks streaked with tears, it didn't look like Aria had moved on at all.

9

ARIA

*S*omething woke me up so unbearably early, it wasn't even light yet. As I tried to get back to sleep, sounds of Owen moving around in the room next to me caught my attention. How the hell he managed to function at this time every day, I'd never understand.

A yowling sound pierced the dreadful morning dark. Piña. The hellspawn was probably what woke me. Scratching joined the yowl and I heard Owen open his door. Murmurs hummed through the wall as he soothed the cat.

Piña hissed. Her commotion was unreasonable, not to mention inconsiderate. She was throwing the kind of tantrum magic might inspire, and if it wasn't me—*crap*. I sat up, reached for my phone and brought up the grimoire app.

I had plans to avoid Owen today. Demanding he acknowledge how much I hurt him and continue to feel my absence in his life hadn't been my finest moment, and I'd liked to pretend it never happened. Part of my apology was motivated in nursing my own hurts about what I'd done, and failed to do for him. It was selfish, but I didn't know how to separate my crap from the need to apologize just for him.

I had to accept that Owen didn't need my apology as much as I'd expected. He'd gotten on without me, and if he didn't want the past to be a big deal, I had to let him take that view.

The cat yowled again. I threw the warm covers back and was blasted by an uncommon chill. The wood under my bare feet was unexpectedly cool. The weather was typical of summer, but suddenly it felt like winter.

I opened my door and was greeted by the faint tingle of active magic. Owen was holding an agitated Piña, wearing nothing but boxer briefs. Cosmos save me. Was the man never dressed?

"Sorry, did we wake you?" The cat leapt from his arms and took off toward the living room. Gooseflesh covered Owen's entire body, and for once I wasn't looking out of poor self-control.

"Are you cold?" I asked.

"Fucking freezing, right?" Owen reached one glorious, tattooed arm across his chest and grabbed his other glorious, tattooed arm.

I turned away and crept down the hall. "Is the air conditioning on?"

"Shouldn't be. I never use it up here. Only in the cafe."

We went to check out the thermostat in the kitchen. The air conditioning was off, but Owen poked at the buttons anyway.

So the cold was definitely magic, but how and why? I took half a step back from Owen so I could swipe the grimoire app without him seeing what I was doing. I searched *haunting* and *cold*. Results were plentiful. I didn't have time to trawl through scores of possibilities. I added *banish* and *dispel* to my search and tried again.

I looked up at Owen while the app took a moment to filter. He had tattoos on his back I hadn't seen before. His last name was written across his shoulder blades in the obligatory font for those sorts of tattoos. It was oddly comforting seeing the name Sanchez surrounded by lush floral designs.

"This thing must be broken." Owen turned away from the thermostat. "No way is it above seventy degrees in here."

"Why don't you go shower. Get ready for work and I'll—um—see what I can do?"

Owen looked surprised at the offer. "Okay. Thanks."

I scrolled the app once he was gone. Every result recommended a seance to deal with a haunting. Solutions ranged from contacting the presence for an exchange of intentions, to complex banishment magic. It was all interactive spell work, also known as a guaranteed failure in my unpracticed hands.

Even if my ability was up to the challenge, I didn't want to have an exchange of intentions with a sentient paranormal presence from beyond this plane. Instead, I looked up a diagnostic spell. It was a start, assuming the more information I had on the haunting, the closer I'd get to making it go away.

Casting a diagnostic would tell me exactly what the haunting was doing with its magic. Making the room cold was more likely a symptom than the purpose of our incorporeal intruder. In theory a diagnostic was an easier, roundabout way of discovering intent, but it was still an interactive spell, not a simple cause and effect like summoning. I didn't have any experience in reading interactive results, so I hoped it'd be intuitive.

Relative subtlety was another point in this spell's favor when seances required a range of materials beyond the basic elements. I slept with my crystal rings on, and almost never took them off, so I had everything I needed.

I glanced around the living room where the cat was pacing back and forth. I kneeled down, away from her, and placed my palms to the floor. The app said I needed to touch the affected object, which I figured was the building. I read out the incantation and felt my rings activate as they focused the power flowing through me.

Nothing happened.

In case I'd done it wrong, I tried again, concentrating hard. Saying nothing happened wasn't quite right, I could feel my magic linking with something. Only the interaction didn't mean anything to me. It only gave me an uneasy, jittery feeling.

I gave it one more shot, opting for as much power as I could manage on my own. I added the words for calling on my birth signs to the incantation. Piña came up to me and hissed. The tattoos on my knuckles tingled and burned white hot. Damn, I hadn't used my stars like this in a long time. Sweat broke out on my forehead, but the intensity didn't bring any more clarity.

I let my magic ebb away and picked up my phone. Maybe I needed a revealing spell? I didn't particularly want the paranormal presence revealed, not knowing what form it would take, but I was running out of options.

As I muttered the revealing incantation the temperature dropped sharply. Piña did a little cat scream and jumped at nothing. Cool. Fine. No need to panic. I was only making things worse.

Out of ideas, I reached out with my magic like I'd done in the cafe with the milk. Just like before, the magic vanished. The temperature shot back up to normal and Piña looked around, confused.

I mean it worked, so win? But I didn't see why the haunting was so opposed to a faint touch.

Things would be normal when Owen got out of the shower, so I'd take it. Worst case scenario, I could reach out and poke the haunting with my magic every time it popped up.

Too bad I wouldn't always be around to cast makeshift defensive magic. I needed a more permanent solution.

I collected my phone and went back to bed, intending to rise again with the sun. I had more Mortal magic shop items to list, but it looked like my day was going to be spent researching seances, keeping an eye on the cafe and trying to solve this before Owen noticed magic in an irreversible way.

I ACCIDENTALLY SLEPT PAST NOON. So much for keeping an eye on the cafe in the morning.

When I arrived at Coffee Cat it was busy with lunch-goers. Owen was nowhere to be seen, neither was Tristan. Tess, whom I'd encountered during my snooping the other day, was running the espresso machine. She wasn't a Witch, and neither was the guy working the register.

There were no Witches in the cafe other than me. Not surprising, since a haunting didn't necessarily mean a Witch was involved, but I wasn't ruling anything out.

I ordered a cold brew and a crisp puff pastry oreja and set up at a table by the window for a day of skulking and keeping an eye out for magic. The cold issue from this morning was still solved going by the cafe's temperature. Everything was normal, the atmosphere inviting and distinctly not-haunty. I wasn't mad at it, but pleasant normalness wasn't helping me solve any problems.

I killed time reading up on seances. The forum section of the app was unusually disappointing. The discussions were often full of tips, tricks and things to watch out for, making the grimoire app so much more than a spell book. It was a vital feature for Witches like me, who weren't in a coven or at the top of their game. No one had posted with tags to seances or banishing sentient paranormal activity in more than a year, and all the old posts were theoretical discussions.

Rare magical problems were the very worst kind.

I looked up from a deep dive into haunting history I wish I hadn't taken, to find a crow staring at me through the window. I stared back. It cocked its head, cawed, and hopped closer. Several more landed on the sidewalk behind it, as the first crow eyed me, standing almost unnaturally still. I turned away for a few minutes, focusing on my phone, and looked back. The crow hadn't moved, but its entourage had doubled.

It wasn't entirely normal, but also not outrageous or beyond the realms of usual crow behavior. Encountering a group of bewitched crows was as rare as a haunting, and I'd normally not have thought twice about the birds. For an enchantment on an animal to override free will, and make it do someone else's bidding, it had to be very powerful, and a haunting didn't necessarily affect animals. Maybe I was paranoid, but I had to check.

I let my magic brush up against the bird, who was still staring me down, giving me some serious attitude. Yep, it was an enchanted crow, as were its fellows.

This magic didn't recoil like the haunting. It gave me a little jolt, like it was pushing back. Outside more crows landed and began to caw, closing in on the window like reinforcements following their beady eyed leader.

I felt a wave of panic. Not because the crows scared me, but because their behavior was odd enough to draw attention. Mortals didn't need to wonder why the birds were acting weird. No one needed to entertain the idea of magic around me, least of all groups of Mortals. Not when the Authority had already deemed me irresponsible. This was the sort of thing I had to keep from happening for fear I'd be blamed if anything went wrong.

"Shoo—go away," I whispered at the birds through the window. I poked at them more forcefully with my magic and they scattered, taking flight noisily.

"Talking to yourself?" asked a familiar voice.

I turned to see Tristan smirking down at me. He wore a bright, flatteringly fitted dress shirt today, and was carrying a folder and a laptop, so not likely here to work the cafe's register.

"No, I was talking to the birds," I said with dignity.

"Right. Because that's better."

To my horror Tristan sat down opposite me and placed his things on the table. He leaned back and stretched his long legs out lazily, glancing out the window. "Damn, that's a lot of crows, though. Right?"

The number of birds seemed to be growing exponentially. At least they were across the street, darkening the branches of the jacaranda tree, and not congregating on the sidewalk.

"I dunno, what constitutes a lot?" I tried to act natural as a dozen more birds landed.

"Enough that it has you thinking *shit, that's too many birds.*"

"Uh-huh." Desperate to get Tristan's eyes off the crows, I changed the subject. "What's with all the papers?"

Tristan turned back to me. "Resumes. I'm doing the hiring for our new kitchen staff this afternoon."

"Everything's good with the cafe?"

"Yeah. Perfect. Why?" He narrowed his eyes at me.

"No reason. You guys have done such a great job here. It's a lovely place."

"Thanks. I mean it's Owen's cafe. I just help out."

I doubted Owen saw it that way but wasn't going to comment. Movement outside flickered at the edges of my vision. I ignored it, keeping eye contact with Tristan. If I didn't look, neither would he.

Tristan seemed to take my keen attention for an invitation. "So how's it going with Owen?"

"What do you mean?"

"The reunion. Are you two hashing at all out?"

I shifted in my seat, angling away from the window. "Um—"

"Owen talked a lot about you when I first met him. I imagine there's a lot to work through."

"Why are you asking me?" Shouldn't he be interrogating Owen and ignoring me?

"I'm nosey," Tristan said, unashamed. "And wondering what you're trying to get out of all this. You must really be in a tight spot if you're here after avoiding Owen for so long."

I experienced a wave of sadness and wished everything were different. I wanted to explain myself in a meaningful way and couldn't. That was why I was so upset yesterday. Owen making peace with a half-baked version of our past felt disorienting and lonely.

"Sorry," Tristan said when I didn't respond. "I didn't mean to poke at you for having nowhere to go. That was shitty."

"It's fine." I crushed some crumbs on my plate. "Owen's handling the unexpected reunion better than I am."

Tristan considered me with empathetic eyes. "You're not as happy to see him?"

"It's complicated." I bordered on sounding miserable. I had a feeling Tristan would be a good person to talk to if I could. I wanted to try, but not if most of what came out of my mouth was a lie. I was sick of halfhearted connections and holding back.

"Complicated? You don't say. I'm not looking for drama, so please, ignore me. There's no need to explain." Tristan leaned his elbow on the table, cupping his chin in his hand, and gave me an exaggerated look of interest, at odds with his words.

I appreciated his playfulness and tact in taking the conversation back to a light place. It gave me an out.

"I'm pretty sure drama is the reason you sat down," I said, managing to match his light manner. "Go on. Do your protective friend thing, because I'm sure that's the other reason you're here. I don't mind."

"Well, that's no fun." Tristan was all eyebrows and looking

down his nose at me, apparently trying to be stern while his lips twitched as he tried not to smile. "I'm supposed to threaten to make your life hell if you hurt him, and you're supposed to live in fear of my wrath."

A laugh startled out of me and Tristan smiled. "I'm glad Owen met you."

"Same." Tristan stood and collected his work things. "I'll see you around, Aria."

THAT NIGHT I DID A SEANCE. After the thing with the birds, I couldn't delay. While Mortals have a great capacity for framing magic in explainable ways, reckless magic can be shocking enough that even the most hardened skeptic sees the truth.

Seeing as I'd discovered the haunting, I bore some responsibility for keeping the resulting magic hidden. I could look after the problem myself or alert the Authority, so they could come in and deal with it. Anything less would be negligent, and a punishable offence if any Mortals came to harm. But I couldn't tell the Authority where I was, that would ruin the lucky break of no one noticing I was ignoring my court conditions. If I called I was in guaranteed trouble. Covering up magic's existence on my own meant I could still sneak away in the end, bureaucratic Witches none the wiser.

I waited until Owen went to sleep, which wasn't hard because the man went to bed appallingly early. Tristan's plan for security cameras was taking time to execute, so the logistics of this B&E were straightforward. All I had to do was grab the cafe key from the peg in the kitchen, sneak past Piña and let myself into Coffee Cat through the interior back door.

I left the lights off and had a quick look around. In the dark, the colorful walls were muted. Long shadows cast by the street-light outside stretched across the floor. The ever-present smell of coffee tickled my nose, but I couldn't sense the tell-tale tingle of magic as I crept into the kitchen and set my bag on the counter-top. Everything was peaceful and as it should be.

Seances were complex even in their simplest form and after a day of research I wasn't brimming with confidence. I pulled a candle out of my bag and set it on the counter, then reconsidered and moved it to the floor. I pulled up the app and checked the set-up guide, feeling like a child. It had been years since I'd delved into magic beyond my familiarity.

Magical ability was a hereditary trait some people were born with that allowed them to connect to mystical forces, and interact with the world beyond what physical senses allowed. Some Witches were born with affinities to certain elements and if they were strong enough you could be gifted with rare abilities, like my psychic sense, which came from a strong air affinity.

A spell to call forth a paranormal presence from another plain of existence required the use of all four magical elements. Fire, earth, air and water. At least two elements were required for all spell casting, most commonly air and earth, or incantations and conduits like crystals. There were rare Witches who had such a strong air affinity they didn't need external elements to harness their magic, and could cast on words or thought alone. These people were more legend than anything, not something I'd ever encountered. There was only one such Witch alive today and I didn't fancy meeting him.

I definitely needed all my external elements if I was going to pull this off. I had my candle for fire. To bring about new beginnings, or you know, call forth sentient paranormal presences into the physical realm. My air element, as always, would be the words of the spell, brought to me courtesy of the grimoire app. For earth I had my crystal rings, and a sizable quartz, which I set on the floor to the right of the candle.

Next I needed water. I glanced around the tidy kitchen. A shelf above the counter held a myriad of metal bowls and plastic containers. I stood on tiptoe and reached for a bowl. I didn't realize it housed several, smaller bowls, and when I tipped it toward me, they slipped out and went crashing everywhere.

I froze, clutching the large bowl to my chest. Crap, that better not have been loud enough to wake Owen upstairs. I cautiously picked up the little metal bowls and returned them to the shelf.

After a few cautious moments in which Owen didn't barge in, I filled my bowl with water from the sink and set it to the left of the candle. The water's purpose in the spell was receptivity, giving the entity summoned the opportunity to appear reflected in the water. It wasn't the afterlife I was calling, you couldn't actually commune with the dead, and anything flitting between this plane and the other wasn't human.

I figured since this particular paranormal pain in the ass was popping back and forth all the time, they wouldn't have any trouble occupying the room in some form, but water was here to lead the way.

I sat on the floor in front of my items, crossed my legs, and balanced the phone on my knee. I lit the candle with a flick of my ring clad fingers, the only spell I could regularly pull off without speaking aloud.

It was show time.

What would I do with the entity I brought forth? I wasn't one hundred percent sure, but I'd chosen a seance geared toward questioning intent, finding resolution and a path to release. So fingers crossed, my spooky friend would appear, convey a sense of why they were wreaking havoc on the cafe, and be reassured and prompted to move on and not come back around.

Hopefully.

And if not, I'd try begging.

The incantation took the form of a melodic chant. As I

spoke, I could undoubtedly feel my magic at work. The three elements in front of me came alive at my words and released their essences as requested. The air became tangy, tingly with power, the heat of the candle a beacon with depth that transcended the physical world, while the crystal kept me grounded.

Trying to connect with something not entirely of this world unmoored me. But nothing else happened. I could feel the magic within me conversing with an abstract plane of existence, but I was left hanging, floating and yearning. No one answered my call.

Eventually I stopped and checked the spell. True, it was the most basic seance on the app, but I could only work within my means. Maybe I wasn't using enough power? The entity I'd been contending with was no small magic. Maybe I wasn't up to going head-to-head with whatever it was. I wasn't the most impressive Witch, maybe it didn't deign to answer my call.

Typical. Magic was so up itself sometimes. Pretentiousness was a quality I couldn't stand. It pissed me off to no end, especially when it was Witchy. Of course some *important, powerful* entity from another plane would ignore my pitiful call. It could probably tell I never went to college. Why would it bother with the likes of me? The judgmental prick.

But I had more power than I'd used, and now I was pissed off at being slighted. Maybe I was projecting my own issues, but fuck it, and fuck paranormal things that thought they were too good for me. I had my stars to call on.

My astrological tattoos were inked when I was sixteen, in a ceremony with Luca. Most Witches don't connect with their stars in this way because the ritual involves rebirth magic. It was an ordeal and a half, but at the time I was still excited about my powers. I felt lucky to have the opportunity to connect to something beyond the four elements, and I'd never have let Luca down. Being twins gave the two of us the rare ability to link our magic together, and to our stars. We were half drowned in the ritual and then tattooed with a substance that wasn't ink, but the power it unlocked was undeniable.

The symbols on my knuckles were my only magical tattoos, everything else was Mortal and esthetic only. In all honesty I hadn't been brave enough to get more magical ink. Of course Luca had; the backs of his hands pictured pure power.

The next opportunity for twin-tattoo-magic-linking-nonsense came when we were thirty-three. I wasn't looking forward to it, but would be there for Luca.

For now, I could use my well-earned link to the stars to increase the potency of this seance. I tried again, adding the words of my stars to the chant. The process was painful, as the tattoos always were when used. Star power burned, it was part of the sacrifice for harnessing such things.

The result was woefully the same. Exhausted, I had to accept this magic was beyond me, or I was being snubbed. Unfortunately, I didn't know any way to get rid of a haunting without first communing with it.

The only remaining course of action was to call Luca. If we tried together, power and skill wouldn't be a problem. He might even be able to help me do one of the more complex seances. It was infuriating to have the only possible solution involve other people. It meant explaining myself, and admitting my failure.

I blew out the candle, stowed the crystal in my bag, and dumped the water.

A clicking sound came from out in the cafe. I abandoned the bowl in the sink and quickly grabbed the candle from the floor. A door opened and shut. *Shit.* I looked around and lunged for the walk-in fridge. Anywhere to hide. I had my hand on the handle when my candle flickered back to life.

The small flame wasn't my doing.

"Aria?"

I turned to see Owen in the doorway to the kitchen. He turned on the light and I shut my eyes with a wince.

"What are you doing down here?" He wasn't amused, there was a sharpness to his tone I wasn't used to.

I blinked away the bright lights. "I was just—um—looking for conchas?"

Owen scowled. "By candlelight?"

I blew out the candle as if that would help hide it. "Yes? Didn't want to turn on the light."

"You stole my key and came down here to raid the kitchen?"

"I'm sorry. I don't know why—"

Owen looked around the kitchen, scrutinizing everything. "We sell out of pan dulce most days. You won't find anything that doesn't need to be baked before you can eat it. You can't be down here while the cafe is closed. Living with me doesn't mean—"

"I know. I don't know what I was thinking."

The candle clutched in my hand flickered back to life for a second time. Owen's eyes snapped to the dancing flame. I didn't think and reflexively blew it out again. I met his eyes, afraid he could see my guilty panic.

Owen looked from me to the candle and back a few times. "How did it do that?"

"I—I don't know," I said with confidence because it wasn't an outright lie. While it was probably our haunt, I didn't know for sure.

"Candles don't just light by themselves, Aria."

"I must not have blown it out properly."

A sweat broke out on the back of my neck as an old anxiety swept through me. Owen was watching me too closely, his eyes too sharp and calculating. I could practically hear his mind spinning.

"I think this place is haunted," he whispered.

"That doesn't sound probable." *Not a lie, hauntings were improbable as fuck.*

Owen looked at me unblinking and way too serious for a Mortal talking about the paranormal. "Do you still believe?"

"In—?" My voice was a waspy breath. I prayed the candle wouldn't come back on, I was scared to death of what we were standing on the edge of.

Owen deflated, calling attention to how tense he'd been. His suspicion gave way to weary disappointment. "In high school, all that stuff you believed in. Your stories. The stars. Fortunes. Forces. Do you still believe?"

My heart pounded. "No. Not like I did. I believe in manifesting, power of the mind and all that." I waved my hand in a jerky shewing gesture. "I don't believe in things that aren't possible."

Owen looked at the candle again. "Come back upstairs." He stepped out of the doorway and gestured for me to walk out in front of him.

I hurried past.

"Piña woke me," Owen said as we climbed the stairs back to the apartment. "She was throwing a fit. Then I noticed the key was gone."

"Sorry. I was being selfish and stupid."

"Just don't do it again." Owen held out his hand for the key. He didn't return it to the peg in the kitchen. "You really don't think anything weird is going on? I'm silly for wondering about hauntings?"

"You're not silly, but nothing's haunted."

The look of disappointment on Owen's face hurt to look at. I shouldn't care. This was good. My Witchly duty. He needed to believe my lies.

We parted ways in the hall, neither of us saying goodnight.

10

OWEN

*T*he next morning I found a note from Aria in the apartment kitchen.

Sorry, I'm an idiot.

It shouldn't have made me smile. There was no excuse for Aria breaking into the cafe. She'd never been overly concerned with rules when we were young, but we were adults. There were boundaries. Could she be so oblivious as to think sneaking around the cafe was okay?

Aria's motivations distracted me as I baked the day's batch of pan dulce. I wasn't alone, my remaining kitchen hand Jason was here to take the pressure off, and I tried to settle back into my usual routine of enjoying the early morning, sweet smells, music, and the quiet yet busy time in the cafe before we opened.

But I couldn't get Aria out of my mind. She frustrated me in too many ways. I felt stupid now for bringing up hauntings. She said I wasn't silly, but come on. I'd been tired and confused and shouldn't have said anything. Of course she didn't believe in that crap anymore.

The morning dragged until the bulk of the baking was done. I had some admin tasks to tackle while Jason and the other staff handled the breakfast torta orders and the rush on coffee, so I retreated to my tiny office. I set a fresh concha on my cluttered desk to give to Aria later. It was a perfect chocolate and vanilla one, with the iconic crackled crust blending brown and white.

There was a note on my keyboard from Tristan saying he'd emailed the contract to our new hire. He'd also sent me security camera packages to read through. I wished he'd let me make him an official partner in Coffee Cat, but I understood Tristan wanted to pursue copywriting as his main career. He managed to do so much for the cafe, all while building a successful freelance business.

Tristan said we shouldn't mix family and business and that was why he didn't want a share in the cafe. He didn't have any more family than I did, we were both only children without parents, though for different reasons. Our relationship was the most important thing to me, and if he didn't want money and business mixed in more than it was, I wasn't going to push it.

After that drunken night twelve years ago, Tristan continued to show up for me. He became my best friend when I thought I'd never have anyone again. He led me out of a destructive phase and carried me through the things I couldn't manage on my own. He even helped me sort out my dad's affairs. We sold my dad's house the summer after freshman year and I came away with an uncomfortable amount of money. It was funny, the Belmontes acted like my dad and I had nothing, when by usual standards we did well. Not mansion well, but a two-bedroom handed down from my grandparents and a life of careful savings was far from zero.

By the time the sale went through my poor decision making had corrected. I knew better than to blow through the money and had tucked it away. That was where the funds to start Coffee Cat had come from. The whole cafe was a labor of love dedicated to my dad, using his recipes to create the menu, bringing love through food to friends and strangers to create community.

Making Tristan a partner wasn't about repaying his kindnesses. I'd done that in more meaningful ways, but I never wanted to pass up an opportunity to show gratitude, or acknowledge his strengths and the amount of work he put into everything we'd created together. This cafe was as much an ode to us as it was my father.

When I was a kid I never imagined I'd be a baker. My plan took shape slowly over the years, as did Tristan's own plan to pursue writing. Through all of our phases, the future was always us. I could rely on Tristan, I knew he'd stay in my life even if no one else would. He pushed me to pursue my culinary talent when I'd only seen it as a hobby. Coffee Cat was a cafe for Tristan to write in while I baked. It was all the good things from my life in one.

Tristan's resistance to shareholding in the cafe came, in part, from me paying off his student loan debt with a portion of my dad's estate back when we graduated. You took care of family. To me it was as simple as that. Dad's death gave the two of us this crazy gift to lead into life ahead of anything we'd dreamed. After that, Tristan squirmed at the thought of taking anything else from me. I never could convince him it wasn't taking when we built this all together, but I respected his need for a bit of distance from the cafe and for something separate and all his own.

Sometimes it felt like all aspects of my life were overwhelmingly caught up in Coffee Cat. This place was loss, and the light that came out the other side. It was every gesture my dad or Tristan made for me, and everything I tried to do for them in return. The life I had now wasn't something I'd ever trade another day with my dad for, but it wasn't a place I'd have ended up without his death. That's why I kept going back to hauntings and superstition. I felt my dad all over this cafe even though he'd never seen it. I didn't believe in God or an afterlife, but part of me clung to the fantastical stories of my childhood, like the magic world Aria and I created was real.

The cafe wasn't haunted but part of me wished it could be, in a way that connected me to my dad. It was a wish so desperate I searched for him in anything, in every little disaster that plagued me. I was unable to discount hope. It was like I was still looking for his help, knowing he'd always be there for me.

But he wasn't here. I knew that.

With a sigh, I got back to work. I turned to the notes on security Tristan left, picked the option he'd labeled as the best value, and settled myself into looking at the cafe's accounts. I was weighing up the cost benefit of switching to a newly established local roasting company for our beans when a knock on the office door startled me.

Olive, a college student who'd worked for me for the last six months, poked her head in. "Sorry to disturb, but we have a situation."

"What does that mean?"

"Something is up with the polvorones."

I looked at her blankly, my mind still on numbers. Olive blushed and looked away.

"Sorry," she said to the doorframe. "It's just they taste off today. A customer came back and wanted a refund."

What the? I'd tasted the batch this morning, and it was the same as always. Perfect.

I stood and followed Olive to the front of the cafe where my other employees, Jax and Carlos, were looking after the register and coffees. There was a box of polvorones off to the side, a piece broken off each one like they'd been tested. I grabbed a pink polvoron out of the display cupboard and took a bite. It was bitter in a way that made no sense.

Not wanting to spit out my own food in view of customers, I quickly swallowed the bite and pulled the rest of the polvorones from the display.

The change in flavor was baffling. The batch tasted fine before. At the risk of being cocky, the polvorones were always better than fine. External sources had called them excellent.

I grabbed one of each of the other pastries and took them all back into the kitchen, thanking Olive for alerting me. I tasted each variety. Everything else was okay, so I tried another polvoron to be sure, and spit it in the trash. One of the ingredients must be off, baking should never taste like rotten lemon juice, or bad milk.

I meticulously checked all the ingredients in the kitchen. I didn't find anything out of order. Nothing neared expiration when I baked consistent quantities each day and had our supply schedule down pat. We had a stellar health rating.

I experienced a chill of unease but knew better than to let my mind go down that path. I was distracted this morning and had screwed up somehow. Nothing mysterious about that.

The polvorones went in the trash. A pretty rainbow of wasted effort.

Even if there was an explanation for the bad batch, which of course there was, I couldn't afford to have things like this crop up. Our appointment with MyFavoriteEats was approaching. If Cindy ate these polvorones, we could count the good publicity goodbye. Even the word of the customer who had to come get a refund could set us back.

As I made my way back to the office, I felt an uncommonly cold draft. The AC was really working today. All we needed was to take the sweltering edge off, not plunge our customers into the arctic. I checked the thermostat and found it set to the correct temperature.

"Oh no, oh no. No!" A muffled voice from the bathroom

stopped me from reaching the half-finished accounting. I rapped on the door.

"Yeah, come in!" Carlos called.

I found him staring desperately at the overflowing sink. He'd managed to stay dry, unlike Tristan, but he looked panicked.

"I swear it wasn't me."

I pushed past him and tried the tap. "This happened the other day. Don't worry. I'll fix it."

Carlos dithered, making an unconvincing offer of help, before going back out front. Despite telling him I had this under control, I couldn't for the life of me get the water to stop. The drain must be clogged, in addition to the unstoppable steam raging from the tap, for the sink to be overflowing this aggressively. Questions like *how* and *why* were only unnecessary distractions until I stopped the water. I was trying to turn everything off at the wall when Carlos came rushing back.

"Sink in the kitchen isn't looking great, boss."

I groaned and heaved off the floor, soaking wet. "Call a plumber. I don't know what's going on."

"Which plumber? Do you have a number?"

I was about to say *any plumber* when Aria appeared behind Carlos.

"I'll call someone." She was already scrolling on her phone.

"Where did you come from?" Unexplained relief rushed through me.

Aria nudged past me, closer to the sink. "I was here having a coffee and saw your staff in a panic."

"You don't have to—"

"Go see about the kitchen," she ordered, pressing the phone to her ear.

I hurried to the kitchen, Carlos in tow. It wasn't so bad in here with the huge sink taking longer to overflow and drain in the floor, but it was still a mess. Jason had stopped all torta preparation under the water onslaught and tried in vain to help me put things right.

Aria came rushing into the kitchen. "I got the bathroom fixed."

"What?"

"Don't look so shocked, Owen. I called a plumber and they told me what to do. Here, move." She pushed me away from the sink and crawled underneath. "Why don't you all go double check the bathroom and the piping to the coffee machine?"

That was a good idea. Jason, Carlos and I left her to it.

Nothing at the front of the cafe was amiss, and by the time we got back to the kitchen that too was back to normal. I immediately started mopping up the remaining water so no one tripped, and Jason got back to the food.

"Was the sink blocked?" I asked Aria.

She looked almost confused for a second. "Oh, no. Once the water stopped it started draining."

"Does the plumber need to come look? I can't have this happening again."

"I didn't think to ask." For someone who solved my problems, Aria didn't appear to have thought about the situation much.

"I should call them back. Or call Jenn. Something is up with this building at the moment." I extracted my phone from my pocket and unlocked it.

"I'll call Jenn." Aria reached out and covered my phone, touching my hand in the process.

"Why?" My tone was harsher than I'd meant it to be.

Aria snatched her hand away. "I'm trying to help."

"You don't need to. This isn't your problem."

"I know. That doesn't mean I can't help. I should call Jenn anyway, say thanks. I might not be able to cook, but I can do something useful while I'm around."

"That's really not necessary." I ushered Aria out of the kitchen so we wouldn't be in Jason's way.

"Owen, you don't have to do everything. I can do you a small favor."

I showed Aria to my office and shut the door behind us. "I don't do everything. I have a whole team here."

"Why is this bothering you so much?"

"It's not. Don't you have your own stuff to worry about? Do you have all your stuff listed online yet? Made any sales?"

"No. I'm getting there. No one wanted to buy that shit in the shop, it'll be a miracle if it turns into something now." Aria glowered at me, clearly not happy I'd brought this back around to her.

"I don't want to add to your stress."

"You're not. You don't need to worry about me. Let someone else help you out for once."

"Fine. Here." I grabbed the concha wrapped in a napkin and thrust it at her. "Thank you for helping with the sinks."

"Oh." She took the bundle and peeked inside, then raised it to her nose and took a long appreciative sniff. "I wasn't helping in hope of free treats."

"And I didn't save a concha for you for any other reason than I knew you'd smile like that when I gave it to you." That came out more sentimental than I'd intended. I felt myself blushing which only added to my embarrassment, creating a mortifying feedback loop.

Aria reached out and squeezed my arm. "Thanks, Owen. You're sweet."

I hadn't meant to be, had I? A weird noncommittal sound came out of my mouth as I turned back to work.

Aria left without another word.

11

ARIA

I wasn't paying attention as I re-entered the apartment later that afternoon. Luca hung up on me after agreeing to come solve my magic problems, but not before lecturing me and leaving me with homework, which I was busy scrolling through in outrage, nose glued to my phone.

A controlled yet ragged exhale caught my attention as I stepped into the living room. I looked up from my phone, reflexively searching for the source of the sound. Owen was at his work out bench doing silly things with weights that made him all sweaty and taut.

Of course he had his shirt off.

"You're staring." Owen set his weights down.

How long had I stood in the doorway? Too long to pretend I hadn't been ogling him.

"I was not." I slammed the door and made my way across the living room. I wasn't blushing or running.

"Aria."

I stopped before reaching the hall and turned. Owen sat there, smiling the most wholesome smile. He was evil. No one should look like sex and then be able to make that earnest face. Owen was comfort, care, and the stuff of wet dreams. His unconcerned gaze cut through all my defenses. I was doomed.

"You can't stop looking at me. Can you?" he asked.

I looked away. "Yes, I can."

He laughed, sputtered and almost choked on the childishness of my response. Owen drank some water from a metal bottle. "It's okay. I don't mind. As long as I'm not making you uncomfortable."

"You're not." If anything I was too comfortable, my mind plagued with desires to get even more so.

I turned abruptly and left to hide in my room.

A familiar tower of boxes and unsold junk greeted me. My plan to sell everything online and scrape together rent money was slow going and in danger of failing to meet my two-week deadline. My back-up plan, for a magically influenced yard sale, was somewhat illegal and completely desperate. Topics Luca had not held back his opinions on when I'd called to explain the cafe-haunting-Owen predicament.

I flopped on my bed and stared at the ceiling. Luca was begrudgingly arriving to help me with the haunting tonight. I'd suggested he wait until the weekend, but he scolded me for allowing the problem at the cafe to get this out of hand, and insisted he'd fly down from San Francisco tonight. The man was rich and organized, in other words a menace. Luca made it clear he was sacrificing valuable time and personal plans for my foolishness.

The background reading he texted to me was total overkill. I'd already delved into seances, reading a few more historical accounts wouldn't make any difference, so I decided to skip Luca's condescending advice to do more research. We need power, which we twins had. Luca already knew everything, reading all afternoon wouldn't get me up to his speed when I was more than a decade behind.

I had other priorities, like doing something about Owen. He couldn't keep catching me out. It wasn't fair he turned me into a flustered mess so effortlessly.

I set about concocting a plan to make Owen as much of a blubbering sex addled fool as I became around him when he was under-dressed. Which was disturbingly often now I thought about it, like he was deliberately flaunting his wares. I knew he wasn't, which only made it worse. It was Owen's combination of genuine good-natured intent and that body that really fucked me over and made me want.

But, but, but, I'd realized what the problem was. *I* was always wearing an appropriate amount of clothing. The solution was simple, and now I'd thought of it, I needed to take action. Immediately.

I'd never have hyper-focused on Owen and his inconvenient effect on me if I wasn't procrastinating. This wasn't even about him. It meant nothing. I was stressed, okay? I needed release, but not like that.

I went through my drawers until I found a pair of wine-red lace panties. They were the kind of thing you wore when you knew you were going to get laid. Scratch that, they were the kind of thing you wore when you knew someone was going to see your underwear.

Conveniently ignoring how long it'd been since I'd worn such things, put them on and found a black cotton tank top. It clung to all the right places. I dunno, I'd do me in this outfit. Not that action was the desired result, I just wanted to make him squirm.

Now that I was less-dressed, I hesitated. If I went out now, it'd be obvious what I was up to and the whole game would be ruined. I dithered around my room, gave in to being productive and listed a few more Mortal magic items online.

Eventually I emerged from my room and walked slowly to the kitchen. Owen was in the living room. I wasn't going to walk right up to him, that was too obvious. I'd make tea and dally in the kitchen until he came in and—

"Cute panties."

My back stiffened and I whirled around to see Tristan. "What are *you* doing here?"

Tristan gave me an amused once over. "Owen invited me over for dinner. You know, 'cause we're friends."

"Where is he?" There was no one else in the apartment. I'd checked with my Witchy sense.

"He's picking up dinner. You'll have to wait for him to get back. Don't want all this to be wasted." Tristan gestured at me with a flourish.

"All—what? It's nothing. I thought no one was here," I lied.

"Uh-huh." Tristan did that looking down his nose at me thing I was starting to find annoying. "What are you up to, Aria?"

"Nothing." I blushed almost painfully, but persevered. "I'm just walking around my home. I was napping and needed tea. Owen's always going around half undressed. I don't see why there should be a double standard."

"No double standard, I wouldn't dare. I'm well aware of the state of summer Sanchez undress. I lived with the man for more than ten years."

"Why don't you live here?" I asked, curiosity the only thing to cut through my wish to melt into the floor.

Tristan shrugged and came into the kitchen. He opened the fridge, pulled out a La Croix, and popped the tab. "I used to live here. I moved out to move in with my boyfriend."

It seemed we were now ignoring the fact I was in my underwear, so I proceeded to make tea. "Surprised I haven't seen him around with you."

Tristan leaned his hip against the counter and sipped his drink. "We broke up. I mean, it lasted a while the first time, then it was kinda on and off. I could've moved back with Owen, but thought my ex might stick around the next time we were on-again, and didn't want to give up my loft if he moved back. Now I'm stuck with the lease."

"Sorry, exes suck," I offered, only to add, "Except for Jenn. I can't in good conscience disparage her. Oh, or Owen. Obviously. Uh—I'm sure Owen would love to have you move back. He said he didn't like living alone."

Sadness flickered across Tristan's features, giving way to thoughtful consideration. "What's really going on with you and Owen?"

"What do you mean?" I turned back to my tea and removed the metal diffuser.

"Something's up."

"It's none of your business if it is."

"Fine. It's not my business but I'm butting in. Nosey, remember?" He heaved a breath, preparing to tell me things I probably didn't want to hear. "Owen is the most steadfast guy I know but he's different with relationships—"

"There's no relationship. I'm not even sticking around." I sounded too defensive, giving away my desire for neither statement to be true.

"Okay, but still. You were together, that will always be there. Don't discount how much history complicates the way people act. Owen isn't as unaffected as he likes to think."

"I'm not trying to—" Well, I was trying to mess with Owen, but only playfully. "—to hurt Owen."

"I didn't think you were, but that doesn't mean you won't."

"Tristan, I've done that already. Do you need to hear that I regret it?" All the good humor leached out of me, and not just because my silly plan was foiled. "I'm not interested in repeating the past. Or messing this up any further. I want—never mind. I'm taking my tea back to bed." Cup in hand, I left the kitchen regretting just about everything.

I RAN into Owen in the hall later that night.

"There you are," Owen said in mock surprise. "You should have joined Tristan and me for dinner."

"I was tired." More like embarrassed and stewing in my questionable decision making. "I'm just going to brush my teeth, you go ahead."

We were both attempting to get to the bathroom. I was dressed in my usual pajama shorts and large T-shirt, pretending to go to bed even though I was meeting Luca later. Owen was mercifully in track pants and a shirt of his very own.

"I'm here for my teeth as well. Share the sink?" He gestured for me to go into the bathroom.

"Sure." I slipped inside and grabbed my toothbrush.

Owen followed, his smile sweeter than sugar. "It's like a sleepover."

"We never had sleepovers." My parents never allowed such things growing up, especially with Mortal children.

"I know." Owen reached across me to get his brush and toothpaste. "Imagine how much fun we'd have had." He laughed.

I nodded half-heartedly.

"Hey, you okay, Aria?"

The water from my brush dripped onto my shirt. I was worried about the haunting and apprehensive about seeing Luca. I was also thinking about what Tristan said. He'd forced me to think past my petty reactions to Owen and examine what I was doing.

Owen and I only had a small window to be in each other's lives. I wanted more but needed to stop acting like that was a possibility, even if it hurt.

"I have a lot on my mind," I said, unable to share any of my real problems.

"You're having a tough time. Of course there's things on your mind." Owen abandoned his toothbrush to give me his full attention. "Not having somewhere to live would be stressful."

"Oh. Yeah. But I do have somewhere now."

"Have things been like this for you for a while?"

I could have pretended not to know what Owen meant, but I liked having him talk to me like a friend.

"Sort of. I've moved a lot over the years. My chosen employment isn't the most stable. But it's not all bad, and I did, you know, choose it."

"You're happy doing fortunes?" He looked genuinely curious, his face completely devoid of the judgment I usually received.

"I do like it." A smile tugged at my lips. "For the people who believe in it, what I do is important. That makes it important to me. I'd rather bring a bit of happiness or sense of security to strangers by reading fortunes than make money chasing someone else's dreams."

Owen nodded, full of understanding. "I know your parents wanted you to go into law, but I get why you didn't. You've got something you find meaningful. It's more valuable."

"It's nothing as impressive as Coffee Cat." I turned away from Owen. "I know your dad would have loved it."

"He would have."

We brushed our teeth in relative silence and exited the bathroom.

I said goodnight, but before I could turn away Owen reached

out and swiped a bit of toothpaste from my chin and wiped it on his shirt.

Owen pulled me into a crushing hug. He smelled sweet, like his baking permeated his skin. I hugged him back reflexively, full of warmth not entirely due to body heat. It didn't last nearly long enough.

12

ARIA

$\mathcal{L}$ ater that night I met Luca at a park three blocks from Coffee Cat. I was sitting on the swings, feeling very high school me, when a black SUV rolled up. Luca stepped out, wearing an impeccable suit and carrying a brief-case like this was the most uppity drug deal, or some spy shit. To my surprise he wasn't alone.

I slid off the swing and hurried over.

"Aria." My brother extended his hand like we'd never met. "Glad to see you're on time."

We shook, the matching tattoos on our hands giving us both chills.

"Marci?" I peered at the casual but trendy woman behind my brother.

She squealed and rushed forward, bracelets clinking, and hugged me. I glanced helplessly over her shoulder at Luca.

He ran a hand through his hair in the most put out way possible. "I told you I had plans tonight, Aria."

Marci pulled back from the hug but didn't let me go. The band of crystals in her curly, dark hair twinkled in the street-light. "When Luca said he was meeting you for a seance I just about swooned. This is way better than cocktails on my roof. It's been too long!"

I hadn't seen Marcella Mendez since our time as teen Witches at the night school. She was the inventor of the grimoire app and dubbed colloquially as queen of modern magic, though she'd been wearing her crystals set in a circlet atop her head like a princess since we were twelve.

"Marci insisted she come along." Luca's tone revealed how little say he had in the matter.

"You can't get out of spending time with me, Luca. Once a month, it's the minimum friend requirement. If you'd left me behind for a seance I'd never have forgiven you."

"Here I am, another plan thwarted. However will I die alone?" Luca said, prompting indignant noises from Marci and me.

Luca and Marci had been rivals growing up. He'd never gotten over the fact he wasn't the top Witch of our cohort. I'd commended him for personal growth several years back, when he'd resigned himself to Marci's friendship, acknowledging the rivalry was only ever one sided.

"Oh, Aria." Marci grabbed my arm in excitement. "You should join our coven."

"You two are in a coven?"

Luca said "No," at the same time as Marci said "Yes!"

"Two people isn't a coven." Luca checked his watch as if the conversation was causing an unreasonable delay.

"If Aria joined we'd be three." Marci was still holding onto my arm and shook it for emphasis. She was either oblivious to Luca's impatience, or more likely, used to it and ignoring him deliberately.

I squirmed, overwhelmed by the suggestion. "I'm not up to your level of magic. Besides, I live a bit far to make coven meetings."

"But you're moving in with Luca." Marci let go of me so she could link arms with Luca instead.

I glared at my brother. "Since when?"

"What? Are you staying here? With Owen?" *Stars*, his disapproval face looked just like our father's.

"Come on, let's go." I walked off, leading them back toward Coffee Cat. "You up for some B&E Marci?"

"Always," she trilled. "But, it's not technically illegal. We're breaking in in the pursuit of keeping magic secret, not to mention Mortal welfare."

"We've got a lawyer on hand in case anything goes wrong," I said.

"Only if I agree to represent you." Luca sounded even more haughty than usual. "Not that it matters. We aren't going to do anything outside the law. Right, Aria? Or have you already done something?"

I made a show of groaning. "Luca, I almost felt like I missed you. Thank you for correcting me."

"You love me," he deadpanned. "And I love you, which is why I'm saving you from this disaster."

"It's not a disaster."

Luca stopped, grabbed my arm and pulled me around to face him. "Aria, be serious for half a moment, *please*. This is a code red disaster. You tried to Tell Owen about magic, and now the second you're back in his life, he's about to find out all over again!"

"Not because of me! I have nothing to do with the haunting."

"So what? You're still here, meddling in his life. This is a mess. Do you realize how much trouble you could be in? You should have called the Authority and let them deal with the haunting the moment you suspected it."

"I'm not meddling, Luca."

"You're not being smart either."

"You're the smart one, idiot. We can't both be."

"Oh my god, take this seriously!"

I let out a screech of frustration and turned back to the park.

Luca was wrong, the current situation was nothing like when we were kids. I'd learned my lesson about crossing the Authority, but he'd never stop seeing me as a screw up. Seeing all the ways my life went wrong and veered off the path he stayed on. Luca didn't even have to compare me to Marci to see me as a failure. I was a Witch good for nothing but risking magic's secret and therefor putting Mortals in danger without considering the consequences.

Judgment from other Witches I could take. Luca was different. He was supposed to be on my side unconditionally.

Luca caught up to me when I reached the park. "Aria, wait."

"Go away, Luca. I already know what you think. I don't want to hear it."

He grabbed my hand gently. "Sorry, Aria. But you can't run away. You need my help."

"That is a terrible apology."

He tugged on my hand. "Ugh, *sorry*. I'm trying to look out for you."

"By telling me how much I'm screwing up?"

"By stopping you from repeating the past. You're coming to live with me right? I put an offer on that house today."

We started walking back toward Marci, who was waiting half a block away, tactfully pretending to be interested in someone's mailbox rather than watching us argue.

"I might. If I can't work out my own rent situation." The illusion I had any real plan other than going to live with Luca was crumbling, but I wasn't ready to let go.

"Why bother? Just fly back with us tonight," Luca said.

"Because disappearing in the night isn't suspicious."

"Oh. Good point. Come this weekend. Why wait? We can rent an Airbnb if you really can't stomach mom and dad."

I looked away from Luca's inquisitive stare. I couldn't tell him I wanted to mend things with Owen, be his friend, sort out these feelings that weren't just friendly. "I have a plan to figure things out myself, get my own place."

"I don't have to be a last resort, you know."

I looked back at Luca to see him hurt and uncharacteristically emotional. He wasn't even glowering.

"You aren't a last resort, Luca."

"Then don't wait. Get on with your life. I miss having you around, it could be—" He sighed. "—fun. There's that internship too."

"Ah." I marched on until we caught up with Marci. "I know you think I'm wasting my psychic power, but I like what I do."

"Aria, I never said you were wasting anything. Never in all these years. I do have my own opinions, separate from our parents. You're letting their limited views blind you. There's a lot of good you can do. My firm represents Mortals and Witches, helping them, not prosecuting them. I think you might actually like the work. Psychic ability isn't all about catching people out."

I suppose I knew all these things, but had never really considered them. I'd been set on pushing Luca away along with everything else. "I'll think about it."

"Will you really, or are you shutting me up?"

"Geez, call me out. Okay, Luca. Yes, I will seriously consider it. Send me an email." The unsettling thing was, I wasn't lying. I liked being a Mortal psychic but how long could I keep it up when it didn't bring me the stability I wanted? Fortunes could be a hobby. And the offer of Marci's coven was tempting in a whole other way. My life had too many gaps I wanted to fill.

Luca clapped me on the shoulder. "Great."

"I agree, it's an excellent idea," Marci said. "What are you staying here for anyway?"

I ignored her under the guise of letting us into the building. The three of us paused at the bottom of the stairs in front of the cafe's back door. I gestured silently to the lock and stepped out of Luca's way.

Luca used a quick spell to let us in. I manually relocked the door behind us as Luca and Marci cast silencing and concealing spells over the cafe. If I'd thought to do that before my seance attempt last night, Piña wouldn't have given me away. With the spells in place, no magic would be detected from outside, except by an experienced Witch.

I led my companions to the kitchen. We still didn't want to be seen from the windows if anyone walked down the street. Invisibility wasn't actually achievable, though a strong diffusion charm was almost as good.

Luca settled easily into a cross-legged position on the tile floor and clicked open his briefcase. "Three small circles please." He handed me a bag of tealights.

"What am I, your assistant?" I asked.

"No. But are you planning to sit around and watch? Not even offer to help?"

I grumbled and made three circles with the little candles. Inside each circle we placed a crystal, a bundle of dried sage, and a thimble full of wine poured out of a hip flask.

Luca tucked his hair behind his ears, exposing a row of crystal earrings. "You two sit on either side of me. Aria, we'll call it forth, then Marci can banish it."

Marci let out a delighted squeal. "I can't wait to share this on the discussion forum."

I sat flush to Luca's side, facing the opposite way so we could link our tattooed right hands. Marci sat on his other side, hands folded in her lap. Taking Luca's hand felt like a shock as our magics echoed one another. We sat for a moment getting used to the feeling before we called upon our stars. I didn't need a copy of the incantation used in the seance—when we did magic together I felt the words through our link.

As we began the incantation the tealights in front of us ignited. A split second later a larger ring of fire encompassed the three of us. Flames danced in the air, hovering above the tile floor. The air crackled with a bitter tang. I fell into a magic haze after that. I wasn't driving the spell and got completely lost in the combination of Luca's power and the call from beyond the physical world.

I teetered on the edge of something, not sure if I was going to fall or fly.

"Aria—" Luca nudged my shoulder and I blinked.

"What?" I looked around, dazed. "Did I miss it? Did you banish it?" I stifled a yawn unsuccessfully. Magic was exhausting when you were out of practice. My wrist and hand ached, the skin around my tattoos hot.

"No. Nothing happened," Luca said.

Marci was scrolling on her phone. "Are we sure it's a haunting?"

"Yes." I stretched and stood. "What else could it be?"

Luca began putting the supplies back in his briefcase. "Any number of things."

"I knew a haunting was too good to be true," Marci said.

"Too good—?" I tried to shake the tired, magic induced fog from my brain. "Are we sure it's *not* a haunting?"

"Yes." Marci adjusted her crystal crown absently. "There was no presence. There's magical manipulation at work in the cafe, but nothing obvious or straightforward enough to point to a source. You need someone experienced in diagnostics to investigate."

"Can't you try?" I looked from Marci to Luca.

Luca shook his head. "Investigative magic is more than saying a spell to see what's going on. You need to be able to interpret nuanced results, and select the right spells to parse out answers. Then create a bespoke counter spell. Whatever's causing the cafe's problems is a Witch, not a haunting, but beyond that—what kind of magic and for what purpose—who knows." Luca stood and straightened his suit.

"Maybe the haunting just ignored our summons," I said, clinging to hope. A rare known problem was surely better than a complete unknown.

"That's not how seances work." Luca clicked his briefcase shut. "If an entity was linked to this place, transiting back and forth, it would have made itself known. Ignoring us isn't an option."

"But if it's not a haunting, it can't be sentient. How can it react to my magic?" I looked around the kitchen, thinking of the milk. "The thing runs away from me every time I brush against it."

"Fleeing a passive touch is weird, I admit. You really need an expert, but I imagine a powerful curse could be reactive," Luca said.

"You should call—"

"I am not calling the Authority," I interrupted Marci.

She turned her phone screen toward me. "I was going to say, you should call a paranormal investigator."

"Oh." The screen showed a local listing for Herrera Investigations.

"Don't look so defeated, Aria. You can't do everything yourself." Luca patted me stiffly on the shoulder.

"Yes, but you usually can."

My brother laughed at that. "I'm looking forward to you moving up North. Call me about the internship soon and I'll set up an interview."

"If I decide I'm interested," I reminded him.

"Yes, yes. Will you be okay going to the investigator in the morning? You really can't leave this problem any longer if Mortals are noticing."

"I'll call in the morning," I promised. "You two can go."

"It was great seeing you, Aria." Marci gave me another hug. "Please move back. The coven needs you—do not roll your eyes, Luca. I saw that."

I walked them out, promised to text Luca as soon as the investigator was contacted, and watched them disappear into the black SUV.

13

OWEN

*A*ria was curled up on the couch fast asleep. It was just after four in the morning and I was heading down to the cafe. I almost didn't notice her nestled amongst all the blankets until she whimpered like she was having a nightmare.

I crouched down in front of her. "Aria," I whispered.

She stirred and opened her eyes, blinked at me for a second, then smiled.

"What are you doing out here?"

Before my question was complete Aria reached out and pulled me to her. She hugged me, taking a deep breath, her face pressed against my neck. I leaned in automatically. My hand found its way into her long hair.

"I couldn't sleep," she murmured.

After an extended time holding each other, Aria pulled back and sat up. I had to get going but sat down on the couch next to her. "Maybe I shouldn't have woken you."

"It's fine. I was dreaming about Luca. Really, you saved me." Aria rubbed the sleep from her eyes.

"You and Luca don't get along anymore?" I asked.

"I wouldn't go that far."

"You two are very similar. It's no wonder if you clash."

Aria half turned toward me, propped her elbow on the couch, and took a good look at me. She all but narrowed her eyes. "Really? Most people would disagree, or say we're twins destined to embody polar opposites."

"You two aren't the same, but your differences are only at the surface. At least, that's what I used to think. What's Luca doing these days?"

"Lawyering. Just like he always said."

"That bothers you?"

"Damn it, Owen, how do you always hear what I'm not saying?"

"You aren't exactly subtle." I smiled at her until she cracked and gave me one back. "Look, if your parents, or whoever, make you feel like he's the successful one and you're not, that's a limited view of things."

"Objectively speaking it's correct, limited or not. But I don't really care what people think of me. Luca wants to help my—" She gestured to encompass the situation. "I don't know how I feel about taking it."

Aria obviously cared about the judgments cast on her, but I let it slide. "I doubt he's offering to help with an ulterior motive. Don't resist him for the sake of resisting."

"I'd never do that."

I gave her a look, arched my brow.

"Okay, fine. I'll *try* not to do that this time. You realize that means I'll be moving back North, sooner than later. Luca invited me to say with him." She looked at me questioningly.

Was she fishing for something, or was I only hoping she might be?

"Move if that's what you want to do. Unless there's some reason to stay? I'm guessing your magic shop stuff isn't selling?"

"No. Not really." Aria looked down at her lap.

"Then don't discount other options just because it's Luca and you hate when he's right."

"For the record, I also hate when you're right, Owen."

A warm feeling blossomed in my chest. "I have to get to work."

Aria's hunched posture straightened, like something had given her a boost. "Need help?"

"I—"

I stopped before declining. The new kitchen hand wasn't fully hired yet, and I was working alone this morning. "Sure. But you have to do exactly as I tell you. This isn't cup of noodles."

She put up her hands in surrender. "I wouldn't dream of messing with your dad's recipes. I can wash dishes."

I left Aria to shower and change and went downstairs to get things started.

The cafe was freezing. I cranked the thermostat. The AC shouldn't have been blasting overnight, my power bill was going to be astronomical, whoever messed with the temperature settings was getting a stern word.

I switched some music on in the kitchen and went about preheating the oven before checking the proofing dough from the day before. I was energized and looking forward to the day despite the disasters of yesterday. Every ingredient was scrutinized before use. There would be no inedible bakes today.

Aria arrived in a crew neck sweater and jeans. It was still unusually cold, but the kitchen soon wouldn't be. I grabbed her an apron and rattled off a list of things she could get from the storeroom. I often heard phantom voices in the storeroom first thing in the morning. I half wondered if Aria would too, but brushed the thought away.

Aria was quiet as we worked, not in a standoffish way—she really wanted to get this right and it showed in her concentration. I wasn't surprised she cared, even if it was rare Aria let that side of herself show without sarcasm to cushion her sincerity. Aria was always a caring person. That was what made her ghosting of me so hard to believe and accept: it wasn't like her.

I'd convinced myself Aria never really cared, in an effort to explain her disappearance, but that wasn't true. She had cared, then perhaps she didn't, or didn't know how to handle losing me, but I couldn't deny she cared now. This morning in the kitchen we were so very us, in a familiar way that had nothing to do with what we said, or what we did. It was how we were together, like it'd always been this way and always would.

I knew Aria was leaving. Even if she stayed in town, always having this comfort together wasn't realistic. Things would change between us. The question was, what form might that change take? I almost caught myself hoping for a relationship with her, which was very not me.

I'd never been successful in romantic relationships; getting too invested threw me off. If I was honest, I hated getting left. My early romantic life was full of breakups I didn't instigate. And okay, no one liked being broken up with, but after my dad I'd started handling it poorly. I held on too quickly and crashed too hard at the end, until I was too worried about someone leaving to even get started. My mom left before I even knew her, my dad died, I couldn't expect anyone to stay around. It didn't feel realistic, nothing could be taken as given. It wasn't the way the world worked.

I knew keeping it casual was a defensive strategy, but I preferred that concession to inevitable heartbreak, and never felt I was missing out. I had my life and my important people. I'd never met anyone worth the risk of changing my noncommittal ways, or anyone who wanted me enough to push my boundaries. My longest relationship could be measured in months not years, and Diego had left without a backward glance.

There was comfort in knowing Aria was leaving. An end date

gave me endless possibilities for the now, without risk. If we let the spark between us become something more, I could enjoy us without getting caught up in future unknowns. The fun flirtiness between us combined with how much she still cared was irresistible. I wanted everything with her, even if it was only for a short time.

"It's freezing in here!" Tristan barged into the kitchen interrupting my wayward thoughts.

"I turned up the thermostat." But I couldn't deny how cold it still was.

"I'll double check, because *damn*." Tristan shivered. "Do we have a new employee?"

"I'll accept payment in cold brew," Aria said.

"Yeah, okay. Good to know." Tristan gave me a thoughtful look. "I'm going to watch the milk guy unload everything. I'm not letting it out of my sight. Wanna help me bring it inside, Aria?"

"Sure." She followed Tristan out of the kitchen.

I began transferring fresh pan dulce to the front display. Tess was here as well, writing on the chalkboard menu. I restarted the register. The screen glitched for a moment, but all was well by the time I stocked the change in the drawer.

Tristan's shrieking laugh came from the walk-in fridge. "You're cruel, Aria."

I found the two of them surrounded by milk crates, out of breath and grinning, Tristan reluctantly, and Aria like a devil.

"You could have believed me when I said my hands were literal ice," Aria said to Tristan.

"Yeah, but you can't just go touching the back of my neck to prove a point." He held out his hands, blue glitter polish catching the light. "Look, I'm shaking."

Aria grabbed Tristan's hand and examined it. "That's not my fault. It's cold in here. As evidenced by my icy fingers."

"Get out of the fridge." I laughed.

After another twenty minutes of prepping the cafe to open, it was clear time in the fridge wasn't the problem. Tristan, who couldn't stay still at the best of times, was practically vibrating.

"You need a sweater?" I asked.

"I didn't bring one, it's freaking summer." He clutched an extra-large almond milk latte and sipped it in outrage.

I ran up to the apartment to get him one to borrow. Piña was yowling at the window, but I didn't have time to stop and soothe her. The moment I stepped back into the cafe, sweater in hand, I felt the temperature difference drastically. The stairwell was bordering on sweltering compared to the cafe.

Customers were lined up and Tess was already busy at the espresso machine. I hoped no one would complain about the cold.

"That thermostat is broken," Tristan said as he pulled on the sweater.

"Just what we need." My almost jittery happy mood dipped.

"Hey, air conditioning problems we can solve, Owen. Don't get in your head."

I clapped Tristan on the shoulder and went to poke uselessly at the thermostat. Aria was on her phone, frowning. She spotted me and hastily tucked the phone away.

"Come on. Unless you can fix the air, we should start prepping torta fillings," I said.

The kitchen should have been hot. The oven was still going, and the griddle was cranking as I cooked bacon, chorizo, eggs, and diced poblanos for our breakfast spread. I'd never been cold working in a kitchen before. Especially in summer.

"It's uncommonly cold, right?" I asked Aria as she washed the remainder of the dishes from earlier.

"I want to disagree, but I can see your breath." She was right, I could see hers too.

I ventured out front to deliver a few tortas to a customer. She thanked me and hurried out, clutching the warm paper bag to her chest.

No one sat at the tables. We usually had a decent number of customers eating in, drinking coffee and working, or meeting friends. I'd never seen every single seat empty.

Everyone waiting for coffee had an uneasy, impatient look. Sun streamed in through the front windows. It should have been pleasant in here, a welcome burst of cool air on a warm morning, instead the cold was driving customers out.

"Mr. Sanchez, it's been a while."

I looked around to see our regular, Max standing in the corner waiting for a coffee. It hadn't been a while, unless you counted two days as a while, which nobody did.

I nodded in acknowledgment. "How've you been?"

Max insisted on calling me Mr. Sanchez even after I'd asked him to call me Owen repeatedly, and with diminishing tolerance. Still, it wasn't as bad as Tristan's situation. It was like Max wanted to mess with us for no real reason. Unless it was a social experiment he was writing about.

Max shrugged at my question, maybe detecting my insincerity, and pulled his scarf tighter around his neck. "I'm fine. Nothing new. You were out of oat milk last time I was in."

"Sorry about that. We've had a few minor supply hiccups. All stocked up today."

Max nodded in approval.

Thankfully, I was pulled into another customer's conversation with Tristan. She peppered him with a seemingly endless barrage of questions about oat milk, having only just heard of it for the first time. Honesty, I didn't doubt Max had a hand in this woman's extensive line of inquiry. He was always butting in and giving uninvited suggestions or advice to random people. And he had a thing about oat lattes.

Out of the corner of my eye I could see Max chuckling.

After we made it through the morning rush, an eerie lull settled over the cafe. Not a single customer stayed to enjoy their treats. Coffee Cat was left empty. This wasn't good for business. A bustling cafe drew more people in, a cozy atmosphere got them to stay and order a second coffee. Nothing like this had ever happened before.

Tristan went outside for a break to warm up, and Aria escaped up to the apartment to charge her phone and make a quick call. I cleaned the kitchen as Tess waited dutifully for customers. Time ticked by and not a single person entered the cafe.

"Is it dark in here?" Tess asked when I popped back out to frown at the empty cafe.

"It shouldn't be."

"I know. But it feels dark. Right?"

I looked around. It was blindingly bright outside but the shadows in the cafe were deeper, darker than usual. We had the lights on, it really didn't make sense.

"There are a hundred and fifty thousand crows outside," Tristan said as he reentered the coffee shop. "And I'm not okay with it."

I went to the front window. Across the street the jacaranda tree was covered in crows. You almost couldn't see any green amongst all the feathers.

"Creepy." The sight gave me chills.

"It really is too *The Birds* to be normal." Tristan's expression was serious. "Look at their eyes. I'm leaving out the back later. No need to be pecked to death before my deadline this afternoon. I still need to edit."

"What are we looking at?" Aria snuck up behind us. It didn't take her long to figure out what was up. She sucked in a breath. "No need to stare and make them angry," she said in an attempt at humor before pulling Tristan and me away from the window and shooing us back to where we belonged.

A few customers trickled in here and there, but it was slow enough that Tristan pulled out his laptop and began his edits behind the counter. I was desperately holding out for the lunch hour.

We all let out a sigh of relief when a group of young professionals came in laughing and talking loudly. By the time we'd served them, the cafe was dead silent, like the cold had sucked the life out of everything.

The group left, taking my hope with them. I doubted any of them would be back.

Aria disappeared to make another phone call and Tess had a turn looking at the thermostat. I made everyone lunch and joined Tristan out front to sit and eat. For once my unease rubbed off on him. We were both at a loss, eating in silence.

The lights went out and the music stopped. The chatter of crows outside intensified.

"Tess!" Tristan yelled. "You fucking with the circuit breakers?"

"It wasn't me!" she called back.

Honestly, I was relieved the power was out. Maybe the temperature would return to normal. I mean of course it would, now that the AC was off.

The three of us went to the fuse box. Nothing had blown the breaker. There was no flipping the power back on, this was a job for an electrician. It was all bad luck, nothing more. I would not let myself fall into fanciful thinking.

"Let's close," I said to my two loyal staff. "I'll get someone around this afternoon, fix all this mess and reopen in the morning. Take as much pan as you want."

Tristan wanted to stay and help, but I firmly sent him home. I had Aria, once I found where she'd gone.

14

ARIA

*T*he investigator didn't call me back. I left her a message first thing and tried to get through two more times. Nothing.

To be fair, Juliet Herrera's website described her business as 'private investigation: no problem too big or small.' There was nothing about urgent, on-call services. She was probably busy being the only paranormal investigator in the county, and not prioritizing answering the phone. Apparently it was too much to hope she had anything as mundane as a receptionist.

The magic infecting Coffee Cat was operating on a new level. This morning the storeroom laughed at me, loud and sassy. Which, rude, but more importantly, *why?* Who put time into magic that did that? A haunting-slash-paranormal entity amusing itself with our discomfort was one thing, a spell or curse cast to laugh at you didn't make sense.

Magic was everywhere, no longer subtle or fleeting, but leaking out of the walls. Piña was beside herself until I cast a protective spell on the apartment to keep whatever was going on downstairs from infecting up here. I only had to hold every-thing off, distract Owen and the others until the investigator could come solve all our problems. And if she couldn't, well fuck.

For half a moment I considered giving in and calling the Authority. They didn't have an office in town, the closest was LA. I could have this over in hours. Only the unknown severity of my punishment for breaking my court conditions stopped me turning to them for help. I couldn't invite Authority Witches back into my life. I was stuck.

The apartment door opened. Piña ran past me and threw herself at Owen's feet, mewling. She couldn't feel the magic up here anymore but hadn't forgotten her trauma.

"Aria, here you are." Owen reached down to pat the cat. "We had to close up. Power outage."

"I've called someone to come take a look." I checked my phone again in vain. "Hope they can get here soon."

"You noticed the power was out too?" Owen picked up Piña and came over to me. When he got near the cat twisted and leapt out of his grasp. She disappeared down the hall.

"She doesn't like you, does she?"

"Cats never do." I didn't pretend to be sorry about it.

Owen flopped onto the couch and ran his hands through his hair, tension visible in the set of his jaw and flex of his arms. He took a few deep breaths. "What's that smell?"

"Sage. I—had a candle going."

Owen closed his eyes. "I don't see how all this bad luck is hitting at once."

"That's the thing about luck. Good or bad, there's no logic."

"Maybe the malfunctioning air conditioning caused the power to crap out," Owen said more to himself than me. "That doesn't explain the birds."

Thankfully we couldn't see the bird-infested tree from this side of the building or else I'd have drawn the curtains. The birds were the most frightening things about the situation, other than the possibility magic would reveal itself. I didn't trust magically altered animals. Whatever Witch cast the spell on the crows was strong, and not someone I wanted to mess with.

I checked my phone in vain for any missed calls. Owen had to be distracted until I got a response. He didn't need to be thinking, worrying, questioning explainability, or calling Mortal repair people.

"Remember the bake off at school senior year?" I said at random.

Owen opened his eyes. "How could I forget?"

I joined him on the couch. "Your cake was so cool."

"A stack of books was pretty boring in retrospect."

"Not at all. The punny titles. It was cute."

Owen blushed. He was gorgeous with that hint of rose creeping out from under his beard. "Your cake was good too."

"Please. A sheet cake poorly decorated with stars and sprinkles?"

"Better than Luca's."

"He was being contrary that day. *This is not a cake* was so him, and so annoying."

The bake off was a fundraiser where the cakes entered into the competition were raffled off. I ended up winning two cakes that year. Owen and I took them back to the field at my parents' house and ate until we couldn't move.

"I really wanted to kiss you that day," Owen said.

My breath caught. "Oh my god, I'm so glad you didn't. I felt sick and couldn't look at sugar for a week. Even the memory—"

"No, not then. I couldn't function after all that cake. It was earlier, when we were walking to the bus stop and you were bemoaning too much of a good thing."

"So complaining and almost dropping cakes all over the sidewalk was it for you?"

"No, you were."

"I—" Oh hell, what could I say? That was months before we actually got together, a whole lifetime ago. How could the memory of that day be so fresh when I hadn't spared it a thought in years? I remembered the way Owen looked at me, a bit like he was doing now.

"You always made the best of a bad situation. You still do. Remember what a bad morning I'd had that day? And look where it ended."

I'd forgotten that first half of the story. "No, I don't know—" I felt myself flushing and growing hot all over. "I cause problems, I don't fix them. All I did that day was distract you." Much like now, though this wasn't the discussion I had in mind.

"You don't have to fix everything to make a difference," Owen said. "I know you care. That's what counted, then—now."

I became more aware of how little space lay between us. My knees brushed the side of his leg as he turned to face me, both of us shifting closer. He had a point about our youth, when many problems were beyond our ability to fix. I'd settled for comfort. But now, I couldn't help feeling useless, unable to solve anything when I had more power to than most. I cared about Owen but I wanted to show it in a meaningful, solid way.

Owen slipped his hand around me to hold the back of my neck. "I'm glad you're back, Aria."

I leaned into his touch, hot at the back of my neck, a tingle of potential crawled down my spine. He made me feel like I was enough, just like this. Owen looked at my lips then up at my eyes, he leaned forward slowly, giving me time to stop him.

I should have. Kissing wasn't the plan.

Instead I slipped my arms around him and pulled him to meet me. Owen's lips brushed mine in a sweet kiss. It wasn't familiar, exactly, but it made me think, *oh this is what I've been looking for*. The smallest physical touch was so much more than a meeting of lips. I was overwhelmed with a sense of healing happiness and strange excitement. I'd never had a touch be so clarifying.

I kissed Owen more urgently and he opened his mouth for me, my tongue slid along his and he groaned. Owen's beard was perfect against my cheeks, rough and tactile under my needy fingers as I held him to me. His hands found my hips and pulled me onto his lap. I leaned against him, feeling everywhere we touched, and not feeling enough with clothing in the way.

We parted, breathless. Owen smiled like someone who had everything and it scared the hell out of me.

"Aria—" He stilled his movements. "I've never seen your eyes so wide. We don't have to do this. I'm sorry if—"

I kissed him. "It's not that."

"Okay." He cradled my face in gentle fingers. "What has you looking so scared to be happy?"

Oh, *fuck*. My heart quivered. Owen's offer to confide in him was all I ever wanted. It was as if, in his presence, I could abandon all concept of fear. But his question opened up possibilities I couldn't entertain.

My hands ran rampant through his short hair and along his rough jaw. "Owen. We can't—there's so much mess between us already. And I'm leaving. I can't change that."

"I know. I'm not asking you to make any promises. I don't generally make any of my own beyond casual arrangements. But if you want to talk, we can. If you want to kiss me, and I want to kiss you—or let's be honest, I want to do way more than kiss you —does it need to be any more complicated?"

"Can we just decide it's that simple?" Owen had such command over his emotions. The past wasn't a big deal, we weren't complicated. Saying it made it so if you were Owen Sanchez. I didn't think it was that straightforward. I wasn't afraid to be happy, I just didn't trust everything would remain untangled. "How I left before—I don't want to hurt you again."

Owen smiled. "You won't, Aria. We can make this simple if we want to. You're leaving, I'm staying. There's no expectation beyond. Maybe we can have this—" He gestured to us, entangled in one another. "—because we never had it before. I can't deny how much you've been on my mind, how I've imagined kissing you, or what giving in to all my other desires would be like."

"That sounds like moving on. Like goodbye sex."

"Maybe it's closure—I don't know."

"I want the things we never had." I pressed my lips to his. I wanted more than a goodbye, more than the physical intimacies we never shared. I wanted this to be the start of something new, but it couldn't be.

I wasn't afraid to be happy, I just knew we couldn't be together.

I couldn't be here, I couldn't stay, but sure, we could have this. I'd settle for it gladly. This kiss. Closure and expression of pent-up feelings. I wouldn't disappear without a word and ruin it. We wouldn't taint it. We'd part like any two people who didn't quite fit but cared more for each other than anyone else.

"I missed you, Owen," I whispered into his kiss.

"I missed you too. So much, Aria."

My fingers found the hem of his shirt and dipped behind the fabric. He shivered and arched into my touch. Needy man, oh I liked that way too much. I smiled against his mouth, kissed him with a soft bite, eliciting a gasp. Then I leaned back and pulled his shirt over his head.

I took a moment to look. Nothing I hadn't seen before, sure, but now he was panting because I made him breathless. His eyes were wild watching me look at him. He liked it. A lot. My gaze. That made me ache, heat pooling between my thighs. It was a sensual connection not tied to touch or words, just letting someone see as you came undone.

Letting out a shameless sound, I gave in to touching him. I ran my hands over his chest, savoring the feel of him. He leaned into it. His hips rolled beneath me as he tried to ease the strain of his arousal. Owen's hands slid from my hips to cup my ass. I rocked into him and he gave me a feral grin. My fingers passed over his nipples and his mouth fell open in a perfect silent gasp.

Our touches blurred into one another. Owen was nowhere near close enough even as I felt him hard between my legs. There was too much fucking denim. I made a desperate noise only to find he echoed it in a shaking almost-rumble. Owen shifted me off him. I lay back along the couch pulling him with me.

"Can I take these off?" He fiddled with the waistband of my jeans.

I lifted my hips. "I feel that's the best course of action."

Owen chuckled and my jeans disappeared in a disturbingly fluid motion. His hands ghosted over my thighs, down my legs and back to my hips. The couch itched, contrasting with the smoothness of his touch, sharpening my awareness of skin on skin.

I wasn't wearing red lace today but couldn't have cared less. Owen's breath tickled my navel. I ached and maybe twitched my hips, or did something equally desperate, because he moved to kiss me over the fabric of my panties, open mouthed and unabashed. I moaned and he was there to steal the sound from my mouth.

Owen moved like a dancer, all strength and beautiful fluid motion, everywhere at once. He redefined rhythm and my body bent to his tune. He let one hand travel down my body as we kissed. He took a moment to toy with the edge of my panties until I begged him to touch me.

"I love hearing you say you want me," he said into my ear as his hand slipped between my legs.

I told him I wanted him, needed him even. Nothing lay between my thoughts and my words. It was loose, honest lust and I was drunk on getting what I wanted. Owen didn't tease me, he let his finger circle my clit with a steady pressure designed to undo me.

He pulled back from our kiss to watch my face. Our breaths mingled. The reflex to hide how emotionally naked I was only lasted half a moment. His own expression was as stripped as I felt, filled with unimaginable desire with a wonderful edge of disbelief.

I writhed under his touch, held steady by his gaze, grounded by his body pressed along mine. Owen slipped his fingers inside me, giving me pressure with the heel of his hand. I moved against him and he watched me splayed out on the couch until I came in a bursting release, pleasure tearing out of me and leaving me raw.

Owen nuzzled his face against my chest. My hands found their way to his hair, trembling, holding him. Owen undid his jeans and let out a sigh of relief as he freed his cock. He gave himself a firm tug, the reverberation of his single stroke sending a renewed jolt of lust through me.

"I want to see you touch yourself," I said in a rush.

Owen picked his head off my chest and looked at me. "Really?"

"Yes." I could feel his erection pressed into my hip and wiggled against him. "Is that okay? If I watch?"

Owen shivered and his eyes flashed a radiant brown shadowed with unrestrained desire. "Yes, Aria. I'd fucking love that."

His words gave me a crazed kind of trill. This wasn't my usual beat, but with my thighs firmly clenched I'd never been so into the idea of looking.

Owen sat up and tugged his pants and boxer briefs down to his knees. He let his head fall back against the couch as he palmed himself, eyes fluttering closed. His whole body was toned and put on display for me. Brown skin, dark ink. Fuck.

"I'm going to be thinking about you coming apart for me forever, Aria."

Oh yeah, I like this a lot.

Too greedy to sit back completely, I pressed myself against Owen's side, on my knees, and ran my hands over his chest. His eyes opened, finding mine as my fingers grazed his pics.

"Do you like knowing I'm going to think about you?" he asked in a strained whisper.

My eyes left his and traveled down. "Yes." I felt a renewed, urgent neediness between my thighs. "Show me how you'll think of me."

Owen stroking himself was one of the most captivating things I'd ever seen. He was wanton and fearless. His cock strained against his hand, beads of moisture leaking out, but he didn't pick up the pace. He was enjoying drawing this out, torturing himself just a bit. The intimacy of watching gave the sense of a private moment shared. My eyes on him were as sure as touch, if his reaction to my gaze was anything to go by.

"Owen you're gorgeous," I breathed in his ear.

He let out a whimper. I teased one of his nipples. He gasped a strangled sound and leaned into me, half burying his face, his hand moving more frantically. His muscles were taught, thighs and abdomen straining. I let my hand wander down past his belly button to the carefully groomed hair framing his erection.

Owen was a work or art from his beard to his tattoos, to the way he moved and touched himself. The tattoo on Owen's hip was a swirl of stars, waves and stylized lines. It framed him perfectly, drawing your eyes to the tight muscles of his groin. I traced it with delicate fingers. He lifted his hips off the couch, a silent request. My hand joined his on his cock. Owen covered my hand with his. I pulled him tight against me as we moved together, kissing, breath mingling. He came with a sharp intake of breath.

We held each other a while. I kissed Owen's cheek and felt a wide grin stretch over his face. He grabbed a throw blanket and wiped us up, then pulled me against his chest and lay back. I pulled another blanket over us and nestled, with no plans to move. Ever.

15

ARIA

*W*e must have dozed. The next thing I knew the afternoon light stretched low in the sky. Owen's arms cradled me to him perfectly, our legs tangled together. I hadn't been this ruthlessly snuggled in a long time. I was only half aware of anything that wasn't him.

He let out a cute little snore.

Piña hissed somewhere at the other end of the house, pulling me out of my half sleep. She shouldn't be able to feel any magic through my protective spell on the apartment.

The cat hissed again. A heavy thump came from down the hall.

Owen twitched. "What was that?"

"The cat, I think."

He ran a hand down my back. "Probably chasing a fly."

There were two more loud thumps, like someone banging on a wall.

"That's not the cat," Owen said, more concerned now.

"I'll go take a look." I hurried to sit up and reached for my jeans.

"It's okay, I can—"

I pushed Owen back onto the couch. "Really, I'm sure it's nothing." I swiped my phone off the floor and hurried down the hallway.

Piña was crouched, tail twitching, hissing at the bathroom door. Another loud thump came from inside. I couldn't sense any magic behind the door, but the cat seemed to, and somehow I trusted her judgment over mine.

I didn't want to open the door. There was no denying my lack of success in dealing with this situation. Another thump, followed by a loud reaction from Piña, left me no choice. Whatever was going on, I didn't need Owen coming to check it out. I cautiously opened the door to an empty bathroom.

Something crashed into the window with a thud. Piña hissed. I stepped forward while the cat stayed in the hall. There was commotion outside the window. Flashes and shadows you wouldn't expect to see on the second story, with no one able to walk by.

I peered out. Across the street the jacaranda tree was overloaded with crows. Even more birds flew above it, circling endlessly. Every crow in town might as well have been here. One broke away from the rest and flew directly at the window. It hit with a bang. I flinched. The bird bounced back, unfazed, and circled back to the tree.

They were trying to break in.

I unlocked my phone (still no word from the PI) and opened the grimoire app. I needed to stop the enchanted birds but had no idea how. I typed *crow attack* into the search. Nothing came up.

Another bird hit the window.

"You okay?" Owen called from the living room.

"All good." *Shit, shit, not good.*

I typed *cursed animals* into the app. The results were complex. I needed to know the nature of the curse, if the problem with the birds was even a curse, before I could counter it. Maybe I could strengthen the glass on the window and drag Owen out of the apartment until I had a better plan.

As I searched for a strengthening spell, more birds hit the window. I clicked on the first result and started muttering the words, hand outstretched toward the glass. Across the street the crows rose from the tree as one. I muttered, faster and faster as the crows took a wide turn and circled back toward the apartment.

They were headed straight toward the window, their aerial formation unnaturally compact. I ducked not a second too soon. The glass burst, and birds filled the bathroom. Piña leapt at them as they flew past, spitting and baring her claws. The crows flew out the open bathroom door and down the hall. I could hear more hitting the side of the building, the window too small for the onslaught, as dozens continued to fly inside.

The cat chased the stream of birds as it made its way down the hall. Owen yelled. I scrambled up and chased after the hurricane of feathers as even more birds flew in, cawing and flapping. Wings hit the side of my face, claws scraping my arms and tangling in my hair.

I reached the living room. Owen stood, stunned in front of the couch. The birds became chaotic as they filled the space, breaking out of their stream and flying erratically around the room. Piña didn't know where to turn as she tried to catch them all at once, a furry pinball amidst a torrent of feathers.

Just as I worried we'd be pecked to death by the ever growing number of crows, they burst through one of the living room windows. Now there was a path of escape, the birds made a beeline for it. A rush of icy air whipped past as more birds came through the hall, into the living room and fled out the broken window. Like a crow highway of destruction.

Piña almost caught one. She bounded off the furniture and

leapt, reaching out like a diver. Her claws made contact as she followed a crow out the broken window.

Owen yelled and scrambled as the cat disappeared from sight. We both rushed forward, birds flapping around us. Piña tumbled on the ground, struggling with the bird. They scrabbled across the sidewalk and into the street. A car was coming, fast enough I knew it wasn't going to stop in time.

I didn't think, I only saw the tragedy of the dead cat about to unfold and chose to stop it. I yelled my trusty summoning spell and Piña flew into the air, away from the street and oncoming car, and zoomed right into my arms. She was stunned into silence, too disoriented to protest the use of magic in saving her.

The bird onslaught mercifully subsided. The last crows escaped to join their fellows darkening the sky around the building. The air in the apartment turned still.

Owen grabbed Piña from my arms and hugged her to his chest.

"How did you do that?" Owen asked, his voice too filled with awe to make me comfortable.

Shit, fuck, goddamn it. I really screwed up. Blatant magic use. In front of a Mortal. But I couldn't have let the cat die, I wouldn't regret this.

"I didn't do anything," I said, not looking at Owen. "She jumped."

He was silent for two beats. "She jumped *out* the window. She was about to get run over, then she—she flew back here. To you."

"No, she didn't."

I could feel Owen thinking, processing. I was numb with panic. Lies, I needed more lies, better lies. But the truth was, I always hated this balls-out gaslighting of Mortals.

"Piña jumped and I caught her. That's all," I insisted half-heartedly.

Owen reached out and grabbed my shoulder. He turned me to face him. "That was magic. You used magic to save her. This is *all* magic."

"No." My voice was too quiet to have conviction.

It was too late. The realization broke over Owen's face. He looked at the cat in his arms, at me, and around the feather strewn living room. I felt the faint click of a Mortal mind shifting.

"That was magic," Owen said again, his voice more confident and a little giddy.

I felt sick, almost faint. I was in so, so much trouble. I'd revealed magic, without any plan or organized forethought, to the one person I was never supposed to expose it to. There was no covering up a Telling. The Authority already knew. The enchantments monitoring Mortal knowledge sent off alarm bells, that faint click might as well have been a booming beacon, revealing our identities and locations.

I tried to push worries of consequences and court away. I opened my mouth to ask Owen what he was thinking, if he was okay, but nothing came out.

"The cafe really is haunted." Some of the color drained from Owen's face.

My heart cracked at the sight of his fear. "Actually, I don't think so. No—I'm not denying magic. It's too late for that. I thought the cafe was haunted too, but Luca thinks it's more like a curse."

"Luca knows about magic?"

"Yes. We're both Witches. Our parents are Witches. There's a whole secret community of Witches."

Owen nodded, thoughtful, fear gone now he was distracted with revelations. He stroked Piña's head. "I thought it was me being fanciful. But there really are disembodied voices in the cafe? The milk really vanished? *Oh my god*, I have to tell Tristan!"

"No." My voice was sharp and he looked at me in confusion. "You can't Tell Tristan. Magic is complicated. I wasn't supposed to Tell you."

"You didn't really tell me, more showed me, and were really bad at lying to cover it."

"Same end result," I waved his words away. "You can't Tell Tristan, literally. There are inherent enchantments on Mortals preventing them from ever Telling. If you tried, you'd open your mouth and nothing would come out."

Owen looked aghast. "You've enchanted me?"

"No. No." I was doing a terrible job explaining. "All Mortals —people without magic—have enchantments and magical laws acting on them from birth. No one cast them on you. It's the world itself that's enchanted. I've never cast any sort of spell on you. It's illegal to do so without your consent, and you couldn't consent because you didn't Know."

"I kind of knew," Owen said, dazed as he reprocessed all his memories through this new lens. "You were always hinting. That's why I was so caught up in everything happening to the cafe. I always half thought—hoped—some sort of otherness was real. Why didn't you just tell me? Back when we were kids?"

I didn't know how I expected Owen to react, but he was remarkably calm. You hear cautionary tales of Mortals who go into extreme shock after being Told. Then again, sometimes the panic doesn't come until later. Owen was so close to believing for so long that the final tipping point wasn't a stretch for his mind. It should be a relief he wasn't scared, or feeling betrayed, or going into an existential crisis because the world was not at all what it seemed.

There was still time for all that.

I led Owen back to the couch. "I did try to Tell you when we were kids."

He looked at me, searching. I grabbed his hand and braced myself. I'd wanted to tell him the full story for so long. Now we were here, I feared it wouldn't be worth all the trouble, truth wasn't the bandage to fix everything.

"Telling Mortals about magic is strictly regulated. Most Witches never Tell, and it's against the law to ever Tell a minor. I knew all that growing up, but never liked it. I didn't like hiding so I shared magical things with you in fragments, as stories and imagination. But I don't know—I was young and didn't think things through. I liked you and didn't like lying. So, at that party, when we were drunk and my inhibitions were down, I gave in, ignored caution, and Told you."

"What? No you didn't." Owen looked confused, his tone bordering on harsh, as if he didn't want to hear something that contradicted his version of events.

"I did. You didn't believe me. To you it was just another of my stories. Just drunken silliness. But I wanted you to believe. I wanted everyone to know, so I went around Telling the other kids. I caused a scene and everyone laughed. You obviously don't remember."

"I wondered about that night so many times." Owen rubbed his eyes until they were red. "I missed the most important detail —focused on the wrong things—but I do remember being made fun of."

"Yeah, 'cause you were dating the weirdo saying magic was real. Then the Authority came, and not even booze could keep me from realizing how bad I'd fucked up."

"Wait—the guy with your dad? I knew that was weird!" Owen perked up, squeezing my hand. Maybe finding a detail connecting what he remembered to what I was saying helped.

I nodded. "I was arrested and taken to court. My Telling

attempt failed, no one actually believed, but lack of success didn't spare me the consequences. The court didn't trust me. They were convinced I'd try to Tell you again. I was too involved in your life. So they forbid me from ever seeing or contacting you."

"That's—I want to say ridiculous, but not in a dismissive way —it's so extreme." Emotions seemed to fluctuate through Owen. His eyes were bright, searching my face, his mouth set in a serious frown. "How could they forbid you from contacting me? How would they know?"

"Ridiculous isn't far off. Witches don't do things by halves. The Authority can use magic to track your actions. They cast a spell on me."

For a moment I didn't think Owen believed me. He scoffed, but when I didn't recant his frown deepened. "That seems wrong. Invasive."

A rush of gratitude cut through my stress. "That's one way to look at it, but I broke the law. I couldn't expect zero conse-quences after being so reckless and irresponsible. They took extreme action to make sure my bad habits didn't grow, turn radical, and continue to risk the secrecy of magic. Chances are, this is going to cause some problems now." I gestured between us.

"Why?" Owen sounded increasingly frustrated.

I understood where he was coming from but didn't think there was anything I could do to ease his mind until I got the facts out.

"Because I Told you for no reason. Because I'm not supposed to be here in the first place, and the fact the Authority hadn't found out already was a fucking miracle."

"I—well—Saving Piña isn't *no reason*." He held the cat tighter to his chest as if to assure her of her significance.

"To the Witches who enforce our laws, saving a cat isn't a

justifiable excuse for revealing magic. I've changed your whole world without a moment's thought for future repercussions."

Owen laughed. "You didn't change my whole world. That's dramatic as fuck. You saved my cat. That's more important to me than whatever weird Witch rule. And I'm glad. Not just for Piña. Aria, I *knew* there was more going on than your parents sending you away. I can't say this makes sense, but now I know. You didn't leave me."

Owen's voice cracked and I hugged him, squishing Piña between us. "I'll never leave you without explanation again, Owen. Fuck, I'm so sorry."

"It's okay." He had his face buried in my hair and sniffled. "I see how it was just as bad for you. I needed to know what really happened. Telling was worth giving me the truth. It pulls the past into focus."

"I'm glad you feel that way, Owen. I'm relieved you're not mad I lied. My parents didn't send me away, but they didn't understand why I hated keeping secrets most Witches didn't think twice about. They saw our friendship as a risk to their influence over my life. That's why they tried to push you away and judged you unfairly. But there's more to magic than our shared past. Now you Know there's all this *stuff*. It changes everything. The laws that I said have been acting on you, as a Mortal from birth, have changed. There's no longer blanket protection stopping magic from influencing you. You can participate in our world and be tripped up by all its pitfalls. You aren't protected by ignorance anymore."

Owen responded to my increasingly stressed tone with comfort, holding my cheek gently in his hand. "Is that such a big deal? I don't know any other Witches. Do I?"

"I don't think so, but I don't know! And you might meet Witches in the future."

"Aria, you're about to hyperventilate. It's okay. It doesn't sound like a big deal." He was smiling now. The more Owen insisted this was fine the more I slid the other way. He didn't understand.

"It is a big deal. I don't know exactly what's going to happen next. Nothing good. Our law enforcers—the Authority—are going to come for me. I probably need to call Luca for advice. He is going to be so pissed."

"Luca is a magic lawyer?" Owen's eyes went wide as I nodded. "How is that possible? How can there really be a whole other *world*? Why can't everyone just know? It doesn't seem fair."

"It's not fair. Magic is the ultimate power imbalance. You live in a world where you don't know all the rules, and the people that do possess more advantages than you even know exist."

16

OWEN

*D*id she have to put it so bluntly? When magic was outlined like that it wasn't such a wonderful revelation straight out of your childhood dreams. It made it sound like I'd been screwed over and didn't even realize it.

"Why is magic secret?" I asked. "If magic is really real, and such an advantage, why aren't Witches in charge? Why bother hiding?"

Aria still looked panicked, but sounded weary. "It's better for everyone if Witches stay hidden. That way we can't subject Mortals to unchecked magical influence."

"What does that mean?" In my frustration, I accidentally squeezed Piña causing her to wiggle away from me in a huff.

Aria watched the cat slink off. "Witches are just people—not everyone's kind and some would take advantage of, or abuse, Mortals. Sure, laws play a part in stopping abuse of power, just as they do in Mortal society. You could argue having magic out in the open, with laws against spelling Mortals in place, was enough protection. But some Witches would settle for manipulation, not breaking the law but using magic, or the threat of magic, to coerce Mortals, exploiting the inequality magic creates. The secret of magic protects you from that because we can't subject you to its influence when you don't Know."

"You make it sound so sinister." I tried for a joking tone, but my head was filled with wicked Witch overlords and a dystopian existence where I lived as some sort of underling.

"I'm not trying to scare you, but you need to understand." Aria looked stricken, not frowny in her usual begrudgingly good-natured way, but more serious than I'd ever seen her.

"Okay. Be wary of Witches. Got it." A lost, overwhelming feeling was sneaking up on me. I didn't really know what was going on. The disorientation of unreal things having been real all along was far from comforting. I found I didn't want to sit and think too hard about it. "What happens now?"

Aria sagged into the couch. "We need to figure out what the hell is going on with your cafe."

"Isn't it illegal? You just said—laws and secrets are supposed to protect me." Anger seeped into my tone. It wasn't right for magic to ruin my business when I hadn't even known it existed. And if the whole reason Aria was cut from my life was to 'protect' me with my own ignorance, then it was crap I was being screwed by magic anyway.

"Yes, the laws do protect you, on a grander scale. If it's a curse it is very illegal. But all the laws and secrets don't make it impossible for Witches to act outside the law. Look at me, trying to Tell you when we were kids."

"Fuck, Aria. This is so—out there—I don't even know why anyone would bother messing with Coffee Cat."

"Me either, but it'll be fine. I'll get it sorted out. You'll be fine, Owen."

I wanted to tell Aria I trusted her, but the words got stuck in my throat. Worry won out as my thoughts flitted from one concern to the next. "Are we in danger, do you think? The bird thing was—" Disaster surrounded us. Broken glass, feathers, a lingering cold on a summer day. I didn't know what I'd do if it happened again.

Aria gave me a hesitant half smile and grabbed my hand. "I don't think our safety is at risk, no. At least not yet. The incidents seem to be escalating. I won't let it get more serious, or allow more people to find out about magic."

Revealing magic was emerging as Aria's chief concern. Hopefully this was out of confidence we could fix the other problems. Or maybe fear that she couldn't. If things got worse in the cafe, I'd have to tell the others something, warn them to not come around if vengeful crows might attack the building.

"I can't Tell Tristan? Or you can't Tell him for me?" I asked again. He needed to know. This cafe was as much his as it was mine. With Tristan in the know we could discuss the madness of the world together, figure out what to do. We always did.

"We can't Tell Tristan. I know that's not fair to you. But I can't."

A sinking disappointment settled over me. If she'd already Told me, what was the big difference in Telling once more? It felt arbitrary. I didn't want to have life-altering information forcibly trapped inside me. I was in charge of my own relationships. Tristan and I didn't do secrets, and that shouldn't have to change if I didn't want it to. He would always be there for me. Being prevented from turning to him in a crisis, however strange, wasn't okay.

"He wouldn't believe you if you Told him," Aria said in a gentle voice.

"No. You'd have to show him. I know—you can't." I looked at her for two long moments, hoping in vain she'd change her mind. I let out a disappointed breath. "I don't want you in trouble. I'm totally focusing on the wrong thing. We need to fix the cafe."

"It's not the wrong thing, Owen. It's natural to worry about how this will affect the most important aspects of your life. That's what I'm trying to say—magic changes everything. We can talk about Tristan again, this isn't the end of the matter if it's important to you. But there's going to be fallout from Telling you. We need to get through that first."

Or she should Tell him before trouble comes. As soon as I thought that, I felt guilty. It was selfish of me, not knowing what this meant for Aria. After what happened when we were kids, I didn't like to think. Witches came down hard.

I hoped Aria's offer was sincere. I'd hold her to it. We'd revisit Tristan later, after whatever ominous fallout she was referring to came to pass. The idea of magic court buzzed at the back of my brain, but I found myself happy to ignore it.

I tried fruitlessly to focus on one of the problems making a scattered mess of my thoughts. "Please tell me you have a plan for the cafe?" If she did, it couldn't be very good, considering it'd gotten this far. "Or are the Witch police going to swoop in on us?"

"I don't know when the Authority will come calling on me. They could be here in a few hours. Until then, the cafe—" Aria went on to tell me about a paranormal investigator she was trying to reach. Her words washed over me like a rising sea. "We could have the Authority fix the cafe, but I think it would be better if we made some progress before they arrive. It might help —Owen, your eyes are glazing over." Aria leaned in to me and ran her hand through my hair. *Oh god.* Her touch was comforting.

"I may need some time to process."

She nodded. "I'll make you tea. Oh! I can make you a soothing draught. Do you want one?"

"Uh—" I almost gave in to her excited expression but wasn't comfortable ingesting magical liquids. "Earl gray will be fine."

I drank my normal tea as Aria put the apartment right. She

used spells to fix the glass and a regular broom and dustpan for the feathers. She talked the whole time but none of the words stuck in my brain. Aria had been dying to share these little details about magic with me, or maybe anyone, for a long time. She felt the need to explain everything now I Knew. Her nervous energy was adorable in its sincerity.

I wanted to comfort her, tell her not to worry about getting in trouble. She did nothing wrong. But I couldn't think of a single thing to say that wouldn't sound false. She knew I had no idea what was going on. I was utterly useless, helpless like I hadn't been since I was child. I hated the feeling.

Aria's phone rang. She shrieked with delight before answering. "Hello—yes. I was hoping to get your help with a Mortal cafe. That's right—somewhat urgent, yes."

What made me a Mortal exactly? It was an odd choice of words.

I left Aria to her phone call with the investigator, relief loosening some of the anxiety gripping my chest. I rinsed my mug and stared at the selection of loose-leaf tea on the counter. Had Aria been brewing Witchy teas all my life, or were these your average varieties? My mind snagged on the thought. Aria was a Witch. I'd been in love with a Witch in high school until we had some dramatic fairytale-esque parting forced upon us.

My current, seemingly simple feelings for Aria turned fragile. Knowing why she really left freed me unexpectedly. Deep down I'd feared I never mattered to Aria, like there was something easily forgettable about me. First my mom stopped caring, and then Aria. It wasn't logical, just an unshakable insecurity. It helped to know Aria never stopped caring, she never ignored me, or forgot me. The rejection I worked so hard to get over never actually happened. Clarity stripped away the last painful pieces of our past.

That didn't mean magic was welcome in rewriting my life.

What if Aria had never been taken away? I was reminded of my teenage longings for great love and forevers, but I didn't believe in the power of romantic love anymore. In an alternate world where she'd never left, would I be a hapless romantic? And what did it even matter; I'd grown into the reality of life. I was easily hurt, and that was okay, not a failing, but I wasn't going to be reckless with myself. I wasn't going to hope Aria would stay, when I knew she wouldn't.

Aria was right, I didn't quite grasp all the implications of a secret world. Magic could cause as great a rift between us as it healed. She hadn't wanted to leave in high school, and that was important, but it didn't stop it happening. The pain I went through was still real. Everything still came to an end. Everyone still left. This one detail didn't change my whole outlook on relationships, or discount all my other experiences.

I was good with what we had going on, I reminded myself. A little bit of sex and moving on. Nothing had to change that.

"Owen—" Aria came up behind me and turned off the forgotten fossette. "The investigator's on her way over."

17

ARIA

*O*wen and I entered the freezing cafe. Two figures stood silhouetted behind the glass front door, framed by the low light of the setting sun. I only expected Juliet Herrera, no one else, so we were off to a great start.

Owen looked at me sideways, hesitating in going to unlock the door. I squeezed his arm, smiled with a confidence I didn't feel, and went to let the Witches in.

"Thank you so much for coming." I stepped aside, pointedly ignoring the crows, who'd reassembled in the tree across the street.

They came inside and I shut the door quickly behind them.

I couldn't help being a little struck by the paranormal investigator. Juliet had soft, rounded facial features and some of the darkest eyes I'd ever seen. She looked my age—but that meant little for a Witch—had brown skin and lush, curly brown hair. She was all curves.

Her expression was a pleasant mask of focused professionalism as she took in the cafe. Seriousness was not usually a quality I was drawn to. Neither was her corporate presentation. Juliet was dressed like someone who happily used the term girl-boss, in an impeccably coordinated pencil skirt suit set, paired with shockingly impractical heels. I wanted to dislike so many of these things on principle but found it disturbingly challenging.

Juliet's companion was a white man with the kind of classically handsome face that was made for looks of disapproval. He was sporting one now, serious in his disdain but like he was about to be bored to death by you. He was dressed like we were shooting a 1920's noir film, fedora and all.

I hated everything about his presence already.

"Aria Belmonte. Owen Sanchez." The man nodded to each of us in turn.

I hadn't told Juliet Owen's name, or mentioned Owen would be attending this meeting. I'd also left out the part where I revealed magic. Of course they knew anyway.

I tried not to let my flash of panic show.

Juliet wasn't paying me any attention. She gave her companion an impatient look. He raised a shoulder in question and she looked away, refocusing on Owen. "I'm Juliet Herrera of Herrera Investigations. This is your cafe, Mr. Sanchez?"

"Yes?" Owen said, lacking his usual easy confidence.

"I'm sorry you've run afoul of someone nasty. Everything will be put right, I assure you, but first—" Juliet gave me a stiff, practiced smile. "Aria. There's a bit more to your story than discovering magic against Mortals, isn't there?"

The two Witches stared at me and I tried not to resent them. "I—nothing else relevant."

Juliet sighed. "It's related at the very least. May I introduce Mr. Bickel, my occasional associate who works for the Authority."

My eyes snapped to Mr. Grumpy-and-Handsome. I was so beyond screwed. I'd heard of him, *everyone* had. He was a legend, the most powerful Witch alive today. He didn't need conduits to cast even the most complex spells, and it was rumored he could bend time. I didn't even know what that meant in practicality. More to my concern, Bickel was known for ruthlessly enforcing the law. Sending him after me was a new level of overkill.

"Telling isn't really in my repertoire," he drawled. "But we were concerned you might not stop at Telling one Mortal. I was asked to follow up. Urgently. No one else could get here fast enough."

Bickel had the unique ability to teleport, it was the most legendary thing about him. Why wait for some lowly Authority Witch to travel up from LA when they could send this nightmare after me? The Authority's reaction was beyond dramatic, like I was some sort of out of control Witch going through town with a megaphone decrying magic's existence and leaving a trail of curses in my wake.

"Was that necessary?" I asked. "I'd never Tell anyone else. This was an accident. The whole cafe is a mess of magic, surely you can feel it. There's no reason to think I was planning to Tell more Mortals."

"No?" Amusement lit Mr. Bickel's eyes without touching his unfriendly freckled features. "It's not like you have a history of trying to Tell a whole group of Mortals at once."

I willed myself not to go red. "That was a long time ago. I'd never do that now."

"Forgive us for not trusting you, Aria. Especially when you're back to old habits." Mr. Bickel scrutinized Owen.

I followed Bickel's gaze. Owen had the guiltiest look on his face. After a confused moment I realized, *shit*, Owen didn't need to be thinking about Tristan right now. I had no immediate plans to Tell Tristan, but wasn't lying when I told Owen I was open to the discussion. I'd do anything for Owen, but Bickel had me reconsidering the implications.

Bickel couldn't read minds, but he wasn't clueless. "Owen, is Aria considering Telling anyone else?"

Owen frowned at Bickel. "No."

The dapper Witch looked back and forth between us before turning to Juliet. "This is why you need your own psychic, so you can tell unequivocally when they're lying."

"I don't think he's lying," Juliet offered.

"Perhaps," Bickel said. "Aria would you agree? Is Owen telling the truth?" He stared at me with piercing blue eyes, casually letting me know he knew all about me and my psychic abilities. There had to be some magic in the way he was looking at me. His stare drilled beneath my skin, planting a seed of fear.

"I'd never read Owen without him knowing." I said, not trusting myself with a blatant lie. "Can we please focus on the problem?"

"I always do." Mr. Bickel blinked and glanced away. The absence of his stare was a relief. "Imagine my surprise when I arrived in Juliet's office to discover she was on her way to see you, Aria. Imagine her surprise to learn you'd just revealed magic. Why didn't you call about the cafe's magical malady sooner?"

"I mean, in hindsight I should have. But we're here now. Owen knows. He's fine, right Owen? Or are you dragging us off to court now?"

"No, I won't do that," Mr. Bickel said. "I'm merely here to ensure a mass Telling isn't about to occur. That you have no radical plans. Your situation with Owen Sanchez will be examined at a later date. Procedure must be followed."

"Yes, all right." Juliet cleared her throat. "With that concern satisfied, we might as well ask Mr. Bickel to stick around as we look into the problem of your cursed cafe, Mr. Sanchez. Or may I call you Owen?"

"Uh—sure. Do we have to keep him around?" Owen gave Bickel an unfriendly look.

"No one ever has to agree to anything they don't want," Juliet said with exasperating seriousness. "But I find him very useful."

I looked more closely at Juliet. She must have quite a relationship with Bickel to imply he was available at her whim. Why had he stopped by her office before coming to grill me about Telling if he didn't know I'd hired Juliet? I'd never heard anything about Bickel and Juliet Herrera being *occasional associates*. Okay, I wasn't the most informed Witch, but I had heard of the Herrera family. If only I could remember why.

I'd likely invited more problems into my life. I couldn't even get asking for help right. This was a new level of hopelessly screwed up Witchery on my part.

Juliet continued her chat with Owen, the problem of Bickel's presence clearly forgotten in her mind. "Will you tell me what's been happening with your cafe? Only if you feel up to it, of course."

Juliet was being kind, I knew many Witches wouldn't bother including Owen in the conversation, but I couldn't help noting the undertone of condescension. Like Owen was a child to be coddled.

"Why wouldn't I be up to it?" Owen asked.

"You've only known about magic for what, half an hour? I'd understand if you want to leave this to us."

"I can take care of my own business," Owen said with force.

Juliet winced, her professional politeness slipping into worry. "Sorry. Of course you can. I didn't mean to imply— I see that wasn't a helpful offer. Please excuse me?"

"Uh—" Owen was as baffled as I was with Juliet's awkward, overly sincere reaction. "Don't worry about it."

Juliet looked relieved before her composure snapped back into place.

Owen took her around the cafe as he explained the myriad of problems he'd been dealing with over the past few weeks. She was attentive, her tone with Owen having lost all hint of superiority. Juliet touched various objects and parts of the building as they talked, magic sparking between her and the cafe as she assessed it.

Mr. Bickel and I trailed along. He was obviously keeping an eye on me, rather than the budding investigation.

"I'm not some ticking time bomb," I whispered to him as Owen explained the milk incident.

Juliet was wearing an odd expression of shock, while simultaneously trying not to laugh. She covered her mouth with a perfectly manicured hand adorned with exquisite crystal rings.

Bickel leaned in to whisper to me, his hands clasped behind his back. "I was tasked to take your measure, so excuse me while I do my job. I hear you don't have one."

I glared at him openly. It was a foolish way to act given he was a literal legend, but Bickel was also a total prick. "There is nothing wrong with being between jobs."

"No. However, I find it unfulfilling to have no purpose."

"I don't define my entire purpose through my job title."

"Good for you." He looked away, sounding bored.

I was seething. Bickel's opinion didn't matter. He was unironically wearing a bow tie and matching pocket square, I didn't care what he thought. I didn't need to justify my life, or match it to others' standards, especially someone who's opinions might be as outdated as his clothes. Why couldn't I take his comments and brush them off? I refused to admit I cared about anything these oh-so-traditional Witches valued.

I bet my parents would have loved Juliet and been horrified to hear I was acting so contrary. Whatever. My parents' opinions had nothing to do with anything. Not what I needed to focus on. My life was objectively a mess but I was getting back on track, I had to. I couldn't keep falling and failing forever.

"Aren't you worried you've been caught breaking your prior court restrictions?" Bickel asked.

"No one's cared I've been around Owen for the past week," I said, hiding my unease with anger. "I expected someone to swoop in immediately. Did no one notice? The spell better not have been a lie."

"Not a lie. But we can't monitor every restrictive spell indefinitely. The Authority only has so much manpower. After ten years, if the offending Witch—that's you by the way—hasn't tried to break their spell, we stop actively monitoring nonviolent criminals. Research shows a ninety-nine percent success rate of indefinite obedience after ten years without reoffence."

Of course they'd done studies. Typical Witches, all their ducks in a damned row.

"Trust you to break *all* the rules," Bickel added with an exaggerated, put-upon air.

"What are they going to do about all my rule breaking?" My anger at Bickel's rudeness didn't stop me from trying to squeeze information out of him. His appearance had me worried I'd be whisked away, but if that wasn't happening, I was at a loss.

He only shrugged. "Prosecution isn't my job. I'm only here to stop you from doing anything else stupid."

"Shouldn't be hard. I'm not planning on it."

"This wasn't exactly planned though, was it?" He smirked down at me.

"Why not just lock me up until the court can see me, if I'm such a wild card?"

"Now that's a bit extreme, don't you think? You're only careless, not malicious, as far as we know. It's not like you've turned an innocent person into a toad, or something equally horrific.

Besides, if we locked you up, I wouldn't get to enjoy the California sun while I keep an eye on you."

"I'd rather go straight to court than be stuck with you hanging around." This was brazen, but I couldn't make myself treat him differently than anyone else who purposely pissed me off, even if sucking up was in my best interest.

Bickel frowned at my insult, almost like he was truly offended. Which was weird. What did he care?

"I'll put in a word for you, Aria. Move you right to the top of the list of naughty Witches in need of a court date."

Well fuck.

Juliet mercifully called her associate over to discuss diagnostic spells. After a moment she closed her eyes and muttered an incantation, everything around us began to glow faintly. Bickel watched, thoughtful. Whatever information they gleaned remained unknowable to me.

Owen shifted over to my side. "They aren't how I imagined Witches to be," he said in a low voice.

"Oh?" I was still busy glaring.

"I didn't expect pointy hats," Owen said seriously. "But I also wasn't expecting the paranormal investigator to look so corporate. And why is that guy wearing a vintage three-piece suit? He looks like he's about to bust out a monogramed handkerchief."

I almost laughed. "Who knows. He's old and powerful. Maybe he thinks he's quirky." Or Bickel never got over the end of the Roaring Twenties. Either way, I really didn't care about his personal style.

"Old? He's barely got more wrinkles than I do. He can't be more than forty-five," Owen said.

I was about to say Bickel was a hundred years old, or thereabouts, and then remembered we hadn't gotten to that Witchy tidbit. Now wasn't the time to discuss it and thankfully Juliet called for our attention, her spell concluded. I ignored my sense of relief at dodging the topic.

"The Coffee Cat Cafe has indeed been placed under a curse," Juliet informed us. "I can see why a haunting may have been your first guess, Aria. This is a bafflingly complex curse. It has layers—"

We'd convened in the kitchen. Bickel was poking around a container of leftover pan dulce and noisily opened the lid, interrupting Juliet. She tugged on his sleeve with the air of a mother dealing with an impossible child while the grown-ups were talking. Bickel rolled his eyes at her silent rebuke before closing the lid and taking up position as stony sentinel behind her.

"Yes, well," Juliet tried to act like nothing happened. "Layers. To the curse. Breaking it won't be a problem. Both Bickel and I have extensive experience in malicious magic. Stopping it, not casting. But the matter of discerning the culprit is more complicated."

"As long as magic stops ruining my business, I don't care about the culprit," Owen said.

Bickel frowned. "This sort of thing is highly illegal. We can't let it go uninvestigated."

"I hired Juliet, not you," I said before I could stop myself.

"Thank you, Aria." Juliet interrupted her associate as he opened his mouth. "I'm happy to look into this for you, in addition to breaking the curse, but Authority involvement is unavoidable. I'm bound to report illegal activity. I don't operate independent of the law, as much as I may wish."

Bickel directed a cold stare at me. "We'll look after everything with the utmost vigilance."

Owen rubbed his eyes. "Cool. So can I open my cafe tomorrow? I can't afford to lose more business. Nothing is working, the power, the sinks, the cold air. It's all the curse?"

"We'll break the curse today, and everything will be back to normal," Juliet said. "There is a disruptive spell woven into the curse, which is the root of the problems with your power and water. Discomfort and disorientation are the other key elements. I really can't explain the milk, other than it was the work of the curse, and specifically targeted. The voices were obviously meant to scare you, as were the crows—an impressive bit of spell casting, that. Like I said, layers. The last of which was a responsive spell, causing the malicious magic to escalate in intensity in response to other magic."

I wanted to hide. I'd actively made the problems at the cafe worse by trying to help. It was like a fucking metaphor for my life. "How could I have known that?" I asked in response to the other Witches' attention.

Juliet gave me a reassuring look. "It's not the sort of thing I'd expect the average Witch to anticipate."

"Regardless, you should have called someone sooner." Bickel couldn't seem to help adding.

"That's easy to say now we know what's going on." Juliet turned back to Owen. "Can you think of anyone with a grudge against you?"

"Me? No. Why would anyone target me?"

"It's your cafe. You're obviously the target. Unless there's someone else? The landlord or a business partner? Another tenant?" Juliet took out her phone and a stylus, poised to take notes.

Owen shook his head. "My landlord Jenn is the best. Can't be her. And my business partner isn't the kind of guy you can stay mad at."

"So it must be you." Bickel stepped out from behind Juliet to scrutinize Owen more closely.

Owen crossed his arms, his spine straightening. "Why does it have to be aimed at anyone?"

"Witches don't cast curses for no reason. Especially one so aggressive," Juliet said reasonably.

Owen moved away from the Witches and readjusted the containers of sugar and flour stored near the oven, likely taking a moment to consider everything. Eventually he turned back to Juliet. "I can't think of anyone who'd be this angry at me. I swear."

Juliet frowned. "No rival bakeries? Jilted ex-lovers? Family feuds?"

"You've got to be joking." Owen caught my eye in disbelief and I shrugged.

"Not at all. Mr. Bickel and I need a lead." Juliet nudged her associate with her elbow. "There's no trace of the Witch's identity in their spell casting, and not enough evidence in the magic running through the cafe to point to anyone. The curser actively practiced concealment. Uncovering a motive would help us find the Witch responsible."

Owen's restless hands were back on the flour container. "Okay, I get that. But I'm telling you, I didn't provoke this attack, and it's not like they're going to come back. You do what needs to be done to find the Witch—I don't want worry about this mess any further. As long as we solve the cafe's problems, to me, it doesn't matter who was behind it."

Juliet put her phone away. "You don't have to worry, that I can guarantee, but we can agree there's a lot we don't know here." Her gaze darted around the kitchen, sharp with attention as if she could will the space to give up its secrets. "Since there's no clear motive, I'd like keep watch for any Witch patronage at Coffee Cat, as a bare minimum, until I find something pointing toward the culprit's identity."

"We can't simply ignore what was done here, even if it wasn't personally directed at you, Owen." Bickel adjusted his already perfect bow tie like he was incapable of ignoring anything that might be out of order.

Owen stepped away from his ingredients, rejoining the rest of us next to the container of extra pan dulce. "Right. Well, you're welcome to come into the cafe and investigate all you want. But can we break the curse now? Please?"

"Yes, of course. Would you like to, or shall I?" Juliet asked Bickel.

"You. Then if you're unable, we'll have a better understanding of exactly how powerful this Witch is."

Juliet nodded in agreement with her companion's suggestion. "Would you mind grabbing my herbs and candle?"

Bickel twitched his finders and a bushel of sage and a purple and black candle appeared out of thin air.

"How'd you do that?" I couldn't keep the awe from my voice. Summoning only worked one way. Sending objects, for example Piña, flying through the air. Witches wouldn't make things appear or disappear, or summon objects out of nowhere. Then again, Bickel had a strong enough affinity for earth to allow him to teleport.

Bickel chuckled and ignored my question.

"Don't act impressed or it'll go to his head," Juliet said to me as she set the candle on the counter and lit it with a flick of her fingers.

He did look annoyingly smug.

Juliet ignited the herbs and began her incantation. From what I could tell, she was improvising the wording on the spot in response to her magic's reaction to the curse. It was impressive, even if it looked like nothing more than walking around, muttering.

A white light flashed, blinding us. When it subsided, the air returned to a tolerable temperature and the hum of electricity clicked back on. Owen gave me a look of tentative relief.

"They're not too powerful then," Juliet said to Bickel.

"I'd hope not." Owen sounded exasperated. "I don't see why I'd have formidable Witch enemies. All I do is bake."

Juliet made arrangements to return to the cafe as Owen boxed up a variety of pan dulce for each Witch. Even if he was finding this whole mess overwhelming, Owen was the kind of person who prioritized generosity and the distribution of sweet treats to all.

I was relieved to finally have magic purged from the cafe. The investigators could work on catching the Witch responsible, but as far as I was concerned, that was officially their problem, not mine or Owen's.

"Thank you, Owen." Juliet gave an excited look inside her pastry box. "Oh, marranitos! I'm eating these for dinner. Mr. Bickel, you can go on ahead."

Her abrupt dismissal didn't faze the other Witch. "But I brought you over here. How will you get back?"

"I don't know. If only I was able to get around without you."

Bickel let out an involuntary snort of laughter and disappeared on the spot.

Owen's mouth opened in silent awe. "Can you do that, Aria?"

"No. No one can teleport but him." And boy did I sound grumpy about it.

"Rather unfair isn't it?" Juliet looked fondly to the spot where Bickel had stood. "Can I have a private word with you, Aria?"

I glanced at Owen.

He looked exhausted and relieved to make his escape. "Fine with me. I'm going to check on Piña."

"Check on what?" Juliet asked.

"His cat," I said as Owen departed. His exhaustion was to be expected, but I felt a pang of guilt. Hopefully Owen wasn't too overwhelmed, and if he was, he'd come to me.

"Aria, are you all right? Is there anything you might—need?" Juliet's soft voice interrupted my thoughts. Her brows were pulled together in concern, and her stringent professional air ebbed away.

"What do you mean?" I asked in confusion. I didn't need any more of her services. She'd done a hell of a lot already. Saved my incapable ass.

Juliet shifted her pastry box and looked down. "This situation must be stressful. Do you have someone to call?"

"I—" My first unkind thought was, why did she care? Juliet was an ideal sort of Witch, powerful and poised. Everything I wasn't. She probably pitied me, thought me extremely incompetent.

"I can handle myself fine."

Juliet went red in the cheeks. "That's not what I meant."

Her meaning eluded me and when she didn't elaborate, I said, "My brother is a lawyer. I need to give him a call anyway."

"Oh, I wasn't implying—trouble—more like—well, it seems you have it under control then?" Juliet gave a sigh of surrender.

It hit me then, Juliet was being kind. Stiff, but sincere in trying to check on me. She appeared lost without her professionalism and her role as investigator. I wondered why she felt she needed to offer more if it wasn't in her comfort zone.

"Thanks, I'm good," I said and saw her out.

As I watched Juliet walk down the street in the twilight, I had the absurd thought she was acting like a friend might.

18

OWEN

*T*he front door opened and close with a soft click. I needed to go out and talk to Aria, but stayed in my bedroom.

The Witches made me uneasy. I was grateful, and knew they were here to help, but it would have been better to have a more approachable pair. I didn't like Bickel. He really drove home Aria's point about there being a lot I didn't know.

I heard Aria coming down the hall. We really should talk. I wanted rid of this lonely, overwhelmed feeling. I wanted to be happy the cafe was fixed and to move on from this mess. Go back to normal.

I opened my door as Aria walked by. She startled and laughed at herself, dropping her phone. It buzzed on the floor.

An odd, settled feeling came over me. Thinking about stiff impersonable Witches cast everything in a dreary light, but Aria changed all that. Magic had always been a part of my life, even if I didn't know it. Magic was always part of us. A hidden element pulling us together disguised as childhood stories and shared imagination. Magic wasn't overwhelming when it was Aria's.

She reached out to grab her phone. I caught her hand instead. With a little tug I brought her to me.

"How are you doing?" she asked, arms circling my waist.

Aria was always taking care of me. *Let me read your palm and we'll see how to fix it.* Aria had said a variation of those words too many times to count when we were young. I might not need it so much now, but I loved knowing that part of us hadn't changed. I was always good when I was with her.

"I'm better now." I leaned in and kissed her.

Aria's lips were soft, already familiar. She kissed me without hesitation and I felt myself smiling into it. Kissing was different than it had been this afternoon. I was still full of lust and longing, but something more shifted inside me.

I was kissing someone I'd loved most of my life. Anger and confused loss had never cancelled out my love for Aria, only obscured it. With no hurt left I only felt hopeful. Stupidly so. Kissing had never been this emotional. I was afraid I'd give myself away in how I touched her, recklessly falling into my own feelings, filling her mouth with small sounds and broken breath. Nothing would go back to normal after Aria. I wanted her in my future in ways that never worked. Couldn't we stay in this moment forever, where I could love her and nothing would change? Stop here before time inevitably brought us to our end?

Our kisses pulled me deeper, no amount of telling myself they were finite prevented them from soaking into my heart, making me greedy for more. With Aria I failed to guard myself.

Maybe we can find a way to make it work. I couldn't stop the thought, only push it away.

Aria pressed me up against the doorframe and I groaned, pulling her in tight against me.

"Owen—" She was breathless, speaking against the skin of my neck.

"What do you need?" I sounded gruff and couldn't quite think with her body pressed up against me.

"You," she said in my ear. The single syllable hit me like an electric shock. Maybe I was imagining it, but she sounded as frayed as I felt.

"You can always have me," I said, and meant it like I never had with anyone else.

She bit my earlobe, tugging playfully, sending tingles down my neck which she chased with her lips. "Yes, until I have to leave."

"Then I want to make the most of this." I pulled Aria into my room, ignoring the reminder of the parameters I'd set this afternoon.

"Me too."

It was two steps to the bed. She stood between my legs as I sat perched on the edge of my mattress. Aria had solid thighs and soft curves. I wanted her legs wrapped around me. I wanted to see all of her, find every place she liked to be touched. Her brown eyes almost sparkled, catching the light, warm flecks of gold and amber almost hypnotizing as she leaned in. My hands seemed to be glued to her hips, until she peeled me away and pulled my shirt over my head.

Aria shucked off her shirt and jeans, in a quick stripping display sexy in its eagerness, before turning her nimble fingers to the button on my jeans. I let her strip me completely while she remained in simple black underwear. I was almost panting, hard and exposed and caught in the way she looked at me. I doubted it was actual magic, but it felt like it, a spell of intimacy and desire that had me burning without touch.

I tumbled Aria onto the bed and looked her over slowly, causing her to squirm but not in discomfort. She was stretching and writhing in a way that put herself on display. When my eyes returned to her face, she bit her lip and raised a suggestive brow.

Hot, so fucking hot. She knew what she was doing to me, and I liked that too.

When Aria touched me, shivers erupted over my skin. I covered her in kisses. My lips started at her collarbone, working my way slowly over her as my cock pressed needily against her leg. The swell of Aria's breast fit perfectly under my hand once I had her bra discarded and thrown somewhere across the room.

I took her nipple in my mouth and flicked at it with my tongue. She squirmed and wound her hands in my hair. My name escaped her lips in a shivering breath. I'd never be able to hear it enough. So I did it again. Her hand found my cock but I pulled her away after a few perfectly tight strokes.

I continued my kisses down her body and slipped my fingers beneath the fabric of her panties, but didn't touch her where she needed it most.

Her hips twitched. "Owen, please."

I pulled the fabric away and settled myself between her legs. I stroked her folds, luxuriating in soft wet heat, and spread her before licking up her slit to her clit. I sucked and teased her with my tongue. Aria let out small little whimpery breaths and I didn't hold back my responding sounds. I loved the intimacy of tasting her, feeling her pleasure so acutely against my mouth as she came.

I pulled back and kissed her thighs.

"Oh fuck, Owen."

I laughed and gave her a playful bite on her inner thigh. She squealed and pulled me up by the hair. Her face was flushed and she looked completely debauched. "Fuck me, Owen. Please?"

My lips stretched in a silly kind of smile. Another laugh bubbled out of me.

"Why is that funny? I'm begging for you here."

"Sorry. Sorry. I'm just so happy."

Aria's playful outrage melted into something warm and seductive in its sincerity. "I'm happy too, Owen. I—" She rolled her hips under me, rubbing my cock between her legs. "I want you."

"I want everything." I buried my face in her neck, hiding. Did she know what I meant? Did I want her to?

Aria was murmuring agreement. *Yes, yes, she wanted everything too.* It was sex talk but not. I wasn't sure.

I got a condom and rolled it on, sitting against the headboard, fumbling and rushed. Aria knelt in front of me watching in that spellbinding way of hers. She was gorgeous. Long tousled hair, faint tan lines crossed her body, light brown on dark. A line of small, tattooed stars matching the ones on the underside of her wrist ran up her side from her hip to below her breast. As if sensing where my eyes were caught, she ran her hand along the tattoo before grazing her nipple.

I pulled her onto my lap, my cock trapped between us. "Like this?"

"Oh, yes." She gave me an almost wicked grin before kissing me.

My fingers traveled up her thighs and dips between her legs. The taste of her was still on my tongue. I held my cock steady as Aria sunk down onto me. Watching her take me was almost as good as the feeling. She ran her hands over my face, reveling in my reaction. Aria moaned and rocked her hips. My head fell back against the headboard.

"Owen, look at me."

She brought us nose to nose. I cupped her ass and thrust up to meet her next movement. We found a rhythm and then I couldn't think. She was hot and tight around me and my world was nothing but brown eyes and hot moaning breath. She came with quick, sharp rolls of her hips, rubbing her clit against me, taking what she needed until her head dropped to my shoulder.

I followed, the feeling of her inner muscles clenching around me sending me over.

Oh fuck, oh fuck. Somehow those were my words breaking through the constant moaning, and then we were laughing again, bodies shaking and sweaty, smelling like sex and us and god, I only wanted to do it again.

Aria shifted off me and flopped on the bed while I disposed of the condom.

"I've never laughed this much during sex," I said, feeling giddy as I lay beside her.

Aria tucked herself against me, grin wide, head on my chest, and my arm went immediately around her. "Do you think it's a bit of hysteria? All too much, between cats and crows, magic and sex?"

"Not at all." I hadn't been thinking of any of that. Somehow sex had never been this fun. It was always fun, don't get me wrong, but there was something about being this free with Aria that released an unbridled joy in me. Pure, and I'd say innocent, except well obviously not. I had the urge to put all these giddy feelings into words but couldn't contrive a way to express how I felt that wouldn't end in a declaration.

"We should go to sleep if we've devolved into unexplained laughter," Aria said.

"Stay?" I ran my hand down her back, my giddiness deflating as reality crept back in bed with us. I meant stay in bed, with me tonight, not stay forever. The fact I had to clarify this to myself meant nothing.

Aria gave a one shoulder shrug and kissed my peck. I pulled a blanket over us. We lay a few moments in silence. Instead of sleep and relaxation settling over me, I felt a growing tension. I couldn't ignore my own thoughts. *Stay forever?* I wanted Aria in my life, not as a friend, and not confined by the safeness of

casual, temporary arrangements. Anything short lived felt like a
waste.

Maybe we should talk now. I could test the field, see what
was possible before admitting anything. I wasn't even sure I was
ready to throw out all my safeguards and change what I wanted
in life. Shit, I couldn't discount this as some sex and magic
fueled moment of delusion that I'd get over. And if it wasn't, if
this was real, I needed to know how much magic set us apart as
a minimum measure of compatibility.

"Aria?"

She hummed in response.

"Why couldn't you break the curse?"

This was the first thing to pop into my head other than, *if we
wanted to make this fling more permanent, how would that work?* I
should have gone with that because Aria stiffened at my seemingly innocuous question.

"I'm not as good a Witch as Juliet. She outmatches me in raw
power, but even if she didn't, I'm—kinda bad at magic."

"No, you're not. You saved Piña."

"Yeah." She sighed. "A simple summoning spell. I have no
idea how to do the kind of magic Juliet did today, and had no
idea how to deal with the curse on my own. I stopped studying,
never trained properly."

Aria rolled out of my arms, onto her back. I felt her absence
like a punch to the gut. I wanted to pull her back but didn't. It
felt like a sign, one that made me glad I shied away from any
pronouncements of feelings.

I said, "I imagine magic's like anything. I can't do what an
electrician can. You shouldn't have to be able to do all kinds of
magic. You have psychic skills instead. Is that right?"

"Kind of." Aria stared at the ceiling as I talked to her. "My
psychic ability is something I was born with. The things Juliet
did were learned, so yeah like an electrician. I don't have to learn

everything, but most people choose *something*. I decided to use my psychic power in a less traditional, untrained way."

"Oh. Was Clara at the magic shop a Witch?" I turned on my side to face her.

She glanced at me then up at the ceiling again. "No. I like living with Mortals. Less pressure. But there are Witchy jobs I could do as a psychic—I've never tried. Luca found something for me, actually."

"That's great." I could tell from her tone that she was hesitant, and I wasn't crazy about the idea, but what else do you say? I had no idea what a Witchy psychic job with Luca entailed other than it wasn't going to be here in town.

I wouldn't ask Aria to get a non-Witchy job to stay with me, any more than I'd be okay with her asking me to give up the cafe to follow wherever magic took her. We each had a life. If those lives didn't fit together, then that wasn't anything I hadn't expected from the start. It was the most obvious end. Avoiding this disappointment was the whole point of casual, and it rarely failed me. I'd briefly hoped for a future with Diego, but our lives didn't fit either. This was shaping up to be the same, magic or no, and so casual Aria and I would stay.

"I don't know if taking the job is the right thing," Aria said. "I didn't want to work as part of the magical law enforcement system. I wanted to do something better. What I do isn't better in terms of career or money, and I mostly don't care, but it's wearing. There's drawbacks to living with Mortals. Magic always puts limitations on my friendships, when I can't really share all of me. I can't deny things aren't working out like I'd hoped."

"Sounds like you want a chance to start fresh," I hedged.

Aria nodded. "Part of me wants to," she whispered. "Part of me is tired of being isolated and out of touch. I've been resisting Witchy things for the sake of resisting—I don't think I realized that until now. I'm missing out on community, connection, not everyone and everything I left behind is bad. I'm sick of childish impulses driving me to stay away."

"Why not take the job? It sounds like you want to give it a try at least?"

"Yeah—I should try." Aria finally looked at me with an exaggerated eye roll. "Besides, I need to leave. I can't take over your apartment forever."

"Oh—" I faltered.

Offer for her to stay. But I couldn't. Her life was taking her in another direction. I didn't fit, of course I didn't. I knew I wouldn't. She was always leaving, that was the whole plan. She wanted the job, or one like it. She wanted more than her life was at the moment, and of course that was all tangled up with magic.

"Don't worry, Owen." Aria reached out and ran a hand through my hair. "Getting the Witchy job I was always meant to have doesn't mean I'm disappearing. Never again. I Told you about magic. You can't get rid of me easily anymore."

I pulled her back into my arms. "I don't want to get rid of you."

19

ARIA

I woke up alone in Owen's bed much later than expected. He'd been quiet to slip out without disturbing me.

My intention to help in the Coffee Cat kitchen again was dashed and the disappointment was disproportionately crushing.

I dressed in a hurry and went down to the cafe. It was busy with customers, the sound of the espresso machine mixed with cheerful voices and music. There was no trace of the cold, haunted—okay, cursed—disaster of the day before.

Tristan was busy at the register with two employees I didn't know, other than by sight.

"One early morning more than enough for you?" Tristan asked when I reached the front of the line. He rang up a cold brew before I had a chance to tell that was exactly what I wanted.

"I should have set an alarm."

"No. No. I was joking." He waved my guilt away with glitter tipped fingers. "Owen really appreciated your help, getting someone to fix the electricity. We all do. But he looked particularly happy this morning."

"Did he?" I asked in a very cool, collected way. Not at all eager, or hopeful.

Tristan gave me a sly, lopsided grin. "Yep. *So* happy."

I tried not to let that warm my worried heart, but stars above, even Tristan could tell what Owen's happiness meant to me. I was thankful he didn't say anything more.

I took my coffee and got out of his way. My seat by the window was open, so I sat. A look outside revealed only one, perfectly acceptable, crow pecking at something on the sidewalk across the street. The jacaranda tree was bird-free and looking much less ominous. My Witchy senses told me nothing in the cafe was cursed, haunted, or magically altered. I wanted to breathe a sigh of relief as I sipped my coffee. I deserved to relax, right? The disaster, if not averted, was under control.

Juliet and Bickel would find the offending Witch and wrap everything up. As far I was concerned, my cafe related magic issues were over. If only I didn't have a bunch of other, even more pressing problems to worry about, I might have been relieved.

There were seven missed calls from Luca on my phone's lock screen. I hadn't updated him after hiring the PI like I'd promised. That was why he was calling. There was no way he could know I Told. Still, my skin crawled with the thought of talking to him, and even more so with the thought of our parents finding out what happened.

"Mind if I join you?" Juliet stood before me as impeccably dressed as yesterday, carrying a leather briefcase.

She surprised me. I'd assumed Juliet wouldn't involve me in her investigation from here on in, and so didn't think she'd want to come and talk to me while at the cafe.

I gestured to the seat across from me, pleased about her

unexpected company. Juliet perched gracefully, set her briefcase down, clicked it open, and pulled out a sleek laptop. I watched her diligently begin work. I couldn't imagine what she was writing, and resisted the urge to pry.

"Have you had many cases like this one?" I asked instead, not that I was particularly interested, but I wanted to say something and couldn't think of anything else the two of us had in common to talk about.

"No." Juliet frowned and looked up from her computer. "I can't say I've been called in on many curses where the Mortal didn't already Know about magic. I checked the watchlists for anything remotely helpful. There isn't a serial coffee shop curser terrorizing Southern California. Unfortunately, these things are almost always personal. Do you know of anyone who'd do this to Owen?"

"No, it's hard to imagine anyone cursing Owen. But I've only—uh—recently come back into his life." Juliet only nodded and didn't press me. I continued talking anyway. "So, if you don't have any suspects, are you actually going to wait for the Witch to show up again? How will you find them if they don't decide to re-curse the place while ordering a trim latte?"

I mean, no one expected the curser to come back. That would make even less sense than someone cursing the coffee shop to begin with.

"Observing the cafe is a start, and maybe not at fruitless as you think, Aria. A curse with all the drama of spilled milk and exploding sinks is a spectacle the culprit would want to see in action. I'd wager they've been here a number of times since they cast the curse. Hopefully they're coming back. It'll pay to wait and watch for at least a day or so, before taking more aggressive action."

When you looked at it that way, Juliet had a good point. For

Owen's sake I hoped she was wrong, but either way the investigators had it under control and I didn't have to worry about it.

Juliet turned back to her computer and began typing at full speed. I unlocked my phone, dismissed Luca's notifications and checked up on my Mortal magic merch listings. Someone had questions about the crystal balls. Great.

Mr. Bickel sat down in the chair next to me without asking. I hadn't even seen him enter the coffee shop and so was unprepared for his intrusive presence. I glared as he handed Juliet a coffee, which she took without looking up.

Was his task of watching me the only reason Juliet had joined my table? I was sorely disappointed at the idea.

"I'd have got you something Aria, but you seemed occupied with that comically large iced beverage." Bickel was dressed as ridiculously as yesterday, in a bow tie and a three-piece suit. In summer. It was almost more offensive for being seasonally inappropriate than for being a century out of style.

"It's cold brew," I said, swirling the straw. "And it's not comically large."

Bickel sipped from a tiny espresso cup, his blue eyes regarding me with frightening concentration.

"I like cold brew," Juliet said. "You want a big cup with all that ice."

"Thank you." I saluted her with my drink.

Juliet smiled at me. It was easy to tell her practiced facial expressions from her genuine ones. Her smile was much softer than her glamorous professional looks.

Bickel ignored us. "We're the only Witches here. This is going to be dreadfully dull." He glanced around briefly before adjusting his posture into deliberate nonchalance.

Tristan came over to our table with a plate of pan dulce and a stack of napkins. Bickel thanked him with barely more than a glance. I caught Tristan's eye to thank him as well. He looked slightly pink, and rushed off to do something else before I could ask what was up.

"What are you working on?" Bickel asked as I got back to my phone.

"Selling crystal balls," I said, not looking up.

Staking out a coffee shop was hardly most-powerful-Witch business. Was Bickel really going to watch my every move? I wished he'd go away.

"My neighbor is in the market for a new crystal ball. Should I tell her to call you?" Juliet asked.

My cheeks went hot as I continued to not look at the Witches in front of me. "They aren't real ones. Mortal gimmicks."

The silence that followed was too much. I glanced up to face their judgment. It was better to get it out of the way. I didn't expect Witches like them to take me seriously any more than my parents did. Bickel was laughing with his eyes, his face disapproving, making for an unnerving combination. Juliet looked thoughtful.

"How interesting," she said without mockery. "Is there a good market for that sort of thing? I bet a Witch would do well in selling fake magical trinkets."

"I—it could be better. I mostly do fortunes."

Before I was subjected to their reaction to that, my phone began to buzz. I grabbed it, excused myself, and hurried out the back to the driveway behind the building.

"Hi, Luca." I pressed the phone to my ear, accepting only audio, not video. There was no need to see my brother's face during this conversation.

"Aria. I thought you might have died."

"No, you didn't."

"I could have."

"And that's the tone you'd take? Dry and unfeeling at your twin's demise?"

"How's the PI going? You didn't update me."

"Good, I'm with her now. All under control. About that job—"

That distracted him nicely. "Yes." Luca sounded genuinely excited. "I've spoken to our intern coordinator. They're interested. Be here Monday morning for an interview."

"Monday?"

"What, are you busy?"

"I might be. Just because I'm unemployed doesn't mean I don't have things going on."

"Aria—" I could feel Luca's eyes roll. "Are you serious about this or not? It will be a great opportunity for you to work with other psychics. Make connections. Open up your future."

Breaking my decade-old pattern of resisting the Witchy world on impulse was near impossible. But I did want to give this a shot. Owen was right, this job was a chance to start fresh, and I needed that desperately. There was nothing to say I couldn't still do Mortal fortunes in my spare time. And Luca was right too, damn it, helping Mortals via his law firm was something I'd find fulfilling.

I needed a new direction. I was sick of having nothing but others' disappointment.

"I'll drive up Sunday," I said.

"Excellent. I'm still at mom and dad's. They'll be happy to see you—"

I made an unintelligible noise. "Have you told them I'm interviewing?"

"No. Can I?"

"I guess you'll have to. The thing is—I need some other advice—"

I sat on the steps of the cafe's back door and poked a stray crow feather with my foot as I told Luca about the disastrous bird attack and everything else that happened since. Except for the part where I slept with Owen. He listened without comment, knowing as well as I did that if he interrupted me with critique, I'd clam up.

"Fuck, Aria," Luca growled when I was done.

"Is that your professional opinion?"

"I mean, kinda. This isn't good. You're lucky no one else saw the flying cat!"

"Obliviousness is a blessing—it's fine. But um, it's not actually illegal to Tell without pre-approval, now that we aren't kids. Right?" My voice was uncertain, almost pleading, betraying my fear that it was not, in fact, *fine*.

"Telling is classed as a restricted act, not illegal among adults. The court can grant retrospective approval, once they've passed judgment on your actions." Luca was obviously disappointed, but he still seemed to want to comfort me. "They understand we sometimes get backed into a corner, accidents happen. You just have to show you're being responsible now Owen Knows. It won't be like your hearing in the past, attempted Telling of groups of minors was blatant law breaking. But there could still be legal consequences for Telling Owen now if you're found negligent."

"How likely is that?"

"It all depends on Owen, how freaked out he is. How worried he is about his future now magic can touch him. If the court thinks he's fine, and you've handled everything between now and then correctly, this mistake won't affect your future plans. My firm can still hire you as long as the hearing results in an approval." He sounded frayed and I could picture his head in his hands, curls tumbling around his face as he bemoaned my inability to do anything right. "I can't believe after everything you let this happen. Aria. Don't let him derail your whole life again. *Please.*"

I shot up from the step and began to pace the driveway.

"Owen never derailed my life, Luca. I did that on my own, thank you."

"You ran away from magic and your future, our whole world, because of him."

"No. I ran away because I realized the magic world is nothing but a bunch of power obsessed control freaks who think they're better than everyone, and I didn't want to be part of it."

"Is that what you think of me?"

I winced at the pain in his voice. "This isn't about you, Luca. You're perfect. But I don't have to be just like you to be worth something. I'm not a total failure."

"God, I never thought you were."

"Fine. Sorry. Don't worry. I won't let this *mess up my life*. I'll make sure Owen is as unaffected by magic as possible. I don't want to fail him too." My voice broke a little and for a horrifying second I thought I might cry.

"Do you still have feelings for him?" Luca asked, his tone too gentle for my liking.

"I'll always have feelings for him, but that doesn't matter. Owen's life is here. I'm moving to take this job—if I get it. I do want to try, Luca, really. Improve my skills, do worthwhile work. I'm sick of being adrift. Owen knows I'm leaving. He knows it will be good for me because he's so damn perceptive. He also knows we'll stay friends this time."

"Friends. Aria, are you sure that's all?"

"It is if I say it is." So what if I had secret hopes of working something out. Fitting Owen's and my life together like a glove, letting these feelings grow into the kind of love I'd always wanted with him.

Luca hesitated. "Okay."

There was one more thing on my mind. "They sent Bickel after me," I said in a whisper.

"Shit."

"I know, I *know*. It's fine, he's just lurking. Making sure I don't Tell anyone else."

"Then don't even think about Telling anyone else. I'm serious. If the court thinks this is the start of a pattern—"

My stomach twisted and I tried not to think about Owen and Tristan. "It's not. Everything is under control now that competent Witches fixed the cafe. I'll see you Sunday."

20

OWEN

I couldn't overstate how reassuring it was to have the cafe free of magic. I'd become so used to the unsettling voices and odd occurrences, I hadn't appreciated how draining it was until it was all gone.

My first day back in the kitchen was a relief, the second day even more so. Everything was explained, and more importantly, fixed. It was a load off my mind. Which left me room to worry about other things.

"When did you become a worrier?" Tristan asked on Friday morning.

"What are you talking about?" I was inventorying the dry goods in the now voice-free storeroom with his help, and had barely thought about my present worries, let alone voiced them out loud.

"You keep getting these looks. Like you're happy and then—" Tristan gestured toward my face.

I gave him an exaggerated smile. *See, not worried.* He pulled a face at me in response and we got back to work.

"I saw you and Aria giggling in the stairwell yesterday. Seems like that's going well."

My stomach fluttered at the memory of stolen kisses. "You saw us?"

"Chill. I was on my way out, I wasn't snooping." Tristan paused, then said, "I like her for you."

"Yeah? I mean, me too." My first reaction was happy relief. I trusted Tristan's opinion and wanted him to get along with Aria. Then I remembered it didn't matter. Tristan was the only constant in my life.

He was watching me now, not even pretending to do the stock-take. "But—?"

"But nothing. I like Aria, I kinda always have. It's been good to reconnect and clear the air."

"Uh-huh. You should give it a shot." Tristan poked me in the side.

"A shot at what? This is only a temporary thing."

"Are you actually okay with that?" He looked at me in a way that made me want to hide. Sometimes it was inconvenient to have someone that really saw you, got you, and knew all your tricks. I couldn't bullshit Tristan easily.

"Perfectly happy," I said. "She's moving. I knew she was leaving from the beginning. That doesn't mean we couldn't make the most of the time we have."

"I'm not saying either of you should deny yourselves, if a fling is what you both want. I just think there could be something more. She really likes you."

"Yeah? How'd you figure that?" I made a note to increase our sugar in the next order like Tristan's answer didn't matter.

"Oh, it's super obvious. I can always spot a fellow caring, romantic soul. Even one who's hiding. I've never understood people who pretend not to care, but she so does. Care, I mean. Mostly about you."

Was Aria a romantic under her prickly exterior? I knew she cared but that wasn't the same as wanting a relationship. "Stop trying to push your romantic agenda on me and everyone else."

"Me?" Tristan put his hand over his heart in mock outrage. "If that's what you think, maybe it's your subconscious trying to get your attention. You're *dying* for a good romance, Owen."

"Are you my subconscious personified?"

He rolled his eyes. "Yes. Obviously. Now listen to me—go for it. One of us needs some romantic success around here."

"I've had plenty of success."

"I'm sure you have. And that's not what I meant."

We worked in silence for a few more minutes before exiting the storeroom.

"So, is that why you're worried? Aria—?" Tristan asked.

"I'm not worried. I promise. Everything is going great. I have nothing to worry about."

Tristan could obviously see the lie in my overdone assurances. He gave me a questioning look. "Why are you pushing back on this?"

"I'm not." But I was, and that wasn't like us. My words fooled no one.

He blinked in surprise. "Okay, Owen. If you'd rather do this alone, you can worry in peace."

I didn't know how to respond. This exchange would be nothing with anyone else, but for us, it was an uncomfortable shift. I knew Tristan hated rejection of his support, and he'd never experienced it from me before. I always leaned on him as much as he did me. Shit, I'd even told Tristan I thought the cafe was haunted back when I feared that was ridiculous. I came to him with all my problems. Every worry.

Guilt amplified my unease as Tristan left to see to his other tasks around the cafe. I couldn't tell him I was concerned about magic trials and Witches lurking in my coffee shop—with good intentions, sure—but it was all surreal and uncomfortable. I couldn't tell Tristan the reasons Aria and I wouldn't work out were magically complicated. I wanted his advice as much as always, but had no way of seeking it, and that was just another thing to worry about.

Aria was leaving because of magic, the thing that separated us last time, and sure, this time it was her choice, but leaving was still rooted in Witchery and things that weren't for me. There was no way to counter offer, and if she offered to stay—well, that wasn't going to happen. Why even think about it?

I couldn't explain to Tristan how absurdly Aria's life didn't match mine. I'd have to deal with this like I always did: pretend it was no different. Not full of magic, and not the person I wanted more than anyone else. I'd be damned if I couldn't trick myself into believing my own lies. This was no big deal, goddamn it.

I poked my head out of the kitchen and saw Aria at a table with the Witches again. I scanned the rest of the busy cafe. Max had taken up residence at a table almost immediately after we opened, I was glad to see him gone. I didn't need his little comments on top of everything else.

Aria caught me looking and waved me over.

I slipped an arm around her shoulders and kissed her on top of the head. "Hey, you." Holding back would have been smarter than giving in to the feelings I was trying to deny, but I acted without thinking.

Aria flushed at the casual affection, her arm coming around my hips.

"Anyone noteworthy coming in?" I asked Juliet.

As far as I was concerned, the curse problem was over and no longer hand anything to do with me, but it only seemed polite to ask Juliet how her investigation was going. She and Bickel were welcome to sit here, buy my coffee and pan dulce, and enforce Witchy laws to their heart's content.

Juliet set down her mug. "A Witch was just here, ordering a macchiato."

"Really?" I asked, caught off guard by the reminder that Witches were all around, and always had been.

"Don't get excited," Bickel said, misinterpreting my surprise for alarm. "She didn't do any spell casting. Or anything Witchy. She was only here for coffee."

"Of course she wouldn't do any spell casting, if it's such a big secret," I said.

"Not all magic is showy," Juliet explained. "If the culprit comes in, I'd expect them to at least probe around, it's like feeling your surroundings with your magic. No one would notice them doing it."

I didn't see why the culprit would come back at all. Now that their curse was broken, they had to know someone found them out. "You don't think sitting here gives you away? Maybe that's why macchiato Witch didn't do anything." Not that I thought this Witch had any reason to do magic in the cafe, but there seemed to be a flaw in Juliet's stake-out plan.

Juliet remained patient with me, her tone friendly. "Any Witch can identify other Witches on sight. But most wouldn't be able to sense another feeling out a room, as I've just described. Aria, a psychic, wouldn't even be able to sense it."

"And you can?" I asked.

Juliet nodded but didn't elaborate on how. She left me baffled. On purpose or not, this sort of thing was what made magic uncomfortable. There was too much I didn't know, and nothing I could do about it but hope a Witch would deign to explain it to me.

"Shouldn't you have talked to her anyway?" I asked. I mean, wasn't that the whole reason they were here? They could easily miss something if the culprit was discreet.

"That would be profiling." Bickel picked up a newspaper and

unfolded it, continuing to talk while not looking at me. "We can't accost every Witch with unjustified questions. But if someone comes in, scanning for magic, like they're trying to figure out what happened to their curse, that's suspicious. It gives us cause to approach them."

There was no arguing with that, and no reason for me to keep prying. Catching the Witch wasn't my problem. The curse was gone and I wanted to put the whole thing behind me.

I left the trio to their Witchy stake-out and made a stop by the glass display to check the pan dulce quantities. Before I could disappear into the kitchen, Tristan grabbed my arm.

"He's hot." Tristan waggled his eyebrows in an exaggerated way, shooting meaningful looks over my shoulder.

"Oh?" We shared a conspiratorial smile perfected in our younger days.

At least Tristan wasn't holding on to our earlier disagreement. Relief had never been so welcome. I looked over my shoulder, natural, as if I was only surveying the scene, and stopped short when I realized Tristan was talking about Aria's table. He meant Mr. Bickel.

Objectively Tristan had a point, and I'd have agreed with no lack of enthusiasm if I'd never spoken to the guy, but Bickel gave me the creeps even before Aria clued me in on his legendary status.

"*Ehh.* No, come on he's—" My mind drew a blank and landed on what Aria had said. "—old."

"Rude. I prefer to think of age as a mechanism for distinguished sexiness. He's only what, like forty, I'd bet. Well within my range. Our twenties are over, Owen. Be careful who you call old, soon it'll be you."

I cringed inwardly at myself for taking this to a judgey place, but my gut said to warn Tristan off. I didn't know that Bickel was a bad guy, beyond being kind of a jerk. It was frustrating to be prevented from telling Tristan I didn't like or trust the cold, calculating man, mainly because he was a scary powerful Witch.

"Go talk to him. Personality doesn't match the package." At least that was true. This problem would solve itself. Tristan wasn't into pretentiousness, no matter how pretty. I didn't need this added to my worries.

Tristan considered my words with some disappointment. "Why's he talking to Aria?"

Right. I'd just gone over there like I knew them. "Oh—uh—something about a job?"

"That's good. Maybe Aria won't be leaving." Tristan gave me a meaningful smile before letting me escape.

This really wasn't going to work. I was lying to Tristan too much already, and I was awful at it. Stammering flimsy excuses he'd see right through if he thought for half a moment. Everyone I dated senior year of college was older. And then there was Diego. Saying Bickel's age was a drawback didn't even make sense. Lies and partial truths might start small and harmless, but where would it lead? Tristan and I didn't keep secrets and I refused to let that change because Witches had rules I never agreed to follow in the first place.

A woman dressed in black entered Coffee Cat, causing Juliet to sit at attention and put her marranito down in a hurry. This was noteworthy because Juliet was facing away from the door, and hadn't even laid eyes on her.

Bickel glanced up briefly from his newspaper as the newcomer approached the coffee line. I tried not to stare.

The investigators included me in their stake-out again today. I still wondered if this was all so Bickel could watch me, but I'd come down to the cafe of my own volition when I could have hidden from them upstairs.

The woman in black was a Witch. To my eye she was glancing around the cafe like she was looking for something, maybe meeting a friend and wondering if they were here, but Juliet could clearly sense something more.

"Oh, she's searching for active magic." Juliet's excitement was kind of adorable.

I still didn't know how Juliet was able to tell the Witch was probing her surroundings. This act was too abstract to really count as spell casting and didn't leave the usual detectable magical signature. The Witch didn't 'poke' at us, we'd have felt that due to the direct interaction, like how I thought the paranormal presence could feel me.

Juliet took her first glance at the Witch in question. "We need to talk to her."

"Here?" I asked.

The Witch caught us staring and turned away, her posture hunched.

"We might as well. If she's our curser, she won't come back now we've been spotted." Juliet gave the woman a wave. She tried to ignore us, but Juliet kept waving until half the people in the cafe were looking our way.

The Witch turned and openly stared at us, color leaching from her already pale face.

"Perhaps Owen has an office we can use?" Juliet asked.

I nodded and went to find Owen as Juliet approached the Witch like a professional greeting a colleague at a conference. Juliet even handed the woman a business card.

"Excuse me?" Tristan called as I slipped behind the counter. "Where do you think you're going?"

"Sorry! Um—I need to ask Owen something."

"Ask me what?" Owen popped out of the kitchen.

I glanced from Owen to Tristan. Both were waiting expectantly. "Can we use your office for—the—meeting?"

Owen gave me a confused look. He handed a torta off to a customer waiting beyond the counter. Tristan was still watching, only half paying attention to the pan he was boxing up.

"You know," I said, trying to convey significance with my eyes. "The *friends* I'm sitting with. The other person we were planning to meet is here and we've just realized we need a private palace to talk."

Owen's dawning realization would have been comical if it hadn't sparked further interest in Tristan. I'd be worried about Tristan's keen observation if he wasn't so thoroughly skeptical.

He watched with more curiosity than I thought the situation warranted as Owen led the Witches, including our new 'friend,' to the back of the cafe.

"Good luck with the job, Aria," Tristan called after me.

I caught myself just in time before saying *what job* and blowing whatever lie Owen had told him, and muttered my thanks instead. God, I was terrible at stealth.

Tristan proceeded to give me a sweet, lopsided smile as I made to follow everyone toward the office. What was he so happy about?

Owen was called back to the kitchen, leaving me outside his office. I was wondering if I even needed to be here, when Juliet turned her attention to me.

"Before I go in, can I ask you a favor, Aria?"

"Sure?"

"Would you mind helping me with questioning? Your psychic ability would be invaluable."

"I'm not checking people for truthfulness if they don't know I'm doing it," I said, even as I experienced a confused wave of gratitude, shocked Juliet wanted my help at all.

"Of course." Juliet gave me a somber look of understanding. "I was planning on telling the Witch exactly what we were doing. She doesn't have to talk to us. If she refuses, that's information in itself."

"Refusing to talk doesn't mean she's guilty."

"True. Bickel isn't going to arrest her for keeping quiet. We're reasonable, you know, and not trying to be intimidating. It's fine if you aren't interested. I just thought it would be worth a try."

She seemed genuine. If Juliet wasn't trying to trick anyone or do anything I found unethical, I didn't really have any reason to refuse. I felt resistant, but didn't know if that was only my habit of shying away from this kind of work, or a more substantial hesitation. I'd be taking part in questioning during my internship, I might as well get used to it. And I wanted to be helpful, show Juliet I wasn't a total dud.

"Okay. Sure."

"Thanks, Aria. I've never worked with a psychic, but I can only see it helping, right?"

I shrugged and opened the office door.

Inside the closet-sized space our Witchy suspect was sitting in Owen's chair, while Bickel stood across the desk from her. It wasn't the most comfortable atmosphere with the lack of windows and overcrowding. I was pressed shoulder to shoulder between Juliet and Bickel, and trying not to think about all of us breathing the same air.

"What's the deal?" The Witch slouched further into her seat, arms crossed. "I was just getting coffee."

"We've been hired to ask a few questions," Juliet said. "Will you talk to us knowing my friend here is a psychic, and will be checking the truthfulness of your statements?"

The Witch narrowed her eyes at me. "And if I don't want to?"

"You don't have to," Juliet said. "There's no obligation, but we were hoping you might be able to help with a problem we're looking into."

The Witch glared. "Whatever, fine."

I was surprised at her nonchalant acceptance. Being a psychic, I assumed no one would want their emotions or intentions read in an adversarial situation. I liked fortunes because it was all on the subject's terms, and had the potential to be to their advantage. Interrogation was on our terms. I didn't know why this Witch would open herself up if she didn't have to.

I tapped into my psychic power and focused on the Witch at the desk. It took a minute to get my bearings. I didn't need physical contact to read someone, but it helped. At the moment, touching Juliet and Bickel was actively distracting. Tuning in to my subject in a situation so unlike fortune telling was more challenging than I expected. I'd been lax in honing my skill over the years, and wondered if this might hurt my chances at the job with Luca.

As I focussed I got a whiff of Juliet: she was determined, pleased and hopeful, and working hard to constantly push repressed feelings further down. She had something well buried, but it was all there for my perusal if I wished to pry. I mentally pushed her away. In contrast to Juliet, Mr. Bickel was like a calm sea, though not as genuinely bored as he liked to act, and somewhat preoccupied by feelings of—I pushed him away too.

The Witch in the seat was scared shitless. My stomach dropped.

"What's your name?" Juliet asked her.

"Molly Swan."

"Molly, do you come to Coffee Cat often?"

"No, this is my first time. A friend recommended it. Is that a crime? Do you accost all Witches who come in here?" Molly said all this truthfully, letting her feelings of bitterness override everything else.

"Why were you checking the cafe for magic?" Juliet asked.

Molly looked surprised. "I wasn't."

I nudged Juliet, alerting her to the blatant lie. "I think Molly's hiding something."

"Obviously," Bickel said. "One doesn't need to be a psychic to deduce that."

I elbowed Bickel and he made a strange sound that almost sounded like a laugh. Juliet gave Bickel and me a tight smile. She'd have been an excellent schoolteacher. I felt her rebuke acutely, and not because of my psychic sense.

"Do you want my help or not?" I asked the man next to me. Bickel answered with a challenging look which only spurred me on. "Molly is hiding something, and not just from us. Not just about searching the cafe for magic." As soon as I said it, I felt guilty, even though Molly knew I was digging into her psyche.

"Thank you, Aria." Juliet turned back to Molly. "Now—we know you were checking the cafe for spells. What were you checking for?"

"I—" Molly looked and felt helpless. "I was worried you were watching me. When I came in and saw you sitting there, I wanted to leave. I was worried it was a trap."

"What was a trap?" Juliet asked.

"I dunno. I thought you were trying to trip me up, and now look!" Molly's fear seemed to be intensifying. She had a secret at the heart of all her other emotions, but there was no way for me to tell what it was.

"Why would we trip you up, or want to watch you? We don't know you, Molly."

"Don't know me, but look where we are." She gestured wildly around the office. I had to agree, she had a point. "I've had some trouble with the law and you look like those types."

"What kind of trouble?" Juliet asked.

"Selling produce at the farmers market."

"How is that trouble?" I asked. Molly's words didn't fit with her feelings of resentment and regret, but she was still telling the truth.

"I spelled the veggies," Molly mumbled. She had a bag with her, leafy greens poking out the top.

"To do what?"

"Be addictive?" Molly shrugged. "I mean they're healthy so, so what? I was sick of being outsold by Farmer Green. His real name isn't even Green! So I cheated, got caught, got fined, and you people won't leave me alone."

"What does that have to do with the cafe?" Juliet asked.

"Nothing! I was worried you were after me, so I was checking you weren't doing anything dodgy."

"Dodgy. Says the Witch with magically altered produce." Bickel sounded almost amused.

Molly looked at the greens in her bag.

"You've started spelling the veggies again," Juliet said. "That's why you were checking for magic. You were worried you were caught again."

"No." Molly was completely lying.

"Yes, you have," I pushed.

She glared, but I could tell. She was overly worried about being found out and now she had been.

Detecting lies was an odd thing. I had some insight into why the lie was told, which left the subject more exposed than they might realize. In Molly's case she was desperate. It was her main motivator for everything we'd talked to her about.

"Have you laid a curse on this cafe?" Juliet asked, changing the subject strategically.

When you can't hide your mind, all psychic Witches need to do is get you to think about something to know your feelings on the subject.

Molly was startled in a pure, complete way you couldn't fake. She had no previous knowledge of the cafe's curse. "No. I've never done anything like that," she said truthfully.

Molly wasn't the most adept at hiding her feelings. Juliet probably could have gotten all this information without me. I couldn't help thinking it was arguably pointless to use such invasive power here, but also a relief to know for sure Molly wasn't who the investigators were looking for.

Mr. Bickel asked Molly a bit more about the veggies and told her he'd have to contact the Authority Witches dealing with her case. I pulled him aside—outside the closet—and suggested someone talk to Molly about why she was resorting to illegal magic. I couldn't ignore her feeling of desperation, and that her magic use was only in response to something more serious.

Helping Molly with the underlying problem was a better way to stop her doing this again than fining her. It might actually help her and lead to a positive outcome. Bickel agreed without protest, and I heard him talking to Molly as he walked her out of the cafe.

Juliet and I made our way back to our table. I watched the other two Witches through the window. They were in deep discussion, Molly looking less frightened, and Bickel surprisingly attentive.

"That went well, don't you think?" Juliet picked up her marranito and took a bite.

"I guess. Other than the fact it had nothing to do with the cafe." I was worried about Molly, and that was the other reason I didn't like doing this. People's motivations were complex. Yes, detecting lies and truths told you if someone was guilty or innocent, but I wasn't so keen to give out that information if no one was interested in the larger context.

"He'll help her," Juliet said, nodding toward Bickel.

I wanted to believe her. "In my experience the Authority doesn't do much more than enforce."

"You're not wrong. I don't particularly like working with the Authority, but Bickel is an exception. He sees things more my way. Which I'm beginning to think is more your way too."

"If you say so." I frowned at the Witches outside. It didn't look like Bickel was being a jerk, but there was no way to tell for sure without knowing what they were saying. "I like to use my psychic ability to aid understanding, rather than to collect answers for someone else's agenda."

"I totally get that. Doing the work you enjoy is the nice thing about working privately. I look into varying magical problems, not necessarily crimes. I think you and I might actually work well together, Aria."

"Oh—thanks," I said, half distracted as I watched Molly shake Bickel's hand before taking a business card from him.

When I turned back to Juliet, she was looking at me like a billion thoughts were ticking over inside her head. She almost said something more, but instead went back to her pan dulce.

Bickel arrived back at the table, pausing before taking his seat.

"How'd it go?" I asked.

"Fine," he said, clipped and annoyed. "Nothing you need to be concerned about, Aria."

Fuck, Bickel was rude. Like, *sorry for caring*. No wonder it was hard to believe he'd help Molly out and not just leave her to whatever punishment the laws dictated. Juliet seemed confident in him, but I had doubts. I liked Juliet, and wasn't hating spending time at the cafe with her. If it weren't for Bickel, I could almost forget everything looming over me and pretend I was sitting here with a friend.

"Do we need more coffee?" Bickel asked, ignoring my seething silence.

"That's probably for the best, Edwin," Juliet said, gathering up our empty cups and handing them to her associate.

I couldn't stop the surprised giggle that passed my lips. Legend or not, I didn't actually know the guy's full name. It had a funny ring to it, and I got a sick satisfaction out of uncovering one of his pointless secrets.

"Yes. I'll take a cold brew please, *Edwin Bickel*," I said with a smirk.

"Don't call me that, Aria." His voice wasn't raised but something about it sent a primal chill down my spine. "You haven't been granted the privilege. You may call me Mr. Bickel, just like everyone else." He actually looked like he might murder me if I didn't listen. It was the kind of icy, superior anger deployed to cover something more personal.

"Sorry." I was all for playful teasing and a bit of snark, but I didn't want to make the man uncomfortable. This wasn't a joke for him.

"That's fine. Just behave. And remember who I am. Respect my status; we aren't friends, Aria." His death glare died down to regular, I-despise-you levels.

After an uncomfortable moment of eye contact, during which I felt worse and worse about poking fun at him, Mr. All-Powerful-Witch left to order our coffees.

Bickel was right, I had forgotten who I was dealing with, and forgotten how much Authority Witches liked titles and honorifics. I'd started seeing him as a usual prickly Witch after all this hanging around together. Maybe I imagined someone so powerful filled their time with grander activities. I wouldn't be lulled into a sense of false comfort again.

I had no idea what I'd stumbled upon in Bickel's extreme reaction, and wondered again why he was doing the job of watching me. The Authority could have sent someone up from LA to take over Aria-the-radical-Teller watch. What was I missing here, other than fucking everything?

"That was my fault," Juliet said. "I should have warned you. He likes to keep to formalities with most people. Just be thankful he hasn't been calling you Miss Belmonte."

"Yeah, I'd hate that."

"For heaven's sake, don't tell him that either. He'll start doing it to annoy you," Juliet said in all seriousness.

I was contemplating asking Juliet what the deal was with the two of them but decided against it. "I doubt any more Witches will come in the cafe today. More than two can't be likely. It already seems like a lot of Witch patronage. Maybe the curser isn't coming back."

"I'm not so sure. And given the number of customers coming

through the cafe, our Witches have been in proportion to population. This town has a rather high Witch residency."

I snorted at that. Figured that a wealthy beachside town would be popular. Witches tended to have means. You couldn't create wealth with magic outright, but there were plenty of magically legal ways to get ahead. Witches were disproportionately represented in the upper class and at the heads of industries. I'd told Owen it wasn't fair, which was perhaps an understatement.

Bickel returned, skillfully balancing three coffees.

I grabbed my cold brew and thanked him, surprised he'd bought me anything at all. Bickel ignored me as he handed Juliet her coffee. I wasn't even annoyed by his snub. Oh, damn the stars, he was *not* growing on me. I just felt bad.

"Look at that." Bickel gestured out the window.

Juliet and I turned to look and everything else was pushed from my mind. The fucking crows were back. A dozen or so were in the tree, which wasn't blatantly weird, but there was also a line of them walking down the sidewalk. They looked like soldiers, all in a row, marching in step. As if they could feel us looking, they stopped, turned their heads as one, and stared back.

"We missed something," Bickel said, as if renewed crow presence was a personal insult.

"But there's no magic in the cafe," Juliet said. "The crow curse was linked to all the rest of it—the layers. They shouldn't be back when everything here is fine."

Bickel sighed. "I don't know what to tell you, Juliet. We're going to have to go check out the damn tree. I cannot believe my time here has been reduced to acting as animal control."

22

OWEN

I wished I hadn't seen the Witches outside under the jacaranda tree. Crows were flapping around Mr. Bickel in a persistent and unnatural way that instantly spiked my worry.

"What's up?" I called as I crossed the street to join them.

"We have a minor situation," Juliet said.

Bickel swatted at a bird. It squawked and flew out of reach.

"Is the curse back?" I couldn't control the wave of panic that washed over me and settled in my stomach. Even though the Witches thought the curser might strike again, I'd worked hard to tell myself they wouldn't, that the curse really had nothing to do with me.

"Yes and no," said Bickel, the only person who could remain dignified and dripping with disdain as he shooed crows away from his person.

Aria came over and pressed against me, shoulder to shoulder. "The cafe is fine, Owen. The Witch probably didn't even come inside. But the enchanted birds are back. Obviously."

I grabbed her hand and she laced our fingers together.

"The first problem with the crows was tied to everything

else," Juliet said. "This time the curse seems to be coming from the tree itself. It's attracting the birds and once they land, the magic infects them. I don't know why the Witch would come back to reinstate this and not the magic affecting the cafe directly."

Maybe it wasn't about the cafe at all.

"Guess the stake-out was a bust," I said, not to be rude, but come on. The Witch probably switched things up to avoid getting caught. "I can't keep dealing with this. The crows almost killed Piña."

"They'll figure it out, Owen. I know they will." Aria squeezed my hand again. It was comforting, even if Aria wasn't offering a concrete solution. I trusted her, and she had confidence in the other two. This might not be so bad; nothing was actually happening to the cafe.

"We need to do more than break the curse this time," Juliet said to Bickel. "Maybe analyze it, extract its essence? See if we can find anything to point to the Witch responsible."

Bickel nodded agreement as another crow swooped towards him. There was a weird sensation, like a record skipping, except all around. I tightened my grip on Aria's hand but nothing else happened.

Juliet didn't seem to notice the disturbance. "Take that back to my place, will you?"

Bickel was suddenly holding a stiff crow under his arm, and the bird that was divebombing him seconds before had disappeared.

"Where did—is it dead?" I asked in alarm.

"No, only frozen," Bickel grimaced at the crow. "I need a place to disappear. I'm not taking this in a rideshare. May I borrow your apartment, Owen?"

I handed him my key and told him the PIN to the outer lock, unable to stop looking at the crow. Luckily, Bickel had his back to Coffee Cat so no one inside could see him holding a dead looking bird. Tristan was peering out the window at us, along with a few customers.

"How'd you catch it?" Aria asked, looking around. She'd also missed something, so at least I wasn't the only one feeling like a fool.

The Witch took a moment to decide if he could be bothered answering before saying in a breathy huff, "I froze time and grabbed the damn thing out of the air. Now, if you'll excuse me."

Bickel walked briskly across the street, keeping the crow hidden from view of the coffee shop by angling his body and holding the animal to his side.

Tristan was still watching, eyes on Bickel, but turned away when he noticed me notice him.

"I'm going to need a good lie to cover this nonsense," I said, almost able to ignore the fact that Bickel had stopped time. Even for magic that seemed a bit much.

"How will keeping the crow help?" Aria asked Juliet, both Witches seeming to ignore me. "You can't leave the curse in place while you analyze. What if the birds smash into the building again? Or go after people on the street?"

The crows were more aggressive than before, repeatedly swooping on us and abusing a Jetta parked under the tree. The owner was going to need a new paint job to cover up the peck marks and scratches.

"We can break the curse here, and leave the curse intact on the frozen crow," Juliet said as a bird tried to land on her head. She ducked, keeping her balance even in four-inch heels.

"That's not possible." Aria waved her cold brew at the bird, ice clinking. "A spell affecting multiple things, or crows, is still one spell. You can't separate it out, break part and not all of it."

The bird decided to come for me and I hopped out of the way.

Juliet stepped off the sidewalk into the planter containing the cursed crow tree. "I told you my associate was useful. Bickel's time altering abilities allow him to break some of the usual rules of magic. Don't worry about the analysis, Aria, we'll get it done. Now stand in front of me while I fix the tree. I don't want people staring."

Like they weren't already. We looked ridiculous. Aria and I did as requested and blocked Juliet from view as she laid her hands on the tree trunk.

"Can you put a protection charm on my cafe, or something?" I asked, thinking aloud. "It's just that I have an important meeting Monday. Someone filming and taking photos for a promotion. I can't have magic messing things up."

Juliet was whispering to the tree. Possibly I shouldn't have interrupted her, but I was increasingly worried. The situation wasn't anywhere near as stable as I'd thought.

Aria rubbed my back in an effort to release some of my visible tension. I tried to relax but my own lack of control over the matter was hard to ignore, and even harder to accept.

Juliet concluded her incantation. The crows leapt from the tree and flew away. "Yes, Owen. I can cast a protective spell. Then we really need to get more serious about catching this Witch. Once I get a closer look at the crow, I might be able to devise a way of getting the culprit to reveal themselves."

"Any chance we can reveal them this weekend?"

I tried not to be frustrated with Juliet, she was helping, but I felt so useless, and this was my life. My business. Even if the curse wasn't directly affecting me this time, it was too close for comfort. I didn't want to be involved in this investigation, I just wanted things solved.

"I don't know if we'll have it all worked out that quickly, Owen. I need to learn about the Witch from their spell work. It's more than figuring out what the spell does, as I did when we first met to talk about the curse. It's complicated, intricate work. But—" Juliet raised a hand as I opened my mouth for what would have been a desperate protest. "The protection spell will see you through your important meeting. Aria can watch for Witches, while Bickel and I work on the cursed crow. Then we'll get everything ironed out."

I muttered my thanks.

"Um. Sorry guys. I need to go out of town?" Aria said it like an apologetic question, looking directly at me, even though she didn't need permission. I knew it was for her interview.

"Don't worry about it, Aria. It doesn't seem like staking out the cafe was much help. Juliet will sort things out for me." I tried to project confidence in this plan. Aria needed to go and that was fine.

I must not have been convincing because she looked disappointed before covering it up with an impassive frown.

23

ARIA

"You all good, Owen?" I asked as we made our way back into Coffee Cat.

"Yeah," he said with too much assurance. I eyed him until he added, "Okay, I'm worried, but it's fine."

Owen looked drawn but the smile he gave me was genuine. Worry was normal. He'd taken all this well so far, but we needed to have a more in-depth talk. I didn't want him keeping things balled up.

"Are you almost done working for the day?" I asked.

"Why? You want to meet me upstairs? Give me an hour." Owen gave me a mischievous look. Maybe he really was all right and I was the one overly worried. Or we really just weren't in a place to confide in each other.

Owen kissed me in a quick, hard peck, then left me to wrap up the kitchen for the day.

I felt a wistful pang in my chest. I'd been wary of starting anything with Owen knowing it couldn't go anywhere, but undeniable feelings of *more* were piling up. I tried to tell myself it was just our history tricking me into thinking we had an intimacy that wasn't really there. But that was a lie. History wasn't a trick but a real part of us. We'd been back in each other's lives less than two weeks, but we hadn't started from nothing, only picked up where we left off.

It wasn't so far off to expect Owen to confide in me, was it?

The truth was I'd never let anyone know me the way Owen did. After more than a decade of only ever getting half involved, holding myself back from love and friendships, I was overwhelmed with the feeling of us. I couldn't guard myself. With Owen I found a crucial element of connection I'd been missing all this time.

In the apartment that afternoon Owen and I fell into kisses before the door was closed. He tossed the mail on the floor without a second glance and pulled me flush against him. I lost my resolve to have a conversation. I wanted this instead.

Owen broke off our kiss and pressed his forehead to mine. He wore a serious look, and I was glad I hadn't interrupted us with words. His expression was seductive but not flirty, like these kisses were more than lust and having a good time. This was everything. Big and heavy, and he knew it, despite his insistence otherwise.

In his bedroom I peeled Owen's shirt off without a word. I didn't want to break the moment even though he'd turned more playful. That look he'd given me burned into my mind. It left a shadow on his face, betraying a change in him he let me create.

I didn't waste any of my touches. I wanted to make him melt, show him I saw him, and give him everything.

My mouth was all over Owen, peppering him with light kisses. Neither of us spoke, we were content with sighs and sharp breaths as we stripped each other in turn. It was slow and deliberate. Not frantic or full of giddy pleasure like the other times we'd come together.

I kissed the tattoo on Owen's hip, trailing along and down until I reached the soft skin of his cock. I kissed him, licking, tongue swirling, eliciting beautiful sounds from his mouth before I took him into mine.

Owen had his hands in my hair, firm but not intrusive. I looked up to find his eyes on me, his face flushed. I decided it was my favorite version of him, wearing all his emotions on his skin. Covered in tattoos and gooseflesh and heat, while his eyes gave me everything they could.

"Come up here and kiss me, Aria."

Owen groaned as I released him from my mouth. I crawled over his body and kissed him. His hand slipped between us and touched me as we kissed and rocked into each other.

"Hold me." My request came out raw and revealing. I could have, maybe should have said, *fuck me*. But that wasn't what I needed.

Owen's arms wrapped around me. "I've got you, Aria." He looked at me with a kind of serious sweetness that made me feel open, all my feelings exposed.

This was exactly what I wanted. I wasn't just asking him to put his arms around me. I never wanted to leave this version of us behind.

Afterward, panting in each other's arms, Owen whispered my name in my ear. I wanted to whisper a lot more, and so kept my mouth firmly shut. Everything was clicking into place, but as my mind cleared, I knew I couldn't trust it to last.

Since the Telling disaster Owen and I spent all our time either at the cafe working and distracted by the investigators, or up here drawing pleasure out of each other. It was amazing but didn't leave a lot of time for talking. I kept shying away from words, as I'd done earlier. It was easier to enjoy what we had, but now we'd shifted to a new place and a discussion felt long over-due. There was no denying what we just shared, or that it didn't fit the rest of our arrangement. I wanted to talk about what this was, where it was going. Now more than ever, but it had the feeling of being too late.

The only time I got close to bringing us up was last night and Owen beat me to it saying, "Guess years of unresolved feelings plus casual sex is the perfect match." Remembering his words now made me wonder how much of the deep exposing experience I just had was actually one-sided.

Casual. The word kept me from saying anything as we lay together, and the intense intimacy between us faded even as Owen ran his fingers up and down my body, giving me chills.

We'd said—he'd said—this was *no big deal,* but was it really? Still? Had I fallen for someone I was starting to think of as the potential love of my life, only to be cursed by impossibility in the form of mismatched expectations? The sex didn't feel casual anymore. You couldn't hide that reality behind labels just because you wanted to. Or was I the only one who felt this way?

The Owen I knew in high school wasn't casual at all; was the grown up him really leaps and bounds from that starry-eyed boy? It appeared I was no different than the Aria of twelve years ago. All her flaws and hopes were still with me, and it didn't look like it was going to work out any better this time around.

24

OWEN

*L*ater that night Aria and I sat in the apartment kitchen. We'd ordered in. I couldn't face cooking when I was boneless and blissed out from sex, and the possibility of Aria doing cooking spells that didn't require pots and pans didn't feel real. Maybe my resistance was unfair, but I'd had enough magic for the moment.

I wanted a simple evening. Food, a few laughs and then back to bed. We'd barely finished eating and I knew that wasn't happening.

Our court date had been set. Piña was sitting on top of two identical letters, unfolded, read, and discarded on the kitchen table. We'd missed them in our haste before. A good thing because they were a mood killer.

Piña was doing her part to try to save us from the printed information. I usually tried to keep her off the counters and food surfaces but gave up. My brain didn't have any energy tonight. The hearing was scheduled for next week.

Aria had been quiet since we came home. She'd spoiled me with pleasure, and I couldn't stop thinking about how different sex felt tonight. Then, before we could make sense of the not uncomfortable shift in mood, I found the letters and Aria turned from thoughtful to distant, like having a set time put her on edge.

The quiet currently settled over us wasn't the comfortable kind.

"Luca called," I told Aria after we'd finished eating.

"Called you?" she asked as she cleaned up the plates with a spell. A few words read out from her phone and a poofing sound was all it took.

"It was good to hear from him." I inspected my plates, wishing this cleaning method was one I could implement in the cafe, and had to admit magic had its perks. Maybe a magically prepared dinner would have been fun. "We were never close growing up, but I always considered him a friend."

"What did he say?"

"We caught up. He asked about the cafe. Apologized for lying at the end of high school, not that it was necessary. He said I can call him about Witchy stuff whenever I want. It was—it's allowed me to relax."

"You can always ask me too, Owen."

I rejoined Aria at the table and stroked Piña. "I know. But it's nice to have options."

"You don't think I'm doing a good job of telling you things?" She was obviously trying not to sound hurt, but the stress about court was making it hard for Aria to keep up her usual guard. Or maybe it was more than that, her guard had been down all evening.

"No. You're good, Aria. It's just nice to have more than one person to talk to. Luca said he can come to the court thing. I said it wasn't necessary, but it was comforting."

"Of course. He's a lawyer. You can always trust my brother to get everything right." Aria said, even though I was in no way comparing her and Luca. "I'm glad he called you. I just didn't know you needed it. I should have offered you Luca's details sooner. It wasn't just me that needed his advice."

I waved that away. I'd meant to share this with Aria to ease her mind, not make her feel like she'd done something wrong. I tried to turn the conversation to more positive ground. "Luca invited me up to visit. After he moves. Said I can meet some of his Witch friends." The idea was as exciting as it was daunting.

Aria looked as surprised as I had been when Luca made the offer. "I never thought I'd see the day when my brother initiated social activity. This is good—I guess I'll be up there too. Most likely."

"Yeah, it will be fun—all three of us together." I tried to imagine it. Aria, Luca and I all hanging out as adults. Not in the attic but in a bar, or a Witchy club, if that was even a real thing.

I didn't see Aria and me as a couple in this future scenario. It was a fantasy of friendship, and that shouldn't have hurt, but it did. It didn't feel real: Aria, Luca and I and a bunch of faceless Witches. It shouldn't have been so hard to imagine Aria and me as friends. We were friends. Or were we were kidding ourselves about staying in touch?

Now that I thought about it, Aria hadn't mentioned any of her Witch friends. In an effort to push my feelings of the future away, I asked, "Do you know Luca's friends, or hang out with Witches much?"

"No, not really." Aria sounded resigned.

The conversation was sinking and I didn't know why. Shouldn't we be excited talking about future get-togethers? I knew Aria was isolated, but she could change that. She already was with the job and everything. Things were moving in a positive direction for both of us.

"Hasn't it been nice spending time with our Witchy investigators?" I tried again.

"There's nothing nice about Mr. B hanging around."

"Okay, point about him, sure. But you've all been getting along."

"I hired Juliet, we aren't getting along so much as she's obligated to deal with me. But—I guess it hasn't been *awful*." Aria played it off, like she didn't care about her interactions with Juliet. In this case I couldn't tell if her dismissal was real or not.

"I think you could come up with something better than not awful," I said in an attempt to inject some playfulness into the exchange.

"Maybe—" She cracked a grin. "I hope the Witches at Luca's firm are like Juliet. There better be a few around her age. If everyone but Luca's from the older generations it could be painful."

"Will be good to work with people your age."

Aria grimaced. She paused for a long time before saying, "Juliet isn't my age, Owen. She's like almost fifty—not that it's the same as Mortal fifty." Aria looked at me without breaking eye contact. She was as serious as I'd ever seen her, or I would have laughed assuming this was a joke.

For a moment I panicked, more than I had when I realized magic was real. Magic was already on my radar. This was too unexpected. "How old are you, Aria?"

"Twenty-nine. We grew up together, you can't fake that. But Witches have prolonged life. That's why you're known as Mortals. Three hundred-ish is our average lifespan."

"I don't really know what to say. That's—weird."

"It's not so weird. Living long isn't just extending a Moral life, it's redistributing a life to match a new timeframe. So we look younger for longer. Witches tend to get stuck in life stages for prolonged periods, like as far as mentality goes. It's extended youth, so Juliet really is more similar to me than a Mortal fifty-year-old. When you think about it like that, it might be less weird."

"I guess. Why tell me this now? Or is there still more stuff I'm totally clueless on?" I asked, sounding bitchier than I'd intended.

"That should be it. I didn't keep this from you purposely. It's not the kind of thing I knew how to bring up."

I couldn't decide how much this new revelation mattered. On the one hand, it was hard to process and so it felt like a big deal. On the other, more practically focused hand, Aria outliving me by hundreds of years didn't necessarily affect me. We could still be friends. It's not like we were going to grow old together anyway. I'd never wanted that from anyone, and didn't need it now, especially with her.

This was only another weird, seemingly impossible Witch ability, like stopping time.

I distractedly sipped from my water glass, forgetting I'd already drained it. Aria watched me closely as I set it back down, like she was waiting for me to say something.

I got up to refill both of our glasses. "So there's a bunch of old, youthful Witches out there? Wait—how old is Bickel?"

"Eh—" Aria shrugged, looking relieved. I wondered if she actually felt it. "He's somewhere around a hundred. I'm not asking him to be more specific. He'll probably curse me. He almost bit my head off today—"

It wasn't the answer I was expecting. God, it was like vampire rules in here. I couldn't even concentrate on the rest of Aria's story about how we plebs weren't allowed to call the old Witch by his first name. At least I'd been right when I told Tristan the guy was old.

I returned to the table and took a long drink. "So about Tristan—"

Aria's expression suggested she couldn't follow my train of thought, but explaining that wasn't important right now. I latched on to Telling my friend, needing to regain some control and fix one of my problems. This would be so much more fun, less ominous, if I could laugh about it with Tristan.

"Owen, we can't Tell him. Luca agrees. The court will freak the hell out if they think I'm starting a pattern of Telling multiple people. Witches who try to expose magic on a large scale are one of the Authority's biggest concerns. Radical Telling. That was why my punishment was so severe in high school. They cut you out of my life to hurt me, crush me so I'd never try a stunt like Telling a whole party again. Having no other way to save your cat is one thing. Hopefully they'll excuse it, but this—Telling Tristan would tank my chance at this job. Even worse I could face legal—"

"Okay. Slow down, Aria." My stomach was in knots. "I get it. It's not simple and I don't want bad things to happen to you. I won't ask you to break laws or face punishment for me, fuck. It's just not fair. Talking to you, and even Luca, is all fine. But it's not enough. This is different. Tristan is my life. Lying is already messing things up. He can tell something's up and more lies will only end up hurting him. I won't keep doing it."

Aria looked stricken. Making her upset didn't help anything. I knew she wasn't drawing this line arbitrarily. They weren't rules she agreed to either, I realized, though at least she'd always known they were there. It was an impossible situation, but I wasn't ready to let it go.

"I know I said we'd talk about it." Aria twisted a discarded napkin in her hands. "But I didn't see this 'Aria is going to Tell the world, arrest her' angle coming. To me, Telling Tristan isn't the same as what I did at that party, but to the Witches in charge it's too close for comfort. My past fuck up is still screwing us over. With powerful Authority Witches lurking around, I need to take this seriously. I can't do this for you. I'm sorry. Anything else—"

"I get it, but—" *God*, how could I object without being an

asshole? "I thought we'd be able to discuss it, find a solution. Not, no, full stop, it's never happening. I'm not okay with any of this."

This evening had been doomed since the court letters arrived. The past few days had been fun and bright. Like a fantasy. Endless kisses and Aria stretched out in bed beside me each night. Laughing and moaning into each other's mouths. Sex this afternoon had been frighteningly like falling in love. This conversation was so damn far from that. It felt like the end.

"Things will get better Owen." Aria reached out, to grab my hand or maybe pat Piña. The cat slunk away from her and settled in my lap. Aria's hand dropped limp on the table. "This thing with your cafe will get cleared up. Then there will be no reason to lie to Tristan. The paranormal investigators will leave, and everything will be fine again. Maybe I'll be gone, but either way I won't let this mess up your life, Owen. I promise."

"But I don't want—" *What, didn't want her to leave?* She'd just offered a solution. Everyone magic leaves my life, no more reason to lie. The best way forward for both of us was clear. I should be happy about it, not miserable. "When you say messing up my life—you're not. Maybe I'm being too dramatic."

"No, don't do that. It's not dramatic. Magic is isolating, and I don't like that I've done this to you. Knowing about magic separates you from your peers, you don't fit properly into either world. But if the majority of the Witchy world stays away, the effect on you won't be so great."

Piña curled into me and I snuggled her soft, warm body for comfort. Aria made it sound like I had to pick between my prior Witch-free life, or getting stuck in a no man's land between worlds. It wasn't really a choice was it? Aria was moving. Everything would naturally go back to normal for me. That was good. What I wanted. It should have felt like a relief.

"And we'll stay friends when you leave," I said to reassure

myself. This wasn't abandonment like last time. Not like my mother leaving, or my dad dying, it was just life taking us different places. Not dramatic, and not something that should make my chest constrict.

"Friends?" Aria discarded the shredded napkin. "I thought maybe—I wanted to talk about—I don't actually want to leave, Owen."

"But why stay? What's in this town for you when you want a fresh start? I'm not going to forget about you. We'll keep in touch."

"Of course we'll keep in touch. I know I'm leaving Sunday, but I'll be back soon."

"For court." Piña nuzzled me, demanding more of my attention.

"And for Coffee Cat. I want to make sure it's okay. Not that Juliet can't handle it—"

We looked at each other. I felt like I was missing something.

"You don't want me to stay in town?" Aria asked. "I could find other work. Get back into my fortunes—not leave."

"Is that what you want? What about all the reasons you want to give the internship a shot?" The cat abandoned me and ran out of the room.

Aria watched her go. "But I don't have to. That idea was a lifeboat when I had no other options. I can stay if you want. We can try—"

Try what? A life together full of lies? How would I explain her unchanging age to Tristan, or anyone? Aria's offer to stay made me panic. This wasn't what we agreed. Every relationship was guaranteed to end, no matter who my partner was. That was why I didn't do this. I'd much rather quit now and save myself the agony, and in that way Aria wasn't so different from anyone else, even if my feelings for her were.

"Don't stay here for me, Aria. I don't want to hold you back from jobs or friends, or your life. I don't think I can keep lying about magic. It's not something I want to get used to. You even said leaving will—make things better. I want to go back to normal."

She looked confused for a second. "Okay. Fair enough. It sounds like the right thing for everyone." Aria stood from the table.

"Are you going to bed?" I asked, getting up to follow.

Was this it? I'd made my thoughts clear, but was somehow still surprised to find she agreed.

"I might go for a walk. Don't wait up. I know you have work in the morning. And Owen—" Aria paused at the doorway to the kitchen. "I wonder if it's best to keep some distance? I'll stay in my room. Alone. Until I move out."

"Totally."

I wanted the opposite. I wanted to pull Aria close and kiss her until we both forgot about reality. I wanted to tangle her up in my sheets and feel her come apart around me. I wanted to live out the rest of my life, time frozen, looping endlessly through the past two days.

"Friends then." Aria paused, waiting for something I couldn't identify, before she left the apartment.

I always knew she was leaving, told her it was what I wanted. Aria wasn't disappearing. Hell, I knew she'd be back later tonight. This wasn't another dramatic end to us, but it felt like something more was slipping through my fingers and I didn't know how to catch it.

25

ARIA

The night air felt refreshing against my too hot, agitated body as I escaped the apartment. I stood on the sidewalk, not knowing which way to go. First I needed to breathe. It shouldn't have been this hard to get air in my lungs.

I'd offered to stay and he'd said no. Why was I surprised? Owen said repeatedly this thing between us was casual. I'd worried about his words, but hoped if I offered, if we tried to talk about it, we'd see casual was a lie, especially after an afternoon filled with so many deep feelings.

Apparently they weren't mutual.

We started with a good-bye fuck, and I'd doubted it would be uncomplicated even then. I should have seen this coming, but we kept falling back together and it meant more each time. Or. From his point of view, all we had was a few days of great sex. It was a fling, not us falling in love, finally together with nothing to hide.

On top of my mess of emotions, I couldn't escape the feeling I was failing Owen. This hadn't been an easy week for him. He probably felt like his life was falling apart. Magic was ruining his business and I was putting magic between him and everything he found important, asking him to lie and play by rules that weren't fair to him, and then feeling hurt when he didn't want more of this shit in his life. Of course he didn't want me and the mess I brought wherever I went.

Owen was right about his dilemma with Tristan, me leaving was the best solution. Stupidly I'd hoped when the cafe problem was solved, I could stay, become part of Owen's life, lay low, and he'd have no more reason to lie. I thought he'd want to try at the very least. Instead, he saw no potential in us, as if we weren't worth the risk.

It didn't help I'd totally screwed myself and freaked him out about Witchy lifespans. I wasn't going to lie or ask him to make decisions about us without all the information, but I wished I'd saved that tidbit to the end of the conversation. Not that it mattered. I was here now, alone on the darkened street.

"Evening, Aria."

I jumped out of my skin and swore. A man lurked across the street. I stomped over. "Are you spying on me?"

"I thought we'd established I'm here to watch you." Mr. Bickel was leaning against my car, just out of range of the street-light's glow, fedora pulled down, half over his eyes.

"Are you watching me while I'm inside my apartment?" An uncomfortably exposed feeling twisted inside me. "How long have you been here?"

"What? No—not long." Bickel looked alarmed. "You're entitled to privacy."

"Then why are you here spying?"

Bickel moved his hat out of his eyes exposing his, for once, emotive face. "Aria. I have—morals. I'm not spying on you, or watching without your knowledge. I don't care what you and Owen do in your private life."

Oh god, now I was thinking about *things Owen and I did* in front of this stuffy Witch. "I don't want to talk about him with you."

"Yes. Please don't. It's none of my business. Sorry—I've given the entirely wrong impression. *Hell.* Excuse me—um—I do, however, need to discuss you leaving town."

For a legendarily powerful Witch, Bickel was so fucking awkward. I'd have felt sorry for making him uncomfortable if this misunderstanding wasn't his fault, and he didn't grate on my every nerve.

"Ever heard of a telephone?" I asked at my most snarky.

Visibly relieved to leave comments on my personal life behind, Bickel said, "I remember when my parents had the first telephone installed in our building. It was quite exciting new technology."

"Right. You should know how to use one if you need to talk to someone. You're lucky I came outside or you'd have been here all night, alone, staring at the closed cafe."

"Perhaps staring at the cafe was my original purpose and I was only messing with you when you came out. A mistake, I'll admit, as I seem to have come across as a creep."

I decided to ignore that. Watching the cafe wasn't a terrible idea given the curse situation. "How did you know I was going out of town?"

"Juliet mentioned it. Were you going to tell me, or just leave?"

"Why do you need to know?" I asked, defensiveness creeping into my tone and posture. I might be glad he wasn't spying but I was so over him, this conversation, and everything going on in my life right now.

Bickel looked at me like I was too much to be bothered dealing with. The feeling was fucking mutual. "I'm keeping an eye on you, Aria, and while I don't need to know your every action, I need to know *where* you are."

"And why do you?" My voice rose until I was half yelling at him. In the back of my mind, I was thankful someone so miserable was here to take my anger. "Why you? Don't you have better things to do?"

"Better than be yelled at by you? Certainly. Maybe I should have handed this assignment over once I met you, discovered your glowing personality, but I'm sticking it out. So deal with it. Where are we going?"

"*Argh!*" The only thing worse than seeing my family, was seeing them with an Authority escort. A too-powerful, grumpy-faced reminder that I was a screw up on the edge of serious trouble. "I'm seeing my parents and interviewing for a job. Who are you worried I'm going to Tell? They're. All. Witches."

He gave me a baffled look. "Why are you so agitated?"

"Owen is pushing me out of his life!" I was still shouting at Bickel, and now completely horrified. We both stood, staring dumbly at each other for a beat so long I feared he'd stopped time and trapped me in a personal hell.

"Oh—uh. I'm sorry?" Bickel said, alarmed at having to respond to my accidental admission. "Should I call Juliet?"

"Why?" I snapped.

"She might—I can't help you with this."

"So I should share my rejection with more people? No thank you. Can you just leave me alone? We're driving up North on Sunday."

Bickel opened his mouth, thought better of whatever he was going to say, and disappeared, looking relieved. I glared at the empty pavement.

The worst thing was, Owen wasn't rejecting me heartlessly. He was pushing me to do things that were good for me, that I'd avoided for largely immature reasons. He was right, I did want this second chance at a place in the Witchy world. I wanted a chance at surrounding myself with people I didn't have to hold back from or lie to all the time. I wanted to feel good about making the objectively right choice for once in my life.

Why didn't I?

26

OWEN

*J*uliet came to Coffee Cat at four in the morning the day MyFavoriteEats was due to film. She was a hero for making herself available before general waking hours, and acted as if it was completely normal to check my cafe for magic and leave before sunrise.

With worries of arctic air and exploding sinks out of my mind, I was able to begin the day's baking. Tristan arrived shortly after the Witch left to do checks of his own before Cindy and her crew showed up. I'd be relieved to have this promotional feature out of the way, but actually, it was shaping up to be a perfect day. The protection spell was in place. The pan was baking. Everything was fine.

Except for one very big thing. I hadn't talked to Aria since our conversation Friday night. Her abrupt departure threw me off and I'd been uneasy ever since. I waited up that night, but she didn't come back until I'd gone to bed. I barely saw her Saturday. She came in the cafe while I was working but didn't say hello, and was absent from the apartment all afternoon and evening. Then Aria left Sunday morning while I was in the shower.

I resisted the urge to ask her why, or what had her suddenly so busy. I had no claim to her time, or right to ask her to justify herself. We were only friends. But fuck. It felt like we'd broken up when we'd never been together.

In an effort to bury feelings I wish I didn't have, I threw myself into work. Cindy and her small camera crew arrived before we opened to film b-roll and get shots of the baking process, fresh pan dulce emerging from the oven, coffee beans grinding, and Tristan working the espresso machine.

"I'm more nervous than I expected," I told Tristan as the crew spent time outside catching shots of the cafe in the morning light. I'd spent so much time worrying about magic or ghosts ruining this, I hadn't thought about being featured personally.

"Yeah, actually having to be on camera isn't ideal," Tristan agreed. "My initial thought in reaching out was some staged food pictures and written reviews. Maybe I got carried away."

Despite nerves, Tristan and I made it through our joint interview and photoshoot. This was our cafe, our story, and sharing it gave me warm fuzzy feels. This place was my family and a space for us to thrive, celebrating our community through food and art. It was everything I wanted it to be. I tried to tell myself that was the same as Coffee Cat being everything I needed.

We had most of our staff on deck today, including both kitchen hands, so Tristan and I could be free for the promo, and so far everything had run smoothly. We'd left Cindy to do her solo reviews of the bakery items and were hiding in my office, taking a breather. Tristan was perched on my desk drinking an almond latte and I was slumped, feeling disturbingly boneless, in my chair.

"Remind me I hate having my photo taken before we ever do this again," Tristan said.

"Shit, same," I agreed, and we laughed. "People love the personal angle, but it's exhausting."

I checked my phone for the millionth time. I didn't even know why I bothered. I'd only had one message from Aria. Last night she sent me a picture of the attic at her parents' house. It looked almost exactly as I remembered, only somehow sadder outside my memories. Aria wasn't in the picture and the accompanying text had only said: *Luca says hi.* I'd 'liked' it as my only response.

Now I was wishing I'd said something. Anything. Instead, I'd spent the whole night replaying memories of Aria and I up in that room, talking, laughing, kissing. I wrote out a dozen texts I never sent, and half composed a message where I told Aria she should stay down South. With me. I'd deleted it quickly, knowing it was better to get over these feelings now.

The office light went out, leaving my phone screen as the only illumination in the windowless room. I stood up in surprise and knocked into Tristan's knees.

"Shit, my coffee," he swore.

The light came back on and we looked at each other. Tristan's latte dripped down his hand and onto my desk. I handed him a napkin.

"Any chance that was just the bulb in here?" Tristan asked as he hopped down from the desk.

I shrugged, very much doubting it.

We left the office. Out in the front of the cafe the lights were on. There was a healthy line of customers and the camera crew in the corner. Nothing out of the ordinary. I knew better than to let my guard down, or trust in luck. It should have been paranoid to think the curse was back.

A crow flew past the nearest window, mocking me.

Cindy spotted us hovering and walked over. "I'm thinking of getting a few customer testimonials, if you don't mind?"

"As long as they're okay with being in your posts, sure—" I said as the lights dimmed.

It was slow, not like the power going out, but like the whole cafe was on a dimmer switch. Seriously, how? Juliet was just here to confirm everything was fine. I scanned the cafe for anything suspicious. For once I wished Witches wore pointy hats.

The lights didn't go out this time. They brightened as steadily as they'd dimmed, until they were too bright. Disproportionately bright, but only for a second as they faded back to normal.

"That was weird," the influencer said. "Does it happen often?"

"No." Tristan frowned. "Maybe I should—"

"I'll go check it out if you help with the customer testimonials," I said in a rush.

"Not gonna argue with that one." Tristan gave me a reassuring look as he went with Cindy to talk to the patrons waiting for their coffee orders.

I had my phone out and was calling Juliet as I slunk out of sight toward the circuit breaker. She answered on the second ring and cursed, not unlike Tristan had in the office, when I told her we had a problem.

"That conniving Witch. I can't believe this. Getting around a protection spell isn't easy."

"Right. See you soon then?"

"Of course, Owen. I'll sneak in the back so the other Mortals don't catch on. Break the curse from the stairwell, or your office."

We ended the call. The lights pulsed again as I rejoined the action. As long as Juliet got here before this descended into another uncommonly cold, joy-sucking situation, I'd be okay. The day might no longer be perfect, but it was still *fine*.

I ducked behind the counter on my way over to Cindy and

Tristan. It seemed the customer testimonials had been fore-stalled.

"You really should try it," Max was saying to a woman holding a to-go cup with the lid off. "Oat milk is delicious."

"I'm sure it is," she said. "But it's not what I ordered."

Tristan was looking between the customers and Cindy. "We'll remake the coffee," he said with the air of someone repeating themselves. Why Max was involved was anyone's guess, I doubted he was helping the situation.

Tess was looking stonily at her milk cartons. "I swear I made her a trim mocha."

"Don't worry about it, Tess," I said.

"I'm not. But I know what I did, and I didn't give that woman oat anything." She began making the replacement drink.

This wasn't something to sweat from a customer service point of view, but I had a suspicion it wasn't Tess's mistake. The cafe's curse seemed to have a milk problem.

The woman with the trim mocha left happily, but Cindy had been sucked into a conversation with Max. He was a perfectly fine customer, until he came out with something rude or demeaning. Out of all our patrons, I'd rather not have subjected Cindy to Max's particular brand of off-putting chatter. Surely he'd keep his snide comments to a minimum if he was being filmed.

Tristan too was caught in the conversation, clearly straining not to roll his eyes. Ah—so Max had gone for rambley rather than offensive.

"I'd love to be a part of your program," Max said to an artifi-cially thrilled Cindy as she led him over to her table set up. "I've found this cafe to be very accommodating."

"Good lord, we'll be here all week," Tristan muttered to Tess and me.

The lights began to fade again. More people looked around, and I prayed Juliet was arriving via teleportation.

"What the—" Tess muttered.

I turned to find her holding a milk container upside down.

"I just opened this. It's empty." She threw the container in the trash.

I grabbed another from the fridge. Its seal was unbroken, but when I opened it, no milk was inside. More vanishing milk. This could not be happening.

In the hope no one would ask me for an explanation, I tried to act normal and opened another new milk. The next three Tess and I tried were empty. Orders and waiting customers backed up as we scrambled, getting behind in making coffees.

The lights went out as I finally found a usable milk carton. Judging by the abrupt end to our music, all the power was out. A general lull settled over the room.

"Thank you for your time," Cindy seized her chance to extricate from Max's monologue.

"No trouble. It's great to be part of this lovely cafe." Max got up, waved to Tristan and me, and mercifully departed. "Good day Mr. Sanchez. Always a pleasure Mr. Taylor-Tomás."

The lights still hadn't come back on. Tristan caught my eye and cleared his throat before making an announcement about coffee refunds if the power to the espresso machine wasn't restored in five to ten minutes.

A rushing sound cut through the relative quiet of the cafe. I knew it was the damn sink before I opened the bathroom door. I slipped in, thankful no one was inside, and locked the door. I rang Juliet and hoped she'd pick up before the water spilling onto the floor reached my toes. She didn't disappoint.

"Are you here?" I asked.

"Just double parked outside. Give me three seconds—" I

heard the beeping of the keypad. "Oh yeah, I can feel the magic. It'll be done in a minute." Juliet hung up the phone.

I only had a few moments to freak out before the power clicked back on and the water stopped. My phone buzzed.

"Do you want me to stick around?" Juliet asked when I answered.

"If you don't mind? Sorry."

"No apology necessary, Owen. I'll come in through the front door, shall I?"

"I owe you and Mr. B a lot."

"I don't see it that way. And it's just me today. Mr. Bickel is with Aria."

Aria hadn't told me that. I felt a flash of sympathy for her. After Juliet hung up, I pulled up my messenger app and sent Aria a text: *How's it going?* I waited. No reply came through.

I mopped up the bathroom because it needed doing for health and safety, also to keep myself from staring frozen at my phone. There was still no reply as I left the bathroom.

I didn't like to think about what a miserable time Aria was having at the Belmonte house between Bickel and her parents. I felt a stab of guilt. I hadn't asked Aria how she felt about visiting home. Even if Aria's parents never really sent her away, there was plenty of animosity between them and their daughter. I didn't delude myself into thinking the last twelve years had changed that.

She should have just stayed here. I didn't know if the thought was only about sparing Aria her parents, or staying-staying. I didn't want to know, or dig further into my sinking feelings. I'd told Aria to leave, but what else could I do? Her offer to stay wasn't any sort of guarantee.

Did I want to be with Aria? Yes. Okay? No doubt. But I couldn't see it working. If she stayed she might resent me for asking her to give up a chance at a Witchy career, or asking her to live an isolated lifestyle when she wanted more. That was a recipe for a prolonged, bad end. And if not, I'd resent when Tristan got sick of my lies. I trusted him to be the one who didn't leave me, but that didn't mean I could push him away, treat him poorly, and expect him to stay.

In the end Aria had offered to stay, only to leave without protest. It must have been easy for her to turn away because she'd already made up her mind to go.

People always said things they didn't mean to ease uncomfortable conversations. The only time I'd drifted into a semi-serious relationship was a prime example. Diego cushioned his departure with empty words just like Aria had. What he'd said was for him, not me. If either of them had been serious, I'd have been able to tell. I knew how to spot someone on their way out better than anyone.

So why couldn't I be glad I made the right choice?

Tristan spotted me hovering near the bathroom as the coffee shop ticked along, disaster averted. "That wasn't the sink, was it?"

"Nah." I pulled him over to talk to Cindy before he saw the freshly mopped floor. "Everything's great, Tristan. Perfect."

Cindy was thrilled, and thanked us for showing her the cafe. We gave her a box of pan dulce on her way out and sagged in relief. The day was an undeniable success for the business despite the small bumps. Tristan insisted we go out for drinks after closing to celebrate with the whole crew.

I should have been happy.

All I could think was, this wasn't everything I wanted in life. The cafe and Tristan were more important than anything, but I couldn't slide back into my content, pre-Aria life so easily. I wanted her here, celebrating with me. Instead I'd told her to leave like I didn't care.

27

ARIA

$\mathcal{T}$he past two days had been a test to my patience. Six hours in a car with Bickel almost made me glad to be at my parent's house, but that was yesterday, and now I'd had enough.

I was hiding in the attic, slouched in a bean bag chair. The familiar sights and smells unearthed feelings I'd left behind, transporting me back in time. Sitting here, it felt like nothing had changed since I left over a decade ago, and not in a good way.

I'd done an impressive job of avoiding just about everyone, my trip into the city for the interview with Luca the only exception. Our parents, Marcos and Deirdre Belmonte, were very busy, very important Witches and I'd hoped I could sneak in and out without prolonged contact. They'd foiled that plan, their schedules unexpectedly opening up for dinner tonight. I had a suspicion the last-minute availability was due to the Authority escort I hadn't forewarned them about.

At least I had good news to present at dinner. Possible redemption was feasible for the first time in over a decade, if we ignored Telling, which wasn't likely but hey, whatever. My parents couldn't fault me for getting a job. So I'd focus on that.

I stared at my phone. Owen texted hours ago and I hadn't replied. I didn't know how things were going any more than I knew what to say to him. My impulse to share all my complicated feelings about being back here was misplaced. Owen might be a friend, but I didn't want to fall into leaning on him like a confidant, or a partner.

"Aria—" Luca knocked on the attic door and poked his head in. "You really should come down. Marci's here."

"I can't believe you're subjecting her to this. I thought you two were friends." I extricated from the bean bag displaying zero grace.

"Our parents are not that bad."

I gave him a dead-eyed look.

"*Okay*—I thought the more people here, the less stifling the atmosphere would be. Marci doesn't mind deploying her charisma for your benefit."

I turned away. "Thanks."

We descended the stairs to join the most hodge-podge dinner party ever held. Everyone was having drinks in the library, because yes, it was that kind of house, and way Witchier than I remembered it being now I was unaccustomed. It wasn't modern in the slightest, and defined by too many darkened rooms filled with old shit that should have been thrown out a century ago.

Case in point, our dad had his historic grimoires out. Marcos was a stocky man with thick white hair and dark brown skin. Tonight he'd gone casual in a button up shirt, waistcoat and slacks, silver pocket watch instead of gold.

Marci was showing potentially genuine interest in the grimoires, but I really didn't know her well enough to be sure.

Either way her Marcos Belmonte tolerance was high. Most people didn't enjoy being lectured at.

Mr. Bickel was drinking whiskey, trapped in what could only be described as a pompous contest with Deirdre. It was like a pissing contest but way more insufferable. He'd gone for a white vintage suit, matching hat, and pale pink bow tie. My mother regaled him with a story about New York in the forties as she eyed his hat. She obviously wanted to tell him off for wearing it inside, but he was a guest, and though Bickel was younger, his power left her outranked, so she settled for pointed looks of disapproval as her only reprimand.

If there was one thing the Belmontes liked more than being the biggest Witches in the room, it was making new, more powerful connections. Deirdre was a retired judge, and having only barely survived the disgrace of my arrest twelve years ago, she seemed uncharacteristically content to let my current situation go. I had Bickel to thank for that; his presence was saving me the Belmonte ire. In a sort of blessed twist I hadn't seen coming, Deirdre and Marcos would rather impress Bickel than divert energy into scolding me for doing something so dumb as to require Authority presence in the first place.

Deirdre looked stunning and gothic as ever, in a black dress and sweeping shawl that struck her signature blend of couture and timeless Witchiness. Her skin was lighter than father's but her hair was just as white. She didn't glance my way as I entered the room.

"I worked on a number of high-profile cases back then," Deirdre was saying. "There was talk of nomination for judgeship —not my first, or last—but I had too many commitments I wasn't ready to give up."

Bickel was winning the pomp-off. While my mother tastefully alluded to her achievements, he conveyed his superiority without words. His unique and unequaled power meant he didn't need to do anything other than exist, obnoxiously, to be considered above the rest of us. Really, it made no sense Bickel was an Authority investigator. Witches didn't have their own government, but you could be a lot more involved in the politics and shaping of our world than Bickel seemed interested in.

Not wanting part in either Deirdre's self-aggrandizing stories, or Marcos's history lesson on the evolution of spell casting, I headed to the bar.

Luca followed, poured himself a glass of wine and then abandoned me to relieve Marci of our father's full attention. I copied Bickel and poured a whiskey. It tasted awful, so I knocked it back and poured another. Unfortunately, drinking enough to make the situation palatable would leave me snoozing in the corner, and as much as I didn't want to care about my parents' opinions, I didn't need to add has-a-drinking-problem to their running tally of my flaws.

I hadn't seen either of my parents in years and yet they'd been too preoccupied since my arrival to exchange more than a few words with me. I should be glad Bickel was sparing me Deirdre's undivided attention, and I was, but at the same time, it irked me. I was a disappointment for not visiting enough, but then why the hell would I bother? No one cared I was here. Who's your own daughter compared to a time-stopping Witch?

I made my way over to Marci. Her genuine enthusiasm for my impending move was almost overwhelming. I doubted she was as desperate for friends as I was, but I couldn't resist her bubbly personality.

Somehow we ended up arms linked in comfortable companionship as she listened to Marcos's take on spells as part of the public domain. I was busy tuning it out, staring at Luca unblinking, pulling the most subtle faces, trying to get him to laugh. It was an old childhood game we made up in an effort to have something to do at stiff, Witchy social gatherings. Unsurprisingly, I was usually the one who cracked and was inevitably told off for giggling.

Drinks seemed to last about five thousand years before we were freed from the library.

"Aria—" my mother said as we sat at the long, inappropriately sized, table in the formal dining room. "I hear you had a job interview?" She made it sound like a foreign concept she couldn't quite make sense of.

I gave Deirdre a smile and her hard gaze softened almost imperceptibly. She'd never understood why I hated her demands I stop looking pinchfaced and smile more, while Luca was praised for his seriousness. I gave up on that particular fight long ago. I only had so much energy, and to be honest I was trying to win some favor here. Giving her what she expected was always a start.

"The interview went well," I said, without even needing to lie. The intern coordinator I met with was a personable Witch and easy to talk to. I'd come away confident I had a shot at getting the position, even if I was far from excited about it. "They took a lot of interest in my experience with Mortals. Their feedback was positive. I should hear back soon, hopefully by tomorrow."

"I'm sure you did well, given your lack of experience with professionalism," Deirdre said, as if she believed her words were a compliment. "I was surprised to hear you were even considering it. I hope you did a better job of selling your desire for traditional employment than you ever expressed at home."

My forced smile turned into a tight line. "That was years ago. I'm making a shift in my life because I want to. It wasn't hard to convey my desire for a job I actually want." Okay, that was a stretch. I didn't so much want the job as need it, but it wasn't like I went into the interview intending to self-sabotage or half-ass it.

"It'd have been nice to know you were considering a career

shift—or let's be honest, a much delayed start," Marcos said from the other end of the table. "We should have approached this more strategically. Found you options to leverage. There's missed opportunity here."

My grip on my fork became almost painfully tight. Even when I was doing what they wanted, I was doing it wrong, or too late for it to count. It was always this way, criticism over all else. I felt duped for thinking tonight would be any different.

"It's a new development," was all I said, wariness threatening to overwhelm me.

"It seems to have taken some very desperate times for you to get your life in order," said Deirdre as she swirled the wine in her glass.

"My life wasn't out of order. I've just wanted a change." Maybe I was a mess, but hell if I'd admit it. I still wouldn't have gone back and skipped out on fortunes entirely. Even if I could rewrite my life, I didn't want to.

"Aria, your behavior has been out of order." Deirdre put down her glass. "If you'd been suitably occupied, you wouldn't have gotten back with that boy and revealed magic."

Crap, I was kinda hoping it wouldn't come up, with the Bickel distraction and all, but we were down the road of my disgrace and no example was to be ignored. Luca winced at our mother's words. There was a painful silence, at least to me, for the likes of Marci it was probably more awkward.

"I'm not back with that boy—he's a man with a name, which you know."

"I find it baffling," Deirdre said before I could go on. "That it took you so long to come around to the career path we'd always encouraged you to pursue. Now you're at a disadvantage, taking a job as a glorified assistant. All your colleagues and competition will be educated. Think of the career opportunities you'd have if you'd trained to be a lawyer with psychic power, like we'd planned. Instead you let that boy ruin everything. And now he—"

"Owen didn't ruin anything. He was a good part of my life. He still is."

"Excuse me for not being able to see the good in someone who caused you to abandon everything."

I had to resist seeing red. "That isn't what happened at all. I didn't want to keep living a life separate from Mortals, lying to my friends just because you told me to. I'd decided not to use my psychic power for the courts long before my own trial. I always wanted to do something different. My 'alternate' career path had nothing to do with Owen."

"Well, you made the wrong choice. You see that now, right? You're back where you started. If you hadn't failed to listen to us—"

"Is that all you see? My life hasn't been terrible for the last twelve years. Why do you still insist I blindly follow your instructions? Like it's the most important thing here. Is taking this job now, instead of then, so wrong?"

My mom made a *tutting* sound. "You always take such a negative viewpoint, Aria."

"Me?"

"Yes. And would it kill you to admit you were wrong? Instead of clinging to the delusion you didn't waste years of your life. And the job you're taking now is not the same, it's junior. We've only ever tried to support and guide you." Deirdre honestly believed it too. Which was the always the kicker.

Fuck, this was stifling. I'd been trapped in a variation of this argument too many times to count. Only I'd never tried so hard to do what they wanted.

I couldn't think straight long enough to form a reply. And that was how they always won.

"Trying to control someone isn't guidance," Mr. Bickel said in a surprisingly icy tone.

Deirdre scoffed. "You've misunderstood—"

"Did I? Aria is free to pursue any alternate, Mortal-esque life she wants. Deciding to take her own direction speaks to a much stronger character than cowing to your bullying demands, especially as a child."

Deirdre looked like she wanted to protest, but Bickel had his scary eyes out. He'd cut right to the core of her, said things I'd always been unable to because I couldn't deal with her manipulative denial and shrewd ability to turn everything back on me. I was begrudgingly touched.

Bickel's rebuke shut the conversation down. We all ate for a few moments, my parents probably fretting mutely about looking bad in front of someone powerful, and Mr. Bickel looking like he couldn't possibly give a single shit about anyone or anything.

I swear Bickel smiled at me but it was so quick I might have imagined it.

I ripped apart a perfectly good tortilla and let the pieces fall to my plate. I tried to force myself to eat. The food was good. Not Sanchez level good, a thought that made me disproportionately sad. But I didn't want to be here.

I abandoned my fork for my wine glass.

Marci, bless her, caught my eye before launching into a meandering monologue. After the success of the grimoire app, she was looking for a new venture. Marci and Luca talked at length about the legal and ethical consideration of a magically enhanced dating app Marci was considering creating.

"Marcella, I'm so glad you and Luca are spending time together, fostering each other's careers," Deirdre said. "It will be good for Aria to join in." Because why apologize when you can double down?

"Hoping she'll rub off on me?" I asked.

Deirdre responded as if she couldn't hear my blatant sarcasm. "Yes. It will be good for you to be around successful people again."

"I don't know why you assume I haven't been. Success isn't just one thing," I muttered.

I'd always wanted my parents' opinion not to matter and told myself I hadn't cared in years, but sitting here I couldn't ignore how much I cared. And how mad that made me. I wanted them to see value in me, treat me positively and without constant judgment. Like maybe be happy for me regardless. That shouldn't have been some pie-in-the-sky desire, but to them I would always be less accomplished than I could be, messy and defined by shortcomings. They would never apologize or change, and I was ready to stop pinning my worth on hopes they would.

I took this interview, in part, to push my life into a mold that only held value from other's perspective. When I looked at my life in the wake of the magic shop closure, I saw what I wasn't happy with—lack of people and stability—and what I knew others found disappointing—a Witch wasting a rare gift. But I was focusing on the wrong half of that equation, and trying to fix things with someone else's solution.

Yes, I wanted to stop running from problems and things that didn't work, I wanted to get unstuck, but I didn't know what I wanted out of life. This job wasn't the answer any more than pursuing it twelve years ago would have been. It wasn't the kind of work I wanted to do.

"Aria, check your email." Luca said, calling me back to my surroundings. He had his phone out, and shook it at me in an encouraging way.

I hadn't been paying attention to the conversation for some time, but extricated my phone from my pocket as requested.

"Really, at the table?" our mother protested.

My inbox had a single unread message from Luca's law firm. I opened it.

DEAR MS. BELMONTE,

Congratulations on being selected for...

"I GOT THE JOB," I announced, skimming the rest of the email with a feeling of indifference.

Marci squealed.

Luca beamed at me. "I knew you would."

"A toast?" Mr. Bickel suggested without emotion.

We all raised our glasses. "Better late than never," Marcos said with a booming laugh.

28

OWEN

*G*ot the job.

The text from Aria distracted me as Tristan and I celebrated the successful filming day. The rest of the Coffee Cat employees had moved on after a few hours, leaving the two of us to fend for ourselves at a local brewery. Twilight settled on the beer garden and I found myself tipsier than I'd been in way too long.

Tristan and I opted to stay out for loaded flatbreads, a-k-a hipster pizza, and another round, which he was ordering up at the bar. I was enjoying myself—I was—I just shouldn't have checked my phone.

It was good Aria got the job. I should congratulate her. My phone screen went dark due to inactivity as I failed to text her back.

"Two flatbreads and an assortment of olives coming up." Tristan returned to our table, setting down a number and two more beers, before he flopped into his seat. "I'm fucking exhausted."

"Same. I wish I'd thought about organizing a day off tomorrow." I sipped my beer like it could solve the problem for me.

After Tristan made a dent in his own drink, he nodded to my phone and asked, "Who's the bothersome text from?"

Of course he'd picked up on my preoccupation without me saying anything. "Aria."

"He admits it." Tristan gave me an exaggerated, ah-hah look.

"She got a job in San Francisco."

"What about the one here with Mr. Good-Looking and the woman with the briefcase?"

"Must not have panned out." You know, because it was a lie. "She wanted this other thing anyway."

"Are you still telling yourself it was just a fling? Because this disappointed act says otherwise," Tristan said, his playful demeanor dropped.

I took a long sip of beer. He waited patiently through my attempt at avoidance. "I—fine. It was more than a fling or hook-up. Happy now?"

"Not really, you sound hollowed out."

"I liked her, Tristan. It was stupid. I knew she was leaving. I should have been able to keep myself in check, but I wasn't expecting to get over all our history and fall for her."

"Did you tell her how you feel?"

"You know I didn't. Which is a good thing."

"Um, why?"

"I knew the whole time she didn't want to stay. She doesn't have a life here. This job will be really good for her. She wants to move on, and I'm no reason to hold her back." I hunched over my drink and watched foam slide down the interior of the glass.

Tristan eyed me shrewdly. "Uh-huh. Sure. That's the whole story? She one hundred percent wanted to leave no matter what, so you hid your feelings. She had no interest in you beyond your hot bod?"

I grumbled. There was magic, and blah blah Witchy bullshit, but there was a mundane detail I'd skipped and Tristan had sniffed it out like a drug dog. "Aria offered to stay, but not like *really*. You know, it's always easier to pretend, cushion the end with half suggested options. We weren't going to work out, our lives don't even match up a little bit. No point pinning hope to fantasy."

Tristan shifted in his seat, betraying his restless energy and maybe annoyance with my situation. "If you like her so much why not try? Offering to stay isn't placating."

This was the fundamental difference between Tristan and me. He was eternally optimistic, and while I had a positive outlook on life, I was weary. "I don't trust anyone not to leave me but you," I said, alcohol allowing me to get to the point without worrying about bluntness.

Tristan gave me a sad little sigh. "Your dad didn't leave you, Owen. He died. And you're right, I'll never leave, but shit, why am I the exception? I could die. Then where would you be?"

"You won't. That's not what we're talking about." My words came out quick and sharp.

"No? Okay. It's not like I'm planning on it, but come on. Why am I the only one you let yourself lean on? Why is everyone else destined to abandon you? Why does adding romantic attraction make a relationship inherently untrustworthy to you?" Tristan was firm but not harsh and had a look like he wasn't going to let me get out of answering him.

Now I was the one squirming.

I had to look away but didn't try to avoid answering an any real way. "Whenever I put my feelings out there I find myself alone. I don't like being hurt in that way. It's not like you've never been burned by a boyfriend, but you take it as a reason to try again. I don't think it's worth the trouble. I don't need or want a romantic relationship."

"Not wanting a relationship would be all good, if it were true. If you were actually happy with casual. But you want a partner, which is why this thing with Aria hurts. You can't tell me you're disappointed it didn't work out, while simultaneously saying you don't want any relationship ever. It doesn't add up."

Tristan's challenging tone caught me off guard and I looked up. "What? No. I'm not. I don't. I'm just upset it didn't work out with Aria because I knew this end was coming all along."

"Was it though?"

Did I detect a hint of exasperation in him? Tristan usually understood me better than this. Why was he looking at me like I was the one confused?

I tried to get my thoughts in order. "Yes, of course the end was coming. You were there when Aria first showed up, it was always temporary. I knew better. Falling victim to indulgence was my own fault. That's all that's bothering me."

Tristan leaned in, making it harder for me to look away. "Or —you wanted it to work, despite thinking it was doomed."

I felt like he'd backed me into a corner and trapped me with those sharp eyes. I blustered. "Fine—yes. I wanted something impossible. A situation I'd never have been in, if I'd remembered I don't need relationships. For. This. Exact. Reason. The inevitable end."

See, I'd got back to my point. Why wouldn't he just accept it?

But Tristan dropped his head back, looking like he was about to roll his eyes. "Oh my god, Owen. It wasn't inevitable."

"Yes, it was. But it doesn't matter. You're the most important person I have, Tristan. I don't need anyone else." I was being more defensive than usual, but that didn't make my statement any less true.

Tristan blinked rapidly, all exasperation gone. "That's not— you know I feel the same about you, but you also know I want more. I want a partner, I want romantic love, and that doesn't change anything between us. You can have more than one person in your life."

He turned his drink in half circles, focused on the glass. I nudged his knee with mine under the table and he look up.

"I know that—and I want that for you. I just don't want it for me." I hoped Tristan could hear how genuinely I meant it.

But he only looked more determined than before. "I wouldn't push if you honestly believed that, Owen."

I shook my head; he didn't get it. How could I make him see? I tried to fend off a weird frustrated and confused feeling and pushed on. "The thing with us—I never asked anything of you, it just happened. There was never a time to worry. By the time I realized we had something important I already knew you weren't going anywhere. I know keeping romance casual is a defensive strategy, but I prefer that concession to inevitable heartbreak. Maybe one day someone will come into my life naturally, like you did, and will stick around despite my worries. I'm just not holding my breath."

Tristan pushed his hair out of his eyes in a jerky, frustrated gesture. I was on the verge of defending myself further when the food arrived. One pear and arugula flatbread, the other fennel and goat cheese, and an overpriced bowl of olives. Tristan took a plate and slice of bread, cut in rectangles in an effort to prevent people clocking it as pizza. I helped myself, trying to think of any topic transition that sounded natural and would take us firmly away from my love life.

"Remember Diego?" Tristan asked before I could come up with anything.

"Um, yeah?" I wasn't liable to forget my longest relationship. "He left me for Seattle."

"Did he though? I mean—yes technically—but not in an abandoning-Owen way."

"What are you even saying?" I wanted to laugh but could see this going somewhere I wouldn't like.

"He tried to make it work with you." Tristan started ticking thing off on his fingers. "Got a job offer in LA, dragged you apartment hunting—"

"But his dream job was in Seattle. I wasn't going to ask him to give that up for me, that would be selfish. Plus, he obviously wanted to leave. We were barely seeing each other in the end." I rolled my eyes.

"Because you pushed him away." Tristan gave me an dramatic look I felt was a bit over the top. "People will always leave if you don't give them a chance. That is the only inevitable thing. Diego was the only one trying to make your relationship work, of course he left. You told him to. You didn't try, so he gave up. What else do you expect?"

I frowned, feeling strangely off balance. "That's not true. It was obvious which life he wanted. He chose Seattle before he even brought up other half-options. I wasn't considering moving any more than he was considering staying. Nothing about us worked. He was older, which was fine, but our lives didn't fit."

"Like Aria and you don't fit?"

"Maybe. I don't know. I didn't push either of them away." But this panicked feeling was starting to churn amidst all the beer in my stomach. *Had I?*

"What has you so convinced Aria's offer to stay was insincere?" Tristan picked up a piece of his flatbread.

"She still left," I said automatically.

He put the food down, half of the toppings falling off. "Owen, no one is going to offer, be told no, and stay anyway. You need to give people a chance. You gave me a chance, and I'm still here."

"That was different."

"Yes. But the difference doesn't make it irrelevant."

Fuck. He had a point. Too many points. *Did I really push Diego away?* I was so sure he'd leave me. The moment he mentioned Seattle I'd counted us done, and hadn't been the least bit surprised. I didn't see him trying to build a life with me because I didn't believe he'd ever want to, but looking back it was painfully apparent. All of the distance was initiated by me, getting there first so it didn't hurt too much, or so I'd told myself. Really, I'd been blinded by my determination to get over him and ignored every gesture he made. And okay, I was maybe a bit young for serious-serious six years ago, but now, was it really the same?

No it wasn't. Magic wasn't the same as 'we don't fit because you're a professional with a career and a 401k, and I'm twenty-four.' Maybe I could have worked it out with Diego, but Aria? I didn't think so. So what was the point in trying?

Oh, damn it. Tristan was right, no matter which way I looked at it, I hadn't tried. In either case. Aria knew all magic's complications and still offered to stay. If she meant it, and I shut her down, of course she'd give up and go along with the previous plan of leaving. I'd rejected her, not told her what she wanted to hear.

If she wanted to stay with me, was there a solution to seemingly impossible, magic-induced differences? She didn't present one. She would have if she had any ideas. Unless I shut her down too quickly, forcing her to take all the risk, when I acted like everything *wasn't a big deal.* Like I don't care about her.

I had a sickening feeling that figuring out how to make it work was something we had to do together. Meaning I blew it. It wasn't fair to expect her to present me with a flawless future on a silver platter, and turn down anything less because I was afraid to put in any work.

"My relationships always fail because I let them," I said, not meeting Tristan's eyes.

"Hey. I'm not blaming you for every one. But in these two cases, I'm thinking yeah. Everyone leaving was all you could see, and without room for other options, you made sure the end was inevitable." Tristan made a circular motion with his hand.

"Why didn't you tell me this before?"

Tristan laughed. "I tried, Owen. I dunno, you were having none of it after Diego. I thought maybe he wasn't worth the fight. Or you weren't ready to honestly self-reflect. I figured you'd see it eventually."

"Great. So—maybe I pushed Aria away out of my own debilitating fear of abandonment—" I looked at Tristan for reassurance. It was all there in the way he looked at me. I took a fortifying sip of beer. "But—if I hadn't, if I'd admitted I wanted her to stay, it still might not work out."

"Dude, that's just life. All I'm saying is give Aria as much benefit of the doubt as you gave me when I popped up. I don't think trust in her is misplaced. The end is not inevitable, unless you make it. Who knows, you might end up with two people who'll never leave you."

He turned back to his food and began placing the toppings back on his flatbread.

I slumped in my seat, not quite giving in to putting my head in my hands. "Cool. Thanks for all this, but what if it's too late?"

Tristan shrugged. "I don't have a magic solution, Owen. Just wisdom beyond my years and a supernatural ability to deal with people leaving me."

And just like that he got me to smile along with him. "Your abandonment issues should be at least as bad as mine."

"Maybe. Or, I met you and you restored my faith in—maybe not *people*—but queerkind at the very least. It's this whole romantic agenda I've got going on. Look. New plan. Aria should stay here, be with you, get that job with the hottie and introduce me. Win-win-win-win."

"Who's the fourth win?"

"The hottie."

I shied away from the eager look in his eye. "I may have exaggerated the availability of that job—"

"Hmm—pity." Tristan ate an olive in deep contemplation.

I was almost giddy, but also spinny and lightheaded after revelations that looked woefully apparent now I questioned myself. Or the wooziness was the beer. Either way, I felt like a dumbass but I couldn't fall too far in a whole of my own making with Tristan's relentless ability to look on the bright side urging me on.

Looking for reasons Aria and I would fail meant I placed more emphasis on negatives than positives. My fear made sure I saw magic as an insurmountable problem. I always found a damning impasse, and if it hadn't been magic, I'd have come up with something else.

Magic freaked me out, not gonna lie, but what if I could learn to incorporate it into my life. I didn't know how to work around the Aria-is-going-to-live-for-like-ever situation, but I could at least ask her. I hadn't even considered her feelings on the subject. And tonight, I'd found a way to talk to Tristan without lies about magic getting in the way even when it was at the heart of the issue. Maybe Telling him wasn't the only option. Maybe I could find a balance.

At the very least, I could try. If it wasn't too late.

29

ARIA

*M*onday night I got a text from Owen, saying: *We should talk.*

Less than twenty-four hours later I was completely freaking out about it. Usually this came before the break-up. *Not that we had ever been together.* What could be happening now? I knew the cafe had magic problems yesterday, Juliet had called Bickel to discuss. Was Owen more worried about magic than the last time we talked? Was Tristan pissed off and demanding answers about weird shit happening at the cafe?

I'd responded, asking what was up, only to be told we should talk when I was back in SoCal. In person chats did not bode well. Why say we need to talk, and then not talk?

"Are you okay, Aria?" Luca asked.

I'd dragged him up to the attic as soon as we got back from the city. He'd been kindly keeping normal working hours while I was here, a habit he should adopt anyway, and one I'd try to reinforce when I was around. You wouldn't catch me at the office until nine at night. Oh god, what if they wanted me at the office until nine at night? No, not thinking about it. I had enough doubts about this job already.

Luca and I left Bickel in the city; there was a fancy restaurant he'd been meaning to try, and we twins were not to be invited. Instead, we were entrenched in an old video game.

"I'm pissed you're still better at this than me," I grumbled.

"I cheated." Luca's hair fell in his face as he concentrated on the screen, fingers flying over the controller. "I've been playing again since staying here." He attacked my character mercilessly. "What's really bothering you?"

"Everything."

I hadn't accepted the job yet or told anyone what the holdup was.

Luca had spent the morning introducing me to some of his colleagues, trying to inspire some enthusiasm in me, but I couldn't see myself working there no matter how hard I tried. Then I'd spent a mopey, miserable afternoon with Bickel shopping for pocket squares and matching bow ties. I'd entertained a feral daydream of Telling shopkeepers on Maiden Lane just to feel alive.

I was supposed to sign my employment contract and have an orientation meeting tomorrow before going South to face the court. Instead I was putting off signing and considering self-sabotage. I didn't want the job and couldn't get over my change of heart.

Luca put down his controller and turned to interrogate me just as my phone rang. I scrambled to answer it. To my surprise it was Juliet Herrera.

"Aria, I'm glad I caught you. Do you have a moment?"

"Is everything okay at the cafe?" I sunk further into the bean bag. I'd hoped Owen would call if there was a problem, placing even a tiny bit of trust in me.

"I've had to banish the curse a couple times, which is distracting me from my analysis of the crow, but there's no disaster. That's not why I called."

We sat in silence for a long moment. "—So why'd you call?"

"Oh. Yes. I was hoping to talk to you."

"About?" If I wasn't distracted with Owen I might have laughed. Not at Juliet, just, I liked her stiffness. Not something I'd ever have pegged as endearing, given it was a trait I usually hated in Witches. It turns out cute-awkward-stiffness was a world away from uppity-I'm-judging-you-stiffness.

"I have a proposal for you, Aria. Please forgive me if this is overstepping, but I hear you're looking for employment?" I indicated I was. "Excellent. My proposal is, well, it's a job offer. With me. As my psychic assistant."

"Really?" Sounding shocked wasn't the best reaction, confidence would serve me better, but I was never a game-player and I had the impression Juliet wasn't either.

"I've always wanted a psychic on my team. It would make Herrera Investigations an actual team, not just me poking around on my own with the occasional Bickel. Since my business is private it's not all Witchy crime, not like the Authority at all. I look into a fair few family mysteries and investigate the odd petty grievance, do community work, and take a lot of cases for Mortals who Know. I think that might be of interest to you?"

"Oh—yes—um, actually it would." I was floored. This sounded way more me. And Juliet, a powerful, incredibly skilled Witch, thought I'd be good on her team. It was flattering.

"Oh yay!" She gave a sweet trill of excitement. "We'll discuss compensation and hours. This really can fit you, however you like. And you never have to read anyone you don't want to, and it would only every be to help our clients. I'm not out here sneaking around. How are you with organization and scheduling?"

"Um—"

Juliet hurried on, her enthusiasm not deterred. "I was hoping to get some help with my calendar. Maybe some light office work? If that sounds terrible, please say no. I don't want to push it."

She was acting like landing me as an employee was some sort of lucky break. "I don't mind office work—I've never done it but I can, like, answer a phone and use the computer. I can't imagine we'd need my psychic ability full time. I'm down for other duties." And, if there was ever anything urgent the messages wouldn't go unanswered for a full day while some idiot—me—revealed magic. But that was beside the point.

"Oh, perfect." I could hear Juliet typing in the background. "I'll send an email. Edwin will be so pleased."

That brought me up short. "Why?"

"He'll like working with you too, even if he doesn't show it. He said you've been miserable."

"Was this his idea?"

"Not entirely. I'd been thinking about it since spending time with you." Juliet paused and the typing sound ceased. "He's always said I need a psychic, and I thought you and I would work well together. I was planning to talk to you when you returned, but then I heard you were considering another job, and Edwin said you didn't even want to move up North, so, it was time to ask you. I'd have been disappointed to have you move out of town, Aria. This Coffee Cat business has been—not fun—but it's been something. Edwin agrees."

My mind was spinning. This was so not what I expected, especially from the dapper Witch. "Are you and Bickel—?" I couldn't help prying.

"Are we what?"

"Um. Like a couple?" I already regretted asking.

"No." Juliet laughed. "I have to tell Edwin you asked, he'll get a kick out of it. Anyway. I told you, he's my associate."

"Okay. Cool." I sounded relieved, which was maybe a bit mean. Bickel had been ridiculously nice to me, but I still had prickly feelings toward him. I couldn't trust someone known as the most powerful Witch of the modern day, maybe I was just being biased.

"If you're hoping to avoid him, you'll see Bickel more than any partner of mine, Aria. My dating life is tragic." Juliet said this like she was stating a fact, rather than complaining, but it gave me an urge to reassure her.

"Sorry—I—uh—can't imagine why. I feel like you have a lot to offer."

"Thank you—" She sounded genuinely pleased. "But this is how I like it. Do not try to set me up with any of your friends."

"You're in luck. I don't really have friends, except Jenn and she's seeing someone."

"And me. Though I'm not a friend you can set me up with, so we're safe. Now—are you available to start this week or next? I have a number of things piling up and an extra set of hands would really help."

I was buzzing, like better than drunk, off this conversation. "Sure, the only thing on my schedule is the Telling hearing." That burst my bubble. "That doesn't bother you? What if they find me—negligent?"

Luca's firm had had a few stern words to say on the subject, making it clear I wasn't a catch in their eyes as much as a deserving charity case. They'd kindly overlook my legal trouble unless I was criminally charged.

Juliet somehow gave the impression of waving her hand dismissively over the phone. "*Eh.* I'd be surprised if they do. It's a love Telling isn't it?"

I almost choked. "Love? You think Owen and I are in love?"

"Are you not?"

"I—it's complicated. He's not super keen on magic."

"That's just because of the curse. I promise I'll have it sorted soon. This case isn't my best work, I admit—but Owen will be fine. He seemed smitten."

"Do you think it could work out between us?" Like, fuck it, maybe Juliet had the answers to all my problems.

"Oh hell, don't ask me for advice. I'm hopeless."

"Sorry, that was maybe a bit much." Carried away with her offer of friendship already, cool Aria, very cool. "I can't imagine you're hopeless at anything, Juliet."

"Really? Thank you. I knew I liked you, Aria."

We hung up and I felt a bit like I'd been hit in the face by a tornado.

Luca shifted on his bean bag. "So I was totally eavesdropping—"

I filled in the details, unable to contain my profound relief. This wasn't everything solved, but I didn't want to work for the lawyers, following someone else's path because I had nowhere else to go. I didn't want to use my psychic magic in ways I wasn't comfortable with, and I was only more sure of that now than I'd been in years past.

"Sorry I won't be moving up here. You were so excited," I said to Luca.

"Don't worry about it. We don't have to be joined at the hip, but I will require visitation."

"Deal." I let myself bask in this new possibility for a few moments. "I think I might just not tell mom and dad. Leave town and let them figure out I didn't take the job." Before I would have worried about what they'd think. Now I'd accepted they would frame this as another Aria failure, no matter what I said, and I didn't have to take that to heart.

Luca shrugged. "Or—tell dad you leveraged. Juliet is from *those* Herreras. They'll be impressed."

"Yeah, I'm not gonna do that." I was going to accept I couldn't change how my parents treated me, only how much I let them into my life. After this I was done holding out for acceptance and validation. Maybe we'd have honest conversations one day, but I had to be fine if we didn't. I was too excited about this next step in my life to let their opinions cloud it and I didn't care if they approved of Juliet's family. "Wait, I'm sorry. Which Herreras?"

Luca gave me a look like he thought the answer was obvious. "Judge Herrera in New York, mom's pal. Juliet's her daughter."

"Really?"

I knew I'd heard something about her family. If I'd realized this was the connection, I'd have not come within a city block of Juliet. Mr. and Mrs. Herrera were their own sort of formidable powerhouse. Juliet's friendship with Bickel was suddenly making more sense. If I hadn't already trusted and liked Juliet, her family reputation may have blinded me. They were the kind of Witches I lived to avoid, but Juliet was nothing like that.

I was glad I hadn't put together who Juliet's family was, or I'd have judged her unfairly. I might actually have a bit of a judgment problem between this and Bickel.

"Working with her is going to be unique, that's for sure."

Luca nodded. "You seem excited about this, Aria. You never wanted to move, did you?"

"I mean— It was supposed to be a visit, a time to hang out with you while I figured myself out." I shrugged apologetically. "And when I implied Owen was just a friend, I may have lied."

"No. Way," he deadpanned.

"Oh, screw you."

"*Ugh*. Aria, why do you look like someone popped your balloon?"

"Owen told me to leave. He's not interested—" I spilled my guts to Luca in a way I hadn't done since we were children. I told him how much I wanted a life with Owen, how I didn't know if he'd ever love me enough to try. I spelled out all Owen's hang ups about magic, Tristan, and my fear these were only surface things standing in the way. "He's this Mr. Casual-Guy now. You should have heard how many times he said things weren't a big deal, or weren't complicated."

"Owen has always been crazy about you, Aria. He's just scared. You need to be there for him, be his—*ew* this is cliche—be his rock, his home. Show him you love him."

I narrowed my eyes. Luca wasn't usually one for encouraging relationship advice. "How do you know he's scared?"

"Personal experience. Casual is just fear wrapped up in a cool bow." He held up his hand. "But we are not talking about me right now."

I let it go. "Fine. Any idea how I can *be his rock?*" I poked Luca's knee with my sock clad toe and laughed.

"I wish I never said that." He gave me one of his rare, over-dramatic pouts before returning to safe, serious ground. "We need to propose solutions to all his magical doubts. Then if he still isn't interested, you'll know he just doesn't like you that much."

"Oh is that all? So I should Tell Tristan? I'll get him on the phone—"

"No. You absolutely cannot do that."

I threw up my arms. "Do you have a better plan?"

"No. But give me a minute. We'll come up with something." Luca brooded for a bit, then sat up like he'd been shocked. "This won't help your Telling problem but there's a spell in one of those old grimoires."

"No there isn't."

But actually, there was.

30

OWEN

I was late for court. The Witches had kindly scheduled the hearing in the evening, so I wouldn't miss work. It was creepy they made this accommodation without ever asking me about my schedule, but I'd tried to take it as a positive sign, or a show of goodwill.

And I'd blown it. I'd been running behind over an hour ago.

Court wasn't the only thing I was missing. I'd put off talking to Aria until we could do it in person. My resolve that a face-to-face talk was vital came purely from fear of the things I needed to say, but I had a plan. Sort of. It was more of an idea. Not that it mattered if I missed my chance.

Aria called while I was at work and I'd genuinely missed it, so I texted, asking her to meet me at a bar a block from the courthouse. But it wasn't my fault I didn't shown up.

There was a minor electrical fire at Tristan's loft. I'd rushed over to help, and it was largely fine, no one was hurt, but still a disaster. We had a busy afternoon shifting Tristan's stuff, assessing damage and contacting insurance. I managed to message Aria to cancel and apologize before my phone died, but only just. Standing her up for drinks wasn't the way to start a *hey let's try again* proposal and I didn't know if she'd replied. I couldn't charge my damn phone at Tristan's place with the power off.

I was paranoid this failed attempt at telling Aria how I felt was a sign not to go ahead with my not-quite-a-plan-slash-idea in getting her back. Getting her back, who was I kidding, this was more like telling Aria I wanted a relationship with her in the first place.

"I really have to go," I said to Tristan when we finally got back to my apartment and I realized the time.

"Hot date?" Tristan had a suitcase full of things and his laptop bag. He needed a place until the repairs on his were done and the electricity could be turned back on.

"At this point I think I'm in trouble more than anything else." Never mind romantic plans, the Witches were waiting.

"Don't be so doom and gloom. She's not going to be mad, there was a literal fire." Tristan rolled his eyes as I ran out the door.

I dashed across downtown and found the courthouse locked. It was after hours at, what I thought, was a Mortal courthouse. Maybe the Witches were just borrowing it for the night? A few tourists milled around taking photos of the gardens and iconic architecture. I tugged on the door again, trying to fight a sinking feeling.

For a moment I had the absurd thought it was all made up. Some trick culminating in me outside a locked building, the butt of a joke. The future I wanted with Aria nothing more than a figment of my imagination.

"There you are." Bickel's stern voice was a relief. "Why are you covered in soot?"

"I'm not covered." There was a smear of ash on my Coffee Cat T-shirt, and okay, some on my shoes and the hems of my jeans. Not something I needed to worry about.

Bickel led me to a side entrance. "You might have changed. Haven't you met enough Witches to know better than to show up looking so—*ugh*."

I hurried after him, down the empty halls and into a huge open room that was frankly gorgeous. Like, I was pretty sure people got married here. Muraled walls, dark wood, it was not a bland procedural space.

Everyone at the front of the room turned to look as we came in. I froze. Two corporate-looking Witches were sitting at a large desk. Aria stood in front of them in a suit, complete with dress shoes.

"Fuck," I muttered.

Bickel gave the ghost of a chuckle as he sat himself down in the back row of seats, presumably to watch this disaster unfold.

"Mr. Sanchez," called a gray-haired Witch from the front of the room. "Please join us."

I slunk forward. I'd never have shown up to a real court date looking like this. It was only just dawning on me, this was a real court date. I tried to smile at Aria and failed, giving her a grimace. She looked tense but her return grin was marginally more successful.

The gray-haired Witch, an Authority judge, started talking while the man next to him took notes. My mind was racing. I'd talked to Luca about all this court stuff but it seemed very different now I was here. Words washed over me, but I couldn't focus. I wanted to talk to Aria, tell her I was an idiot before. I was afraid she was in trouble and that I'd made it worse with my unkempt lateness, on top of missing my chance to tell her we were in fact, a very big deal. She was the biggest deal and my insistence otherwise was—

"Mr. Sanchez?" The Witchy judge was looking at me.

"Huh?"

"Before Aria gives her account of revealing magic, can you

tell us, in your own words, the nature of your relationship?"

"Relationship?"

"How do you know each other?" The judge sounded impatient. "We have records indicating a childhood association and —*complications*—how would you describe Aria's return to your life?"

I looked at her, standing back rigid and uncomfortable. I wished I'd seen her before to reassure her at the very least. She'd have been nervous and I should have been there to support her.

"Mr. Sanchez." The judge was losing his patience.

Right, right, his question. "Aria just kinda showed up out of the blue."

"Indeed." The judge narrowed his eyes. "Did you get the impression she was seeking you out? Any sort of agenda in the works, perhaps?"

I laughed, but no one else did. "No, it was all unexpected. I'd never thought I'd see her again, and that was really not fair," I added vehemently, like fuck this court for banning Aria from my life. "But when she turned up, I was so—happy. Surprised and confused, and maybe upset, but I was so glad to see her. It's—" I turned away from the judge to look at Aria. "I'm so glad to have you back. Then, now. And I don't want you to go. I pushed you away because I was scared—"

"Scared of magic?" interrupted the judge.

"No." I didn't even look at him, but instead kept Aria's sweet brown eyes locked on mine. "I was scared because I'm falling in love with you. And I'm really bad at it. I never try. I'd rather be safe in pretending I don't need anyone, but I need you. I needed you before and it wasn't your fault you weren't there. I need you in my life still, now, all of it, always. I want to try, for real, Aria. All that stuff I said was worrying me, I want to do it anyway, even if it might not work out. Um. Unless you don't want to?" My heart pounded, the others in the room of no concern. My world was only her.

"Owen—" Aria closed the distance between us and hugged me.

I kissed her, not too heated with the audience, but I couldn't not. Aria was practically vibrating. I tried to communicate through the kiss that we'd work it out, get through this, I was all in. I didn't know if the message was received, but there was stuff I didn't want to say in front of official Witches. Court really wasn't an ideal setting for proclamations.

"Lovely," said the judge without enthusiasm as we pulled apart. "So I guess we'll note down that you're in a romantic relationship?" He turned to the notetaker who scribbled on his papers.

Good, this was good. I'd gotten it out there, not the way I'd wanted to, but at least Aria knew. We'd try. But the pure joy of her kiss was fading fast. The weird company and setting were anxiety inducing. Yes, the room was beautiful, but the Witches didn't foster romantic vibes or give me confidence we were compatible when magic was still so *involved*.

What if we broke up?

All my doubts came roaring back. Tristan was at the apartment, hopefully not getting accosted by the magic plaguing the cafe. Lying wouldn't be easy with him living there, even temporarily. It still felt like everything was a mess. I couldn't picture a future together, not long term like I wanted, but this time I was going for it, regardless.

I needed to give Aria a chance to stay. I needed to trust her and believe that we could have something worthwhile even if it wasn't perfect or easy. Maybe I was dooming myself to heartbreak but I didn't care about that more than I cared about her.

With effort, I pulled my mind back to court. Aria and I held hands as the judge asked her to explain the events leading to the magic reveal. We told the story, then I went off on a tangent about how important Piña was to me. The tale drifted into cringy territory, as I described her to symbolize my business and love for my dad, but I didn't care. I fucking loved that cat.

"I have a document from Juliet Herrera outlining the curse issues plaguing your cafe," the judge said. His opinion on Piña unapparent. "Everything you say is corroborated and there is no reason to believe Miss Belmonte caused this situation intentionally. I can't say you've acted responsibly Miss Belmonte, but sadly that isn't a crime." After a dramatic pause the judge turned to me, tone shifting from accusatory to monotone. "Mr. Sanchez. Telling is an odd thing. Learning about magic has altered your life, but this change was done to you. Without your permission or consent. Given this, you have the opportunity to request the Telling be reversed if you are dissatisfied with the way magic will affect you. If you take this route, your memory will be altered, erasing everything from the cat flying incident till now. So far, you have not expressed the distress or regret of a Mortal not coping with the new reality. However, if you would like to talk to someone about it, that can be arranged."

I shifted, uncomfortable as he regarded me. "Um. That seems unnecessary."

"Some Mortals don't take well to Magic. It's hardly their fault. You seem to be doing well by all accounts. But please note, reversal isn't an option you can take at any time. Mind alterations are a strictly controlled magic, needing informed consent and court approval. Large chunks of time can't be removed without causing serious harm. That is to say, you can't come back in five years and say you want to start over. So speak now if you have doubts."

"There's no way I want my memory erased." I squeezed Aria's hand. "We'd never have gotten together. Not like this."

"Aww—" The notetaker had his chin in his hand, looking at

Aria and me like we were just the most adorbs.

"Okay. Thank you Mr. Sanchez. The only two items left to discuss are the burden of Telling and Miss Belmonte's tendency to want to Tell large groups of people." The judge scowled at Aria.

"I'd argue it's not a tendency, but a singular incident of poor decision making, made by a teenager," Aria said.

"Mr. Bickel?" the judge called, as if Aria hadn't spoken.

We all turned to where the dapper Witch sat at the back of the room. He didn't bother to stand, and barely looked up from beneath the brim of his infuriating hat as he said, "Aria has exhibited no signs she is at risk of continued, or radical, Telling."

The judge nodded. "Very well. Without evidence of intentional recklessness on your part Miss Belmonte, the court is bound to see this as a single incident and not an indicator of a larger problem. You will be fined for breaking the conditions set out for you at your last trial, but we can't prove any harm in your reconnecting with Mr. Sanchez so I will consider that matter concluded."

Aria made an indignant sound.

"I will, however, give you an official warning. Any further unapproved Telling will not be tolerated from you unless it involves clear life and death risk, or serious mental or emotional harm to the Mortal if you don't take magical action. No more saving cats. Got it?"

"I will resign my post at animal rescue." Aria nodded solemnly.

The judge looked like he might bite her head off, but Bickel laughed from the back of the room, distracting everyone.

"Lastly, the burden." The judge made eye contact with both of us in turn, stressing his point.

The notetaker rolled his eyes.

"Miss Belmonte, you must take full responsibility for the

burden of Telling Mr. Sanchez about the existence of magic. The court will appoint you as Mr. Sanchez's lifelong magical guide. You are obligated to look after him in regards to magic, through continued education and assistance in any and all matters of Witchery relevant to his life. Mr. Sanchez, if you do not trust Miss Belmonte to act to your benefit, or without prejudice, you may object now."

"Uh—nah, I'm good." No one had spelled it out quite like this. Aria's 'responsibility' was a lot more strictly regulated than the general, I'll-be-there-for-you-for-magic-shit impression I had in my head.

"Miss Belmonte. Any lapse in this responsibility is a punishable offense should Mr. Sanchez fall victim to harm, whether through negligence or your ill intent. Do you accept?"

"Yes. Understood," Aria said without a hint of doubt in her voice.

"Perfect. With burden agreement being legally binding, and every indication the Mortal is well adjusted and unharmed, I grant retroactive approval for this Telling. Court is adjourned."

Aria turned immediately and pulled me toward the exit. "Why is there soot on your cheek?"

"What?" I swiped at my face in alarm. I shot Bickel a glare as we passed. "You didn't say I had it on my face."

He fell into step with us. "I thought pointing out you were covered was more than sufficient."

Who cared if I looked like a fool. It didn't affect anything important other than my pride.

"Thanks for having Aria's back in there," I said.

Bickel gave a shrug so lazy it was like even his limbs couldn't be bothered to acknowledge me. "I was just doing my job, Owen. I'd no more lie to screw Aria over than make something up to help her. There's literally nothing to thank me for." He disappeared without waiting for a reply.

31

ARIA

*T*he sun was setting orange and gold when we exited the courthouse.

I turned to Owen. "What do you mean you're falling in love with me?"

"I thought that bit was self-explanatory?"

I laughed, sounding unhinged rather than mirthful. To say I'd been stressed when Owen ditched me at the bar for our pre-court talk was an understatement. To say I freaked out when he didn't show up on time or answer his phone was—oh fucking stars, I'd been a shitty mess.

"Humor me," I said.

Owen ran a nervous hand through his hair. "I'm sorry I told you not to stay when you offered, and acted like what was happening between us didn't matter. I wasn't lying about being happy the moment you walked in the cafe—conflicted, sure— but I've been falling for you since then. I only tried to resist because I'm terrified."

"Me too, Owen."

"I'm sorry I pushed you away, Aria. I've never been so myself with anyone else. And that's not casual. I don't want it to be. I never did. I want all the things I told myself I don't need. I want them with you. I'm flying way out of my comfort zone here, but it's us, and I want us too much to be okay with comfortable."

"You really want to try?" I faced Owen and gave him a hard look. Not smiling and lovey-dovey, I was far too hopeful for that. This was serious, real shit I wanted so bad my stomach hurt.

"Yes." He looked nervous, but adamant. "I know it might not work. I don't see how it can, but so what. I want to give us a shot. I don't want you to move. I'd love if you stayed, but I understand if it's too late?"

"Why do you keep saying we won't work, but you want to try anyway?" Any relief or happiness was simmering under the surface. I wouldn't let it out until I was sure Owen was giving us a real chance.

Owen stroked his beard, thinking hard. "Sorry, I just mean— no relationship is guaranteed to last. Which is obvious. But all my dating life I've been too afraid to accept that basic risk. It was a mistake to tell you we weren't a big deal when I was too afraid to face what we really meant. But I couldn't fool myself. I want you in my life."

"I want to be with you too, Owen." I grabbed his hand and laced our fingers together. "I don't think things are as doomed as you fear. We don't have to be together bracing for the end, or in spite of coming heartbreak."

"Yeah? I know I have hang ups—Tristan is um, now living in my apartment? And I don't care about looking old when you don't. I want to share my life with you, it doesn't matter if that takes a different form, we can do whatever works for us. But it's complicated. How do we share everything when I can't explain your unageing looks? I'll look like a creep at seventy and you're like twenty-five. I can't withdraw from life or keep more secrets if we're doing this for real."

I giggled, still flirting with unhinged. "Sorry. But just imagining—"

"I can't quite see the humor. Maybe we can ignore that all for now? It's so far off. I'm going from nothing to forever, but when I think of us I want it all." Owen looked cautiously hopeful.

"I think ignoring the future is a bad way to start a life together. And that's what I want, Owen. I want to share my life with you too, and so I have some proposals."

"Oh, thank god." His posture sagged in relief.

"Yeah." The serious resolve that was keeping me together cracked into a sweet smile, bringing an inner warmth I felt down to my toes. "First, if we as a couple make it long term, there's a way around the looking like a creep thing. It's some serious, powerful magic, like rare to the point no one's done it in California this century, but a work-around is possible. Luca found a historic spell allowing me to give you some of my power. It won't make you a Witch, but it will give you a lifespan to match mine. Which is madness, by the way. It's one thing knowing how long my future will be, and another thing choosing it. And it would mean one day withdrawing from Mortal society to an extent. I don't expect you to decide you want something like that right now, or ever. But we can do it if we want."

"Oh shit. Yeah that is, like, a better solution than I'd thought possible, but scary as hell."

"It's a mind-fuck knowing centuries will pass you by, and an existential crisis waiting to happen if you think too hard about purpose or progress. But neither of us would go through it alone. Maybe we revisit the spell after we've been together a while?"

Owen nodded. "That's reasonable. I'm guessing being granted a centuries long life is a non-reversible type situation?"

"Yeah, the bonding spell is permanent and can't be done on a whim. Besides, I don't think anyone would perform the ceremony for us right now. They'd make us wait, consider the gravity of it all. I'm not powerful enough to do the magic on my own."

"Okay. Yeah, I'm not exactly jumping for borderline immortality. But I'm glad it's there as an option. There's no expiration date lurking ahead of us. I shouldn't need that assurance, but I do. Thank you."

Owen squeezed my hand and led me down the courthouse steps. We walked quietly for a couple blocks until we reached a park shrouded in the fading light. I sucked in the night air and let myself feel relieved. Court was done. My Authority troubles were behind me. I'd managed to deal with the situation without failing miserably in the eyes of the law, or the man holding my hand. This was success. This was my life falling into place and working out. I could live in this feeling of contentment forever.

"About Tristan," Owen said.

I deflated. "Thanks for not bringing him up on the steps to the courthouse where someone might hear, but Owen, I can't—"

"Aria, wait. I think I get it. You never told me about the legal responsibility Telling places on you." Our walking slowed to a stop. Owen pulled me around to face him.

"I didn't see why you needed to worry about responsibility. It doesn't bother me. I'd support you whether I had to or not. They call it a burden, but it's not. I'd do anything for you."

"Oh, Aria." He blinked rapidly before giving up and letting a tear fall. I wiped it away and felt Owen's smile lift his cheeks beneath my fingers. "I know you're here for me. And now I understand, Telling Tristan isn't a decision to make lightly. It's more than worrying about trouble with the Authority, which the judge made clear you'd be in. I'm not going to make Telling him a condition on us working out. I want to fit our lives together, and that means figuring this one out with compromise. You're right, once we fix the cafe it might not be such a sore point in lying. I just need to get used to it."

"I think lying about magic will be manageable, Owen. I've lived around Mortals for years. And if it gets to the point it's straining your relationship, we'll work it out. You don't have to pick between Tristan and magic. The judge said I can't get away with more unapproved Tellings. If we put forward an application, and go through the arduous process of pre-approval, there's no reason we can't Tell Tristan one day. But like changing your lifespan, it needs to be planned, and Tristan's reaction considered irrespective of what we want."

"I can totally live with that." Owen was beaming. "If you're okay with being responsible for two Mortals, should it come down to it?"

"Totally. I'm on the road to getting my shit together. I'm not going to fail either of you guys. And beyond all this seriousness, we might actually have some fun."

Owen looked at me with excitement and trust, and an openness I'd never seen in him. I was finally relieved of worry. More than that, I was bubbling. Like I was slowly coming to a boil. Everything good was sitting out ahead of us. It was possible. Owen and me.

"You're not moving then, are you?" he asked.

"Oh, hell no. I'd like to say turning down the job was a romantic gesture, that I came running back for you but, um, Juliet offered me a job. Otherwise I'd have taken the one up North. It wasn't what I wanted, but changing nothing about my life wasn't an option I was okay with anymore. Juliet's offer was a weight off my mind. This way, the change feels more like my life."

"I'm glad you didn't come back for me. I wouldn't ask you to pick me over yourself. I used the job as an excuse to push you away, but I do think it's important we're bringing our lives together, not drowning the other out. We could have done a long-distance relationship if you'd moved. That was my grand idea anyway."

"This way is much better."

Owen showed his agreement with a kiss, and his soft lips framed by his coarse beard were the most welcome touch. It was a gentle kiss, because as much as Owen got me going, this kiss wasn't about lust. It was us agreeing to something new and complicated, and so much more.

The warm evening air was sweetened by the park's flowering trees, creating the illusion of a private world as we walked another lap around the grass before heading across downtown toward Coffee Cat.

"Wait, did you say Tristan is living at the apartment?" I asked.

"Yeah—not so funny story—" Owen filled me in, at last explaining the soot. "So, I'm just gonna have to prompt him to pull out the noise canceling headphones when we get back. There's no world in which the we're-back-together sex is going to be quiet." Owen gave me a heated look that built from sweet sexy to pure sin, because as great as moonlight kisses were, lust was still very much on the table.

"Why don't we just book a hotel?" I said.

"Oh fuck. Yeah, that sounds way better."

"Come on, Owen, you've got to be up early to bake all that perfect pan, and there's a number of things I need to do with you before you get any rest."

32

OWEN

*A*t the height of the morning rush, Juliet walked into the cafe, marched right past the line of customers and greeted me where I was re-stocking the display with conchas.

"Owen, I hope you have a moment free." She was poised and purposeful as ever, but a hint of excitement had me hoping for good news.

"I'm due for a break once the tray is unloaded," I said.

"And Aria?" The Witch looked around the cafe. "Oh good, she has a table. It's never too soon for her to start work."

Juliet departed for the back of the line. Whatever she was here for wasn't so urgent she couldn't get coffee first.

Tristan gave me a meaningful look from the register. "Oh my god. Out all night *and* Aria's taking the job here. Look at you two, getting all serious."

"I kind of can't believe it's coming together."

"You're adorable." Tristan gave me his most genuine lopsided grin. "I love being right."

"Yeah, you being right isn't the worst."

I'd been silly smiles all morning, my head full of plans for Aria and me, only some of which were of the sexy variety. I was ready to create the future we wanted. Not even a psychic Witch could look ahead to see where we ended up, but I wasn't afraid it would end badly. I didn't need more assurance than us committing to working it out as best we could. We'd created something worth having, and that would always be worth it.

Aria and I would be back at the apartment tonight, and while the hotel was fun, I was in anticipation of our more mundane couple life. Tristan already planned a home cooked meal and movie night for the three of us. Aria was looking forward to it even more than I was.

After the pan dulce was displayed neatly in the case, I checked on the kitchen staff, and joined Juliet and Aria at a table near the front door.

"I've cracked the crow," Juliet said in triumph as she extracted a small glass vile from her briefcase.

"Is that blood?" I asked, recoiling.

"No, it's the curse's essence. I'm going to use it to trap this Witch." Juliet nestled the vial into the small, decorative potted plant sitting on the table. "Now. Owen, have you had any further thought to who might be targeting you?"

I stared at the plant. "I really can't think of anyone. My professional relationships are all—well professional, low key. I swear I didn't double cross anyone in starting Coffee Cat, and my main friendships these days are Tristan and Tess."

Tristan caught us looking his way and waved.

"They both seem lovely," Juliet said with a frown. "But there must be someone—"

"Should we be talking about this here?" I glanced around to see the people at the nearest tables occupied with their own conversations. But still.

"Don't worry." Juliet pulled a crystal and herb adorned neck-lace from within the folds of her blouse. "This carries a minor diffusion charm, rendering our conversation, not silent, but compulsively forgettable to those around us."

I glanced at Aria, who seemed as impressed by this trick as I was. I loved Aria's low-key Witchiness. It left us on a more even footing, even with magic. Aria would fit into a mostly Mortal life with me without changing who she was. She had a handle on both worlds, shifting between them seamlessly, and I was here for it. Along for whatever ride she took us on.

Juliet cleared her throat, prompting Aria and me to snap out of our mutually daydreamy gaze and refocus. "I learned a few things from my analysis of the curse. The essence gave off the aura of a petty grievance, the caster is looking for revenge, and is by all accounts a mean-spirited person. None of that fits anyone you know, Owen?"

It was hardly a specific character profile. "I mean, that could be anyone. I'm not a petty revenge kind of guy, so nothing comes to mind. How is the vial going to catch them?"

Were we just leaving it in the plant where anyone could take it?

"It's a beacon. The Witch will be drawn to their own curse. It will work best if they come to the cafe naturally, but even if they were planning to avoid the place, this will draw them back over time. I harnessed the magic trapped in the frozen crow and cast my own spell on it, persuading the magical essence to call upon its caster. Magic is always linked to its source. Whenever Witches use magic, we're laying down a piece of ourselves, and with some skilled manipulation the pieces will attract the Witch that spawned them. It's the same inherent link blood has to its source, or say, a tree has to its sap and leaves."

"Uh-huh. Cool. But is that really a trap? How do we know—"

The bell above the door chimed as Max walked in. "Mr. Sanchez!" The man jumped in feigned surprise. "What are you doing sitting down on the job?"

"Don't worry, the pan is baked and coffee roasted," I said with my customer service smile.

"Excellent—" Max looked around distractedly. "I have a lot of writing to do today."

Aria kicked my leg under the table as Max plunged his hand into his laptop bag, rooting around for something while scanning the cafe. Juliet watched him closely.

"Say, Mr. Sanchez, not to be rude, but will you be using that table long?" Max asked, hand still probing the depths of his bag.

"Um—" I glanced at Aria. She was trying to communicate something wordlessly, but I really wasn't picking up what she was putting down.

"We'll be needing this table a bit longer, I'm afraid," Juliet said to the preoccupied customer while fiddling with her crystal necklace.

Max jumped, and unlike his entrance to the cafe, he seemed genuinely shocked to see Juliet sitting in front of him. At his sudden movement, Max's laptop bag slid off his shoulder and fell to the ground.

A large crystal rolled across the tile floor and hit the leg of my chair.

Max picked up the crystal and stuffed it in his bag. "Yes, you're—quite right. I shouldn't have asked. It's just—I have a feeling about this spot today."

I stared at Max. No way. A crystal was hardly a smoking gun, but it was distinctly Witchy, and at the risk of stereotyping, Max didn't have the personality of a Mortal who carried crystals around. And Max was, without any caveats, petty and mean spirited. His constant snide comments, and repeated jibes making fun of Tristan, left no room for doubt.

Max sat in the remaining empty seat at our table as if he hadn't meant to, but couldn't help it. "Maybe I can join you? This seat has good lighting for my—writing." He slid his laptop out of his bag and then adjusted the little potted plant, pulling it closer to himself.

He blinked at the plant and pushed it away again.

"Did you curse my cafe?" I asked Max before I could stop myself.

"Mr. Sanchez, I have no idea what you mean." He patted my arm in the most condescending way. "Don't you have a cake to bake or something?"

"We don't sell cakes."

"Then I'd love an oat milk latte." Max waited expectantly for me to go get his drink.

I crossed my arms and glared at him.

"Cut the crap, Witch," Juliet said in a very Bickel tone of voice.

"Pardon me?" Max's outrage was undermined by his restless hands, which continued to adjust the potted plant.

Juliet pulled a business card out of her briefcase and snapped it down on the table in front of Max. "I'm a paranormal investigator looking into illegal magic affecting the Coffee Cat Cafe. My assistant here is a psychic. You can either talk to us now, or deal with the details after your arrest."

"I pick neither of those options. I don't have to stay here and be subjected to baseless accusations. You can't arrest me." Max slung his laptop bag over his shoulder but instead of standing and storming off as I expected, he reached into the potted plant and extracted the vial. "*Argh!*" He dropped it like it burned him. "What the ever living *hell*—?"

Juliet grabbed the vial before it rolled off the table onto the floor. "That worked beautifully."

"What?" Max scowled. "I've never seen that vial in my life, it's not mine. I have nothing to do with anything."

"The contents of this vial hold proof you cursed the cafe." Juliet waggled the vial and Max snatched at it. She held it out of reach. "Now that you've given yourself away, it will be straight-forward for official Witches to prove your involvement."

"I only came here for a coffee," Max said through gritted teeth.

"You're lying," Aria said.

"People are always lying," Max snapped back. "Half of social interaction is lying."

"You think a psychic can't tell the difference between polite lies and dishonesty? All your deceitful intentions are written out for me to see," Aria said.

"Oh? Then tell me, why did I curse the cafe?"

I couldn't believe he admitted it, but once you were caught by magic, I suppose you were caught, and Max was so arrogant I wouldn't be surprised if he thought he'd get away with this even still.

Aria took her time considering the Witch. "You did it for amusement—and out of—bitterness. You're very angry."

"I'm sorry," I cut in before Max could respond. "You cursed me for amusement?"

"Oh, Mr. Sanchez, try not to be so offended. It was a test. Not on you, calm down. I was testing some new bespoke spells. A real rat's nest of a disruption spell, and some tweaks to enchanted crows I've been playing with for years. I needed to observe all the magical components interacting before I unleashed my creation on the true target. I already spent so much time here writing my novels—it was ideal for observation —and then one day you served me a full milk latte. Full Milk. I cannot stress the betrayal I felt. Such a fine establishment, such a commitment to non-dairy alternatives. I don't even see how one could mistake oat milk for full fat cow swill. Retribution was in order."

"Maybe"—I said through gritted teeth—"You grabbed the wrong latte."

"Oh." Max considered, stroking his chin in an unintention-ally comical way. "Perhaps. I don't recall if other drinks were on the counter at the time. It was weeks ago, you see."

"Meanwhile, my business lost money and you caused unrea-sonable chaos and stress."

"Mm. Unreasonable is subjective, Mr. Sanchez. And I imagine I'll be paying a fine now the game is up. Recompense will be had. You won't be any worse off."

"This isn't a game or any sort of light matter," Juliet said.

"But it has been amusing, and proved my cursing ability is up for the task of striking back against my brother. He has it coming, don't worry. He turned my eyes green. It was a year before I could fix them. Sunglasses in public twenty-four-seven. A nightmare."

"Your eyes still look green." Aria scowled at the man.

"Not the irises. The whites." Max shuddered. "It gave my vision a swampy tint. All the clothes I bought that year were wrong. And—" He held up an entitled finger. "—before you fling more accusations. The curse wasn't supposed to be so dramatic. It was a low stakes test run. How was I supposed to anticipate a Witch coming along and messing with my creation, prodding it with magic, and triggering the escalating effects? Really, the person meddling should be held responsible."

Aria's mouth dropped open in outrage. "You can't blame me for this."

"Without you the effects were hardly noticeable." Max shrugged as if that settled it.

"No, I definitely noticed," I said, remembering the weeks of confusion I'd endured. Max smiled at me mockingly, stoking my frustration. "I bet this wasn't even about getting your brother back. That excuse is weak. You were just being an ass about us getting your drink wrong. If you'd complained we'd have given you a new one. There was no need for any of this."

"But my way was so much more fun." The Witch's eyes flashed.

"No, it wasn't." I clenched a fist. "You've been coming in here to gloat all these weeks."

Max only shrugged again.

"How did you get around my protection spell?" Juliet asked, before I could snap back.

Max leaned in, clearly enjoying this and disturbingly unconcerned with the consequences of his actions. "I planted a link to the curse. A spelled screw hidden under the bathroom sink. The linked object was in place before you cast the protection, which meant *it* resided under your spell. The magic it harbored wasn't an attack from outside. You preserved a key to the curse when protecting the cafe, and all I had to do was come back and activate it. It's a spell I've been working on longer than the curse itself. I didn't honestly know if it would work."

"This wasn't a low stakes test at all," Juliet said. "You'd seen how badly the curse affected the cafe, and kept pushing, coming back for more. I'll have to hand the screw over to the Authority as evidence. They'll want to investigate the loophole you've found."

"It's my creation, you can't steal it." Max seemed angry for the first time.

"You shouldn't have used it against unsuspecting Mortals if you didn't want it confiscated." Juliet crossed her arms looking triumphant.

"He's not unsuspecting. He knows all about magic."

"Because of this whole mess." I gestured around at my cafe.

"No." Max glared at us. "There was no risk of giving away magic. You can't hold me to that."

"That really is for someone else to decide." Juliet stood and smoothed her skirt. "Aria, walk him out with me. I'll call Mr. Bickel."

33

ARIA

ix months later.

"GOOD TO SEE YOU TRISTAN, it's been so long," I said as he joined Owen and me on the couch.

"I know you're being sarcastic, but you love me. And I brought snacks."

Tristan cozied up to my left side and passed a bowl of popcorn and pepitas to Owen on my right. Piña sniffed at the bag of sour candies in Tristan's lap before abandoning him to curl up on Owen's feet for Monday movie night.

"With this warm welcome we should go away more often, Aria." Owen chuckled.

"It was a weekend with Luca, not a cross country trip," I grumbled, but honestly I was loving this.

It was good to be home, and not just because I missed our apartment and the tasteful Witchy decorations I'd scattered around (Luca could learn from my understated style). I preferred our home to my brother's. Owen's and my whole life was full of comforts. Including Tristan's steadfast presence and excellent taste in snacks. Piña was growing on me too, even if she still had attitude about magic.

"Now that you know Coffee Cat won't fall down in your absence, you can go on a real vacation next," Tristan leaned around me to direct his words at the cafe's owner.

"I knew you'd take care of things for me," Owen said, as if he hadn't had minor separation anxiety from his cafe baby while we visited San Francisco.

"Aria would have seen trouble coming though, right?" Tristan smirked at me. "She'll warn us if anything is about to jump out—" He half lunged off the couch with his arms out like a zombie. I pushed him in the shoulder and he flopped back against a pile of pillows.

"I've never claimed to see the future," I said for the hundredth time.

"No, you're just an *online psychic*. When are you going to read my fortune?"

"When you stop calling me a hack."

"Hm. So never?" Tristan pouted. "But really, I get the hustle of needing two jobs. It's just fortune telling can't be that lucrative."

"I'm doing fine, Tristan. Stop trying to get me to work at Coffee Cat. We'd drive each other up the wall. There's such a thing as too much togetherness."

Owen tried to suppress a laugh. He passed the snack bowl back to Tristan and grabbed my hand. "I'd never get sick of having you around, Aria. You helped the cafe before. Your *unique skills* could help wash dishes in the cafe kitchen."

Tristan cracked up.

Owen meant using magic, or I'd have been offended. "Wow. You guys are forgetting the other half of the equation. I don't think Juliet would cope without me. Quitting on her would weigh on my conscience, and I like her better than you, Tristan."

He stuck his tongue out at me. Which I ignored in favor of opening the candies and picking out the ones Owen and I liked best.

My assistant gig with the paranormal investigator was a whole lot more than I'd imagined. In a good way. I didn't know how Juliet had functioned outside her investigations before me, to be perfectly honest. All Juliet's energy seemed to go into doing one thing well, to the detriment of everything else. Where I, on the other hand, could do a bunch of stuff generally okay. Together we struck an oddly harmonious arrangement, filling in each other's gaps.

I'd started off my job helping Juliet regain control of her office space, and was now working on pushing a semblance of balance onto the woman's lifestyle. Juliet was a workaholic, but not in the crushing way I imagined Luca and his coworkers to be. Juliet and I had fun together. I was even improving my basic magic skills without pressure. Juliet never made me feel inadequate or like I was falling short.

I'd have invited Juliet to movie night, but Owen and I were trying to keep the really Witchy stuff away from Tristan so we didn't have to lie about too many things. A plan which was working out nicely. All pressure to Tell Tristan about magic had faded away. He was perfectly skeptical, and enjoyed the fake psychic version of me way too much for Owen to want to burst his bubble.

Owen and I were settled. The cafe hadn't had a single whiff of magical problems since Max was dealt with. I could go off with Juliet and do my thing with the local Witch community and come home to the life I wanted. I hadn't done any psychic interrogating since Max, but I was able to connect with some of our clients and use my skills to help them find clarity on their problems on their terms. I sometimes did Mortal readings, set up on the beach each Saturday. It was a new, happy normal. I had no doubts I'd made the right choice for my future.

I had Owen and shared everything with him. That's all I'd ever wanted for us.

Tristan turned on the movie and we sat back to watch. The evening went quickly, like so many other similar ones before it. After, Tristan wished us good night and left to go back to his refurbished loft.

"Do you think we should go on a real vacation?" Owen asked me as I closed the door.

"Sure." I wrapped my arms around him.

"That wasn't the most enthusiastic response," he teased.

"I'm enjoying all this." I looked around at the apartment.

"Yeah, me too." Owen kissed me.

"Besides, I think Juliet needs me here for the foreseeable future."

Owen laughed. "She's lucky she has you. I don't mind waiting. Gives me more time to plan our trip."

"Plan anything you want, Owen. You've got me pretty much forever."

We both laughed at that. I turned off the lights with a muttered spell and then flicked my wrist to ignite the various candles placed around the apartment.

"Actually, do you want to go on the roof and look at the stars before we go to bed?" Owen asked.

"Yes." I snuffed out the candles and followed him outside. It was a perfect night for us to kiss under twinkling sky and whisper about the rest of our lives.

THANK YOU FOR READING GIVE A WITCH A CHANCE

More from the *Love & Magic* world

KEEP YOUR WITCHES CLOSE
COMING 6 JUNE '23
Juliet Herrera & Mea Dubois

ONE WICKED NIGHT
COMING 10 OCT '23
Tristan Taylor Thomás & Edwin Bickel

Would you like a free **bonus scene**? Head over to my website coletterivera.com and subscribe to my author newsletter. I'll send you a glimpse of Aria and Owen in high school!

Please consider leaving a review for Give a Witch a Chance on your favorite site to help others find magical books they love. 🤍

KEEP YOUR WITCHES CLOSE
Love & Magic Book 2

Can a Witch who trusts no one count on her rival to keep her safe?

Paranormal Investigator, Juliet Herrera has a painful past. A secret. She doesn't need anyone from *before*. Especially not a certain Witch who inspires as much lust as she does loathing.

Unfortunately, Juliet can't seem to stay away from the woman.

Authority Witch, Mea Dubois swears Juliet used to like her. She'd give anything to get their friendship back, and more to follow the spark Juliet ignites... if only Juliet didn't hate her.

When Witch disappearances bring Mea to town, Juliet resigns herself to working together. She didn't expect to become the centre of the case.

A target.

Mea is tasked with keeping an eye on Juliet, who doesn't like what being stuck with Mea is making her want...

Juliet has to decide, if she can't face the threat alone, can she trust Mea with the truth? And what about with her heart?

ACKNOWLEDGMENTS

I would like to thank my wonderful editor May Peterson for her work on this book. I would also like to thank TK for being so supportive and reading early drafts of this story, as well as all the less successful, unpublished books that came before it.

Note: There was, once upon a time, a cafe called Coffee Cat in the town where I spent my teen-age years. It has been closed for a while now, and was the initial inspiration for Owen's cafe. However, the cafe depicted here doesn't resemble or represent the actual cafe in any way, beyond the name.

ABOUT THE AUTHOR

Colette is an award winning author of lgbtq+ paranormal romance. She lives on an island made of books where she creates HEAs fueled by coffee and baked goods.

Colette can be found on Instagram and Twitter @colette_rivera or at her website coletterivera.com.

CPSIA information can be obtained
at www.ICGtesting.com
Printed in the USA
BVHW070318310123
657442BV00005B/264